HELLDIVER

CHRIS ALLEN

BOOKS

By Chris Allen

Black Ops Intrepid

Defender

Hunter

Avenger

Helldiver

For my boys, Morgan and Rhett, for whom I write every word

Vinci Books

vinci-books.com

Published by Vinci Books Ltd in 2025

1

A CIP catalogue record for this book is available from the British Library.
Paperback ISBN: 9781036703448

The Sword Of Interpol

When extremists plunged the world into dark decades of war and nations mobilized for vengeance, the shadow of remorseless terror and unrestrained violence called for a new generation of crime fighter.

The UN Security Council turned to INTERPOL - the International Criminal Police Organisation – to raise a new division of elite men and women, hand-picked from across the globe.

Skilled, fearless and unrelenting - part police officer, part soldier, part spy - they would be international in every way, ordained to fight fire with fire, no matter how dreadful the crime nor how treacherous the adversary.

So it was that INTREPID - the Intelligence, Recovery, Protection and Infiltration Division – came to be.

Above all, we should acknowledge that the collapse of the Soviet Union was a major geopolitical disaster of the century. As for the Russian nation, it became a genuine drama. Tens of millions of our co-citizens and co-patriots found themselves outside Russian territory. Moreover, the epidemic of disintegration infected Russia itself.

—Russian President Vladimir Putin
The Kremlin, Russia
April 2005

The biggest disaster of this century would be the restoration of the Soviet Union.

—Ukrainian Prime Minister Arseniy Yatsenyuk
Washington, DC, United States
March 2014

Prologue

Just as the rain finally stopped hammering the roof of his treasured navy blue 1968 S-Type Jaguar, Lieutenant Colonel Reginald "Nobby" Davenport of the Army Legal Services Branch turned the car right, off Alison's Road and into the vehicle checkpoint at the entrance to Montgomery Lines, switching off the windscreen wipers and Jazz FM as he did. A young paratrooper, a "Tom," dressed in sodden combat fatigues, maroon beret and armed with an SA80 assault rifle, emerged from the rain-soaked surrounds, directing Davenport away from the boom-gated chicane and into a search bay to the left. As Davenport pulled into the bay and shut off the engine, the soldier withdrew, taking up a position from which he could maintain coverage of the vehicle and react, if necessary, with lethal force at the first sign of trouble. Two more identically dressed and armed soldiers, equally as drenched as the first man, immediately appeared from the vicinity of the guard box. If they were feeling the bitter cold they weren't showing it. One of them was carrying a search mirror on an extendable arm. He

1

dropped out of sight and began the process of inspecting the underside of the car. While this was happening, the other man, a corporal, approached Davenport directly. Davenport wound the window down. Icy air filled the car instantly.

"Good morning, sir," the corporal began, his warm breath wrestling against the cold air. He was a Geordie. "Could I see some identification, please." It wasn't a request.

Davenport produced his British Army identity card. "I expect I'm on your list for this morning. Captain Wills at Brigade Headquarters is the contact."

"Alright, sir. Just a moment please." The corporal took the ID card and returned to the guard box to make the necessary calls just as a muted clunk at the back of the Jag told Davenport the search man had opened the trunk and was having a look inside. Davenport was glad to see the regiment was still taking the domestic security threat seriously. The politicians might be talking about a truce with the IRA but this wasn't the time to be letting the guard down. Old enemies die hard and old wounds heal slowly.

Just as the trunk slammed shut the corporal returned from the guard box holding an A5-sized pink card.

"You're all clear, sir. Here's your car pass. Leave it face up on your dash while you're here, alright, and one of the boys will collect it from you when you leave. You know your way around?"

"I do, thank you."

"Right. Well, you're good to go, sir."

Saluting, he returned Davenport's ID and signaled for the boom to be raised. Davenport drove through the chicane, making a series of left and right turns through the narrow bitumen roads of the garrison lined on either side by the imposing, two- and three-story concrete bunkers that formed the headquarters and accommodation buildings for the various units of 5 Airborne Brigade. The gravity of the place and the imposing, fortress-like constructions felt familiar, almost welcoming to him. The old gray barracks, Bruneval, Arnhem and Normandy among them, had been built for purpose. The Parachute Regiment was the sharp end of British policy, foreign and domestic. It was the regiment the government turned to when all else had failed and a sledgehammer was required. It had been Davenport's first and only choice when he'd left New Zealand to join the British Army, and coming back to Aldershot gave him a sense that he had returned home.

He drove past the site of what had once been the 2PARA Officers Mess, now just an empty space with a plaque marking the spot where a car packed with explosives had been detonated by the IRA back in 1972. The explosion killed a Catholic priest, a gardener and five women who were employed as civilian staff. Nineteen others were injured, many seriously.

Within a few minutes he'd parked at the 3PARA Officers Mess, removed the civilian spray jacket he routinely wore over his uniform when driving, donned his beret and camouflage combat smock, and walked through the grounds of his old battalion, past the transport yard and the mortar platoon, and under the covered concourse behind the company offices. As he turned the corner to the battalion headquarters he was met by a familiar figure, apparently waiting for him.

"Young Mr. Davenport. So we actually managed to coax you into a uniform and back down to Aldershot where all the real work's done; although I see that damn beard's become a permanent fixture?"

"Good morning, sir," Davenport replied warmly with a salute and handshake. "No entourage this morning?"

"No. I've sent them all ahead to grease the wheels. Wanted a moment with you alone." Brigadier Gordon Pymble, DSO, MBE, Commander 5 Airborne Brigade, was as tall as Davenport, although more heavily set, with gun-barrel dark brown eyes and closely cropped iron-gray hair visible below the black leather band of his maroon beret. "They can wait for me a little longer."

They began to walk together, slowly.

Pymble had forged his career in the Parachute Regiment and Special Air Service and had been Davenport's commanding officer with the SAS during Desert Storm when Davenport, then commanding an SAS squadron, had been badly wounded by an Iraqi mortar, sustaining injuries that left him with shrapnel embedded deep within his right knee and eventually saw him medically retired from active service. Pymble had personally overseen the then Major Davenport's recovery and, importantly, his continued career in the military. "*We can't afford to lose you, my boy,*" he'd said then. "*Far too valuable to us.*" Under Pymble's patronage, Davenport had completed an extensive physical rehabilitation process and, resurrecting a law degree he'd earned at the University of Auckland years earlier, he transitioned into Army Legal Services, maintaining his rank and seniority. He owed Pymble a debt he knew he could never repay.

"Well, thank you for the invitation. I'm delighted to be back," said Davenport. "And, yes, the beard's permanent; as permanent as anything, I suppose, in this line of work. As I spend most of my time creeping around the corridors of the MOD and Whitehall in a suit, my director general has been kind enough to allow me this small rebellion against Army protocol. Civilianizes me somewhat – that's my argument anyway. I'm sure somebody will make me shave it off at some point."

"Well, it's damn good to see you, my boy, even if you do look like a bloody sailor. Can you come to the house for dinner this evening? I know Catherine would love to see you, and you can fill me in on your deployment to the Balkans."

"That's very kind. I'd be delighted, thank you." Davenport inclined his head toward a group of British and foreign military officers standing across the other side of the parade ground. "I see our friends are gathering already. Care to fill me in before we join them? The request you sent was rather cryptic. Something about assisting you with translating during a CFE visit?"

"It's a little more than that I'm afraid, Nobby," replied the Brigadier. The two men continued slowly toward the others. "I'm sure every one of them bloody well speaks English fluently, they only pretend they don't. No, there's something else I need you for. This is the first of these Conventional Armed Forces in Europe visits we've had here at the Brigade and, of course, I'm happy to oblige; in fact, the CFE Treaty requires me to; but when I saw the list of attendees representing the Eastern Block countries, one name instantly stood out among all the others, and I knew I'd need you to verify whether or not it is the same man."

"Very well," replied Davenport. "Who is it?"

"You'll think I'm out of my mind when I tell you – Zolnerowich."

"Zolnerowich. Are you sure?"

"Not a hundred percent. That's why you're here, my boy. In my position, I can't pay any particular attention to him, but you can."

"Would he be so reckless as to turn up after all these years under his own name?"

"Look at us," replied Pymble. "We're all suddenly friends now. You show me yours and I'll show you mine, and all that rot. From what I recall of the man he'll be relishing the opportunity to stand on British soil as an officially invited guest. Using his own name would just be the icing on the bloody cake." Pymble paused. "Nobby, you were the closest of any of us when we tried to snatch him from Tiergarten back in eighty-five. You were one of our best Russian speakers. You watched him, studied him and listened to his voice for days during the surveillance phase of the operation. If anyone can confirm it's him, you can."

By now the two men had arrived at the edge of the multinational group gathered at the northeastern end of the battalion parade ground. A young captain wearing a maroon beret and the uniform and insignia of the Australian airborne forces separated from the group and approached them. The name tag on his distinctive mustard-colored camouflage uniform read "Collins."

"Good morning, sir," he said, saluting Pymble.

"Good morning, Lewis," replied the Brigadier. "This is Colonel Davenport from the MOD."

"Colonel," Collins replied, shaking Davenport's hand. "Good to meet you."

"Good to meet you, too. You're a long way from home."

"Yes. I'm attached to the regiment for two years; about halfway through at the moment."

"Lewis is currently commanding Patrols Company with 3PARA and he's drawn the short straw to host the visit this morning," Pymble said. "Are we all set?"

"Yes, sir. Although, we're in the hands of the translators unfortunately, but I suspect most of these guys understand exactly what we're saying anyway." Collins guided Pymble and Davenport back toward the group, adding, "I'll make the introductions."

The group totaled about thirty, a half-and-half mix of British and Russian officers and senior non-commissioned officers. Via the translators, Collins began the circuit of introductions, then Pymble gave a few words of welcome, acknowledging the importance of the CFE Treaty. Once the Brigadier was finished, Collins resumed the hosting role, explaining the visit schedule: "… which will include a demonstration by the reconnaissance platoon and snipers, a demolition presentation by the pioneers, and the deployment of the battalion tactical headquarters by the signals platoon within a combat operations scenario …"

As the briefing continued, Davenport took the opportunity to blend into the background, his eyes subtly searching the group for the man introduced just moments ago as Colonel Zolnerowich. He seemed to have disappeared. No, there: wearing the uniform and embellishments of a colonel in the Motor Rifle Division, complete with a papakha fur hat. This was definitely Zolnerowich. Colonel Igor Sergei Zolnerowich. Uniforms don't hide much when you're used to them, he thought. It's a person's presence and physicality that's telling when everyone is in olive drab or camouflage: the set of the shoulders, the crest of the brow, the profile, gait and general demeanor. When you know someone well enough, all of those elements transcend the anonymity of the uniform. He was just as Davenport remembered him, average height, although a little thicker set than ten years ago, with the same light brown hair, large ears and cold, lifeless eyes. Even his wearing of the papakha was telling. Davenport knew enough about the Russian Army, pre- and post-Cold War, to know that the iconic fur hats had recently been banned by President Yeltsin. They were seen by the new Russian leadership as a symbol of elitism among the most senior ranks of the old guard. So, Zolnerowich saw himself as above the decrees of his commander-in-chief. Interesting but not uncharacteristic.

During the late 1970s and early 80s, Zolnerowich had emerged on the radar of Western intelligence agencies as a KGB problem solver, making a name for himself as *istrebitel' predatelei*, "the killer of defectors". He was responsible for the murders of a Czech deputy minister during a trade delegation visit to Helsinki, a Polish bio-weapons engineer in Paris, and a string of others, all of whom had either defected or who had reached out to the West and were in the process of making the final move, including a pilot who'd absconded with a MiG and made it safely to Aalborg in Denmark. Zolnerowich had a knack for appearing just as everything seemed to be all clear. He became known to Western intelligence agencies for ensuring that the murder of every defector was witnessed – a wife, a husband, a mistress or colleague – while doing nothing to mask his identity. At the time Davenport first heard of him, Zolnerowich was wanted for the murder of Major Piotr Adamczyk, a Polish Army officer who had spied for NATO for almost a decade. In April 1983, when Adamczyk was sold out and the KGB began to close in, the decision was made to extract him. An urgent plan was cobbled together, MI6 took point and the extraction went, relatively, like clockwork. And then everything unraveled. No sooner had they managed to bundle Adamczyk safely across the border into West Berlin than Zolnerowich appeared. He shot Adamczyk between the eyes, along with the MI6 officer who had extracted him, and permanently maimed the West German agent who'd established the safe house – thereby leaving his witness. It was a major embarrassment for the West.

Two years later, MI6 reported that Zolnerowich had once again been identified operating within the British sector of West Berlin. It was the first confirmed sighting of him since '83 and the opportunity to capture him was too good to miss. With no notice, as was so often the case, Davenport's team was scrambled from Hereford to Tiergarten. The operation to capture and interrogate Zolnerowich was to have been a major coup for the West.

Davenport involuntarily shuddered against the bite of a cold wind, maintaining his composure despite the sudden resurgence of bitter memories. He looked casually around at the gathered group of former adversaries. Now everyone was suddenly expected to be on the same bloody team, smiling, shaking hands, even sharing secrets – to a point. After almost fifty years of facing off against each other, the paranoia and lies, a dozen dirty little wars, countless deaths and the world constantly on the brink of Armageddon, it was all just swept away. But how long could it last? Political leaders could stand their militaries down and talk of peace, but for those who'd been on the frontlines for decades, it was a lot harder to forgive and forget. Davenport realized his jaw was clenched tight, just as his fists were within the pockets of his combat smock. He let the air escape through his nostrils and resumed his quiet study of the enemy. The old enemy. He noted that, like him, Zolnerowich was also hanging back, under the radar, standing behind the Russian delegation. Davenport decided to make his move, edging discreetly around the perimeter of the group, eventually coming to stand close behind the Russian's left shoulder.

"I see you've come prepared for the cold, colonel," said Davenport in flawless Russian. He indicated the papakha.

Zolnerowich glanced lazily at him, his face expression-less. The black eyes blinked once, capturing an image, assessing it, filing it. "You took your time coming over," he replied in English.

"Well, I'm here to assist the Brigadier," Davenport said, remaining in English. "He doesn't speak Russian."

"But you do and very well. Why is that, colonel?"

"I expect for the same reasons that your English is so good."

"Perhaps you're right," said Zolnerowich. "I suspect we have crossed paths over the years."

"It's possible," Davenport replied noncommittally. There was no humor in their exchange; they were appraising each other, chipping away at decades of ice. "Perhaps during a visit to Berlin – after the wall came down, of course?"

Zolnerowich finally turned to face Davenport, offering a grimace verging on a smile. "No, colonel. I think we both know it was long before that."

Davenport remained silent.

"You see, it interests me that – among all my comrades here – you found it necessary to come and talk to me. Why? Because you recognized me. Now, the only way that you would be able to recognize me is if we had frequented similar circles and, in our line of business, those circles are very small. Yes?"

Davenport only smiled.

"You see, I also know who you are, comrade Colonel Davenport, and I know that you have not always worn the insignia of the Army Legal Services. In fact, I believe you are much more at home here with the Parachute Regiment and perhaps even more so in Hereford with your Special

Air Service, than you are in the Ministry of Defence. Am I right?"

"I'm sure you have me mistaken for someone else, colonel," Davenport replied. "I'm afraid I've only ever been a pencil pusher; never one for the field, as they say. Besides, the MOD does have its charms."

Zolnerowich laughed and patted Davenport on the back. "You see, comrade. That is exactly why I know it must be you. Despite all this pretense of friendship, your first instinct is caution. Why should you suddenly trust a man who has been your enemy these many years? Why indeed. We are warriors, you and I. We know what it is to stand on the frontline and shed blood. War is in our hearts and in our bones. That cannot be changed with just the stroke of a pen or pulling down a wall."

Captain Collins had concluded his briefing and was leading the group toward an area where an explosive demolition display by the pioneers was set to occur. Zolnerowich and Davenport walked slowly, a short distance behind all the others.

"This whole thing," Zolnerowich continued, waving his hand toward the group. "This treaty. Expecting us all to suddenly be friends and walk away from a lifetime of confrontation, of … anticipation of total war. It is a farce."

"I take it you're not a fan of Mr. Gorbachev's legacy, then?" Davenport replied, barely able to believe the Russian's candor. It was as if he had been waiting for the opportunity to vent away from Mother Russia. "His reforms have been almost universally embraced, at least here in the West they have. Glasnost. Perestroika. The Commonwealth of Independent States."

Zolnerowich gave Davenport a withering look. It was

just a flash but it was the same gun-barrel eyes with which Davenport had become so familiar all those years ago.

"*Etot kozel rasvalil stranu!* That goat Gorbachev has torn our country apart. Don't hang your Western dreams of the future on glasnost or perestroika, colonel. These things have destroyed us. Destroyed Russia. And they will destroy you, too, comrade, believe me. When the world begins to fall apart and borders are redrawn based on ethnicity and religion, not nationality, then you will see. For us the first dominoes fell in the Baltic Republics and the Caucasus, foolishly cutting themselves away from the coattails of Russia. And in a whisper of time, everything was gone. But they are mistaken if they think that it is the end of it. The disintegration of Yugoslavia should be a lesson to us all. The Serbs, Slovenes, Croats, Kosovar Albanians, Bosniaks; once Tito was gone it was inevitable. People must be controlled, ruled with strength and power, comrade. If they are not, there is nothing but fucking chaos and carnage. The West condemned us for Afghanistan. You funded and armed the Dushman – the Mujahideen – to kill our helicopters and our tanks. You laughed when the goat ordered our withdrawal. But one day, colonel, you'll wish you left us alone to finish the job. Mark my words."

"You don't believe we can all make this global renaissance work then?"

"Anyone who does is a fool. Fortunately, there are still some of us who believe in true sacrifice; putting one's country before oneself. You are a soldier, you know that." Zolnerowich turned to face Davenport directly. His eyes locked on Davenport's to emphasize his point. "In twenty years, we will be reclaiming every inch of Russian soil back from the separatists and the West will thank us for it."

Chapter One

Alex Morgan cast an appraising eye out over the pristine tranquility of the Pacific Ocean and wondered, not for the first time, how in any version of his life he could possibly have ended up here. In every direction he could see out to the far horizon without even a cloud in sight and only the slightest breath of wind. A seamless transition in cyan between sea and sky conjured the idea of being cocooned within the very center of paradise. He guessed it was a genuine feeling of serenity that he was experiencing. How long it would last he couldn't say, but for now it felt right and he was running with it. He pushed a hand through his thick mop of brown hair, realizing he was way past due for a haircut, and then began stroking the beard he'd been growing for the past couple of months. A very rare thing indeed, he thought; he hadn't had one since the desert. Standing only in a pair of swimmers and sporting a pair of well-worn Ray-Ban tortoise shell Wayfarers, Morgan breathed in deeply, sipped more black coffee and allowed himself the opportunity to thoroughly enjoy the stillness of this particular moment.

His shift wasn't for another hour, but the idea of staying in his lower-deck crew-quarters cabin didn't appeal, despite a standing order direct from the owner that the hired help were supposed to be invisible at all times unless they were doing something they were being paid for. Yeah, right. Morgan wasn't really one to abide by rules imposed by assholes and at this stage, based on the arrogance alone, Zolner definitely qualified. He was going to enjoy his coffee in peace and outside.

Despite his nautical ancestry apparently dating as far back as Sir Henry Morgan, Alex Morgan had never had much interest in boats – or the sea, for that matter. He considered himself more of a landlubber at heart, although he was dive qualified and had turned out to be quite good at it under the expert tutelage of his late friend, former US Navy SEAL Dave Sutherland. In a strange, roundabout sort of way, he decided he could blame Dave for his current situation. After all, if not for the diving experience he'd gained with Sutherland, he never would have got this job. Good old Dave. Bastard. It had been Sutherland who'd really got him interested, dragging him around the world on numerous dive quests when they'd been on breaks between missions for Intrepid. There'd been a lot of water under the bridge since his last mission. Dismantling the human trafficking empire established by Darja Voloshyn, aka the Night Witch, had come at a hefty price, most significant of which was Dave's murder in Hong Kong. Morgan himself had even come close to death in Belize not long after. Over most of the past year he had been through the hell of both personal and professional reconstruction as he dealt with the fallout. It all seemed like a lifetime ago, someone else's lifetime rather than his own.

Shutting down any deeper introspection, Morgan tossed the last mouthful of coffee over the side and, turning his back on the sea, gazed up at the stacked, multiple decks of the *Gemini* that disappeared beyond view into the blue sky above him.

The Superyacht *Gemini* was in every way a super yacht. Almost 300 feet long and 3000 tons, it had a master suite with 360-degree views and luxury that would rival the Royal Suite at the Ritz. Below that were a dozen staterooms, crew rooms, bars, dining areas, three tenders for ship-to-shore transfers, wave runners, a dive deck – everything. With a top speed of 18 knots, cruising at 15 knots, she'd been built by Derecktor in the US and was in a category reserved for the most prestigious private yachts in the world. Even with the fleeting exposure to the A-list standards of luxury he'd enjoyed with Charly Fleming, Morgan had never experienced anything on this scale. The past month he'd been aboard, he'd seen extremes of indulgence he'd never thought possible, or even thought morally defensible. But within the circles frequented by his employer extravagance was the norm, in fact it was expected. Meanwhile the minions, like Morgan, were required to remain below decks and only emerge as and when required. Of course, in fairness, it was slightly different for the security detail.

"Hey, new guy. You're eager." It was Norland, former US Army, who was also security detail 2IC. Morgan liked him.

"Me, eager? Nah. Just getting ready to take over in—" Morgan checked his trusted Tag Heuer "—thirty minutes. You must be ready for a kip. I can take over early if you like."

"Thanks, bro, but no thanks. You know what the bossman is like – if you're paid for twelve hours, you do twelve hours. Whether he's around or not."

"I keep hearing that. Where is he now?"

Norland pointed off the stern. There was a shotline tethered to the *Gemini* that disappeared below the surface and out of sight, reaching all the way down to the bottom, close to the wreck.

"Early dive. He wants to take some more footage of that fucking plane."

"The Helldiver, right?"

Norland nodded. "You've probably guessed, he's got a real thing about them. Tracks wrecks all over the world; doesn't care what condition they're in either. If there's a Helldiver to be found, he'll be there. That's why we've spent weeks out here trying to find this one and why we spent a shitload of time in and out of Indonesian waters last year, just because he heard a rumor there was a Helldiver wreck down there. He didn't find it the first time around but he found it on the return trip. He's obsessed with the fucking things; something to do with his first wreck dive when he was a young guy."

"What happened?"

"Nothing. Apparently he just liked that 'Helldiver' was kinda like his name, you know, the H-D, Hedeon. Now he uses the name 'Helldiver' as a sort of personal brand. Kinda like Madonna!" They laughed. "Anyways, when you've got as much money as he does, you can do whatever the fuck you want."

Morgan turned back to the water. "What time did he go out?"

"About forty-five minutes ago, give or take."

Morgan checked his watch. He knew their employer,

Hedeon Zolner, was renowned for being a damn good diver. He also knew that the Helldiver wreck Zolner was so curious about was submerged under fifty feet of water, hence their current position. With the tanks they were using, and an average consumption rate of around five gallons per hour, at fifty feet he would have around fifty minutes of dive time. "He's right on the limits of his air already. He should be coming up. Anyone go out with him?"

"Shit, no. He hates that, bro. Only dives alone when he's searching for those wrecks. He doesn't like the distraction of us 'incompetent assholes,' or so he says."

"Well, incompetent or not, we can't do much for him from up here while he's down there. Anything could happen to him and we wouldn't have a clue. He should be up by now."

A panicked call stopped everything.

"Help! Somebody, quickly. Sharks! Oh my God. Hedeon is still out there!"

Morgan's eyes locked onto the source of the commotion, the very top deck of the *Gemini*, the owner's deck. He could see Zolner's wife, Kristina, an auburn-haired, brown-eyed, over-indulged heiress, draping herself over the balustrade, waving her arms around to summon the attention of the minions. He followed her gesticulating and line of sight out to the suddenly energized waters above the Helldiver. He could see a definite surge of surface activity along with the fin or two that had drawn her concern.

"Fuck me," said Morgan. "Grab a rifle."

Norland disappeared as Morgan sprinted back to the dive room to grab his gear – Tusa face mask, Mares X-Stream fins and HUB Avantgarde integrated buoyancy compensator, weight, and regulator system. In no time he was back at the platform pulling on his dive booties.

17

As Norland returned with the rifle – a .308 Browning BAR Mark II Safari – Morgan kitted up, managing a quick look in the general direction of the sharks. He estimated that there was probably half-a-dozen of them in the immediate vicinity. It was impossible to tell how big or what type they were but their sudden appearance just off the *Gemini*'s stern and clear interest in whatever was going on beneath the surface suggested a top-end predator. In these waters that meant they were most likely tiger sharks. He hoped not.

"Deal with those if you can, without hitting us," he yelled at Norland, pointing toward the sharks. "I'll get Zolner." Without another word he pulled on his fins, slipped the mask down over his eyes, clamped the regulator mouthpiece between his teeth and dropped into the water.

The explosion of bubbles evaporated as the cool water grabbed him, dragging him down into the uncertainty of the deep blue-green water. He cleared his ears, then twisted around and kicked off, reaching for the shotline. Finding it was a godsend and keeping himself as close to it as possible, Morgan made the line the center of his universe and swam like hell straight for the ocean floor, his speed in check only to avoid over-pressure in his ears balanced by the need to constantly valsalva during the descent.

The threat of the sharks and his reservations over how Zolner might react to his sudden intrusion on the wreck dive dominated his thoughts, but he had to shut all that out and just find his boss. Whatever was happening down there he'd deal with it as it hit him. For all Morgan knew, Zolner was probably fine and already ascending the line, but his gut suggested otherwise and he tended to trust it.

Hedeon Zolner, billionaire, was the son of a former Russian General, Igor Zolnerowich. As a boy, the young Zolnerowich rose through the ranks of the Komsomol, the

Young Communist League, later getting noticed when he began exploring business opportunities during the economic reform era of Gorbachev's glasnost and perestroika in the late 1980s. In the nineties he benefitted extraordinarily under the mass privatization of state assets strategy introduced by Yeltsin. Critics claimed the influence of his father, a respected military figure much in favor with the political elite, saw him ideally situated during the initial privatization process, which, under the second wave known as the loans-for-shares scheme, resulted in the accumulation of vast resources and wealth by a select few who became known as the oligarchs. Consulting Wikipedia, Morgan discovered that he had shortened his name to Zolner in the late nineties when his business interests and public profile began to spill out of Russia and across Europe to England and the United States, an overtly deliberate attempt to distance himself from the association with his father's name and influence. By 2005 he had very cleverly adopted the unofficial moniker Helldiver almost exclusively. And in a world where major news stories lasted only as long as a Facebook feed, most people were oblivious to the travails of the Russian economy of the 1990s, and many didn't know that Helldiver, the eccentric businessman who occasionally appeared in the news, was even Russian. Nor did they care. Why would they?

Morgan kicked hard, the X-Stream fins powering him fast along the length of the shotline. Marine life fled in every direction while he selfishly barreled through their water. As he neared the ocean floor he pushed off the line and followed a short course due west through the coral toward the wreck. Butterfly fish, yellow tang, octopus, manta ray, moray eels; they were everywhere, but every one of them made way for the intruder. He kept checking for the sharks but couldn't make out any in his immediate area. Before he could allow himself the naïveté of feeling lucky, he caught sight of two large bodies passing closely, their size and a flash of their distinctive stripes confirming the species as their tails disappeared into the murk about five yards away. Their sudden proximity was unsettling. Morgan preferred it when he could see them; watching the speed with which they'd vanished into the darkness and not knowing where they'd vanished to or how quickly they could reappear put Morgan instantly on edge. But he couldn't be distracted by it. He had to find Zolner. He had to keep his head down and power on.

As the new guy on the security team, Morgan hadn't even been allowed within arms' reach of Helldiver, not once. Morgan was very definitely aware that he was on trial only and considered backup, an additional pair of hands just in case. As a result, he'd not been allowed to do any diving with Zolner, and as Norland had said, as far as diving the wreck was concerned, not even the most trusted members of the security team were allowed that privilege.

It didn't take long before he saw the wreck. He immediately gained speed, pulling his way even faster through the water. First he saw three misshapen blades of the propeller, and then the barely recognizable engine housing. The wings were basically invisible with just the hint of their span discernible. The tail section was completely gone. All that remained was broken, rusted and barnacled metal amid forests of the spectacular, multi-colored coral that had reclaimed the shell of the long dead beast, submerged for seventy years.

And there in the midst of it all, grappling desperately with something within the cockpit, was a panic-stricken Hedeon Zolner. He was a big guy, around six-four, heavy set, and despite the fact that he was only fifty-one, his hair was completely white. Down among the depths, the shock of white hair was like a beacon. A stream of blood was billowing from beneath him in thick plumes like black smoke, while circling high above, like vultures readying to swoop on a carcass, were the tiger sharks. There was three of them, all at least twelve feet long, one of them verging on fifteen, most likely a female. Morgan knew there'd be more nearby. Not good. He decided it was time to activate his Freedom7 SharkShield. Switching it on, he powered the last few feet straight for the wreck.

Zolner saw him approaching and began pointing wildly inside the cockpit. It took Morgan less than half a second to see that the man had caught his right foot and most of his calf within the collapsed, rusted and barnacled controls of the ancient Helldiver. Blood was erupting from a deep gash in his calf and all of his frantic clawing to free himself was getting him nowhere – if anything, it was making things worse. Morgan could also see that Zolner's diving rig was jammed among the wreckage of the rotting bomber and, worst of all, the gauges on his tank indicated that his air was as good as spent. Zolner had been so consumed by his struggle to get free that he hadn't noticed the sharks or how bad his air situation was, and just as Morgan was about to read the gauges, Zolner's air ran out. Everything was suddenly, painfully slow, everything except the sharks. And as Zolner looked up to Morgan for help, he finally noticed them.

Trying to communicate calmly and logically with a person who had just realized that they were being circled by half-a-dozen predatory sharks and that he had just run out of air was impossible, multiplying the complexity of their predicament exponentially. Zolner's blood was leaving his body in steady streams directly into the electroreceptor path of the shiver of tiger sharks now homing in on his location. Struggling to breathe, Zolner gave up on trying to free his leg and instead began grabbing for Morgan's regulator. Morgan fought to remain composed, deftly brushing aside Zolner's attempts while grabbing the second mouthpiece of the octopus regulator he'd dived with, forcing it into Zolner's mouth. Zolner took hold of it and began to steady his breathing while looking to Morgan for direction.

Then the first of the tiger sharks made an approach, circling within five feet of them. The second and third sharks followed suit. The speed of their movement caused a surge in the water that buffeted the men as the pack began their approach for attack. Zolner's eyes were wide with fear and he began to panic, striking irrationally at Morgan. All Morgan could do was take the beating against his rig while reaching for the six-inch titanium dive knife from the sheath attached to his right calf. The three sharks disappeared again, circling their prey and gathering more speed before the fast return and final attack. Morgan raised a threatening arm to quell Zolner's terror and then turned in the direction he expected the sharks to approach from. Sure enough, in seconds they reappeared, growing in size and menace as their heads and open jaws sped toward the Helldiver. Morgan braced, placing himself between the predators and the helplessly trapped Zolner. The knife was a paltry deterrent but it was his last line of defense. It was in his hand and poised, ready to strike at an eye or snout, wherever he could reach first to inflict an injury. Behind him Zolner was rigid with fear, his hands holding on tightly to Morgan's left arm. The tigers were within just a few feet, in dive formation, gaining speed, getting bigger and bigger. Morgan's breathing was steady but strained, the adrenalin threatening to tear him apart. They closed in fast. Morgan's eyes locked onto those of the leader: the biggest of the pack. His hand curled even more tightly around the knife and his body coiled, ready to counter-attack. And just as he prepared to strike, all three of them suddenly turned away; one, two, three, each in succession had closed in for the kill only to pull away abruptly at the final moment. As the first three withdrew, two more − lower in the pecking order than the others but just as hungry from the scent of blood in the water − made their move, spiraling down from directly above the wreck. By now Zolner was still attempting to free himself. Morgan redirected his counter-attack stance, readying to strike upward into the flesh beneath the lower jaws of the sharks but again, they balked and pulled away.

In that moment Morgan knew that the SharkShield was doing what it was supposed to do. The length of thick antennae cable trailing behind him was creating an electronic field that caused a reaction in the electroreceptors located in the snout of each shark. Once the sharks came within range of the electronic field they were instantly affected by it and withdrew. Sutherland had introduced Morgan to it ages ago but until today, his only point of reference had been the theory. He was fucking glad it worked in practice.

He returned his attention to a thoroughly bewildered Zolner and set to work on getting him free. He began with Zolner's rig, which was caught on strands of rusted metal that had once been the aft headrest for the tail gunner. With the rig clear, Zolner had more freedom to move and, eventually, to wriggle his calf and foot free with some help from Morgan pulling back the offending wreckage that had caused the restriction. A much relieved Zolner finally pulled clear. Morgan cut some strips from Zolner's wetsuit and quickly bound the gash. It would be enough to get him back to the surface and aboard the *Gemini*, but it'd need proper attention soon.

Holding Zolner close, tiger sharks still circling and the SharkShield cable trailing behind, Morgan kicked off, taking them both toward the surface and the clear blue sky.

Chapter Two

Captain Farooq Chaudry watched Honey, the girl he called
his muse, wander naked from the bedroom of his deluxe
suite to the bathroom. He loved the way the muscles of her
ass tightened as she walked and how the butterfly tattoo on
her back flew with the unabashed freedom of her movement. He propped himself up on one elbow among the
pillows so he could enjoy every step she took. She paused
just long enough to smack herself on each cheek before
disappearing to the shower. He loved it every time.

"You tease me, Honey," he called out to her. "It's not
good for my heart. I'm an old man, remember?"

"You're only forty-two," she called back to him. "That's
not too old. Besides, watching my ass is good for you. It'll
keep you young."

He heard the taps squeal and the water bursting from
the shower head. It definitely will, he thought. He lived for
these moments with her and the freedom of being away
from home, as far removed as possible from his responsibilities as a husband and father. Now that he regularly flew out

25

from Singapore he was establishing a second life here. His eldest son was already at university in Islamabad and the other two were not far behind him. All three of them were self-sufficient, living their own lives. And his wife was only interested in the paycheck that being married to an international airline captain provided. She didn't care anymore if he was there or not.

The shower taps squealed again and the sound of rushing water stopped. When he looked up again, Honey was quietly watching him from the doorway. He smiled at her.

"So, have I convinced you to finally leave her and move here to Singapore with me?" she said, water dripping from her naked body onto the carpet in the anteroom. His dumbfounded silence caused her to laugh. "I always know what you're thinking, Fooky. You can't hide anything from me." She lifted her towel and walked back into the bedroom, dabbing the white cotton all over her damp body.

Chaudry was mesmerized by her. He still could not believe his luck; a beautiful 24-year-old Russian nanny, blond and blue eyed, had fallen in love with him, here in Singapore. All in the space of just a few months. But he deserved it. He deserved her. He knew that. Tomorrow he had a Singapore to London flight, via Beijing with a crew he'd never flown with. From London he'd fly directly home to Islamabad and the drudgery of his normal life. But tonight was still his and he had decisions to make.

"Let's go out for dinner and talk," he said. "We'll go somewhere special."

"Oh, so you want me to get dressed now, just so we can go to a silly old restaurant," she said, back near the bed. As she adjusted the towel she shared with him again her beautiful body. "Are you sure you wouldn't prefer to eat in ... again?"

"You're an evil woman," he said. "I'm a respectable man. I can't spend my last night of freedom locked in this den of debauchery with you!"

She laughed at him. He reached out and grabbed the edge of her towel. She let it fall away and climbed back into bed, straddling him. He reached up and pulled her down to him, kissing her neck and breasts.

There was a short, sharp rap on the door. "Room service," a male voice called.

"Fuck!" He whispered in her ear. "Not now."

She giggled. "Maybe I've arranged a surprise for you, Fooky. Champagne, perhaps? Leave it to me. You can hardly answer the door with that thing sticking out everywhere, now, can you?"

Chaudry groaned with frustration. Honey slid off him, retrieved her towel from the floor, wrapped it tightly around herself and walked out to the door. He heard her open it.

"You took your time," he heard her say at the door.

"Get dressed," came the reply. An accent. Spanish? "Do it in the bathroom and stay there until I tell you to come out."

"Honey, what's going on?" Chaudry was standing now, reaching for his pants. This didn't sound right. He couldn't see the man at the door yet. He walked into the foyer. Honey turned to him.

"Sorry, Fooky. It's nothing personal. And face it, darling, you're never going to leave that fat old wife of yours."

"I said get dressed," the accented voice ordered Honey again and then he appeared in the room.

Farooq Chaudry didn't know where to look or what to think. Honey collected some clothes from her suitcase and then disappeared back into the bathroom, and a well-dressed middle-aged man, Latin American, swarthy and immaculately groomed, was now standing in the middle of the room.

"Who the hell are you?" Chaudry demanded. He was unsteady on his feet, zipping up his pants. "Get the fuck out of my room!"

The man didn't address Chaudry at all. Instead he just looked back out into the corridor, and beckoned someone else in to join them.

Two more men entered. One was young, fair skinned, tall and big. He stood at the door until the third man walked in. Then the young guy closed the door quietly, removed a pistol from the waistband of his jeans to stand guard. Chaudry was dumbstruck. Despite the shock of the intrusion, the intimidation of their sudden, unequivocal control of his situation and the appearance of the gun, it was the last man to enter who held Chaudry's attention. He was almost identical to Farooq Chaudry in every way: about five-nine, a hundred and sixty pounds, jet-black short hair with flecks of gray at the temples, a slight paunch around the middle. Posture, physique, everything matched – even his watch was identical. Their facial features were so similar that only someone intimately familiar with Chaudry could possibly tell them apart.

"What is this?" Chaudry heard himself asking. "What do you want?"

"What is this? What do you want?" the third man mimicked.

"Perfect," said the Latin American, who had now positioned himself between them, studying them minutely. "This is the new you. Quite a resemblance, don't you think? He even sounds exactly like you."

A shudder of despair rippled through Chaudry's body. He could see where this was going.

"Wait. I know you," he said to the Latino. The penny had finally dropped. "You're Salazar, the recruiter. But ... why me?"

"You look like him. He looks like you. That's all. Nothing personal. His name was Reza but now it is Chaudry, Farooq Chaudry. Of course, that means you have to disappear. We can't have two Farooq Chaudrys flying around the skies now, can we?" Salazar took a sudden pace forward. He produced a hypodermic, flicked the protective sheath from the needle and jammed it straight into Chaudry's neck.

The last thing Farooq Chaudry was aware of was Salazar forcing the needle into his neck and Reza, his replacement, helping to lower him to the floor. Someone said, "OK, get that laundry trolley in here."

Then, nothing.

Chapter Three

OAHU, HAWAIIAN ISLANDS

The Riva 33 Aquariva was luxury in the extreme. Thirty feet long, ten feet across the beam and capable of a very respectable forty knots at top speed. She was the *Gemini*'s principal tender for the exclusive use of the Zolners and their guests. The high sheen of the painted mahogany hatches, decking and cabinets, set against the rich burgundy of the upholstery and cushions and the stainless steel of the bespoke fittings, spoke of old-world luxury. In a word: classic. Morgan was enjoying every minute of the trip back to Oahu, a much more comfortable ride than the navy boats he'd frequented in his life. His old life. He could actually get very used to this new life he'd found himself. Or, could he?

Twenty-four hours, give or take, after he'd rescued Zolner from a certain death, either by drowning or as shark bait, Morgan had been unexpectedly summoned for a personal audience with Helldiver himself. Morgan didn't like being summoned by anybody, but Zolner was paying him, and Morgan, after all, had willingly accepted the work. Earlier, Norland had been dispatched to find Morgan and deliver the message, *He wants to see you. And grab all your gear; you're going ashore*. With that, Morgan had begrudgingly stripped off the T-shirt and shorts he'd been wearing, ready for some down time at the end of his shift, and pulled on a pair of beige chinos and a navy polo shirt before stepping into deck shoes, grabbing his bags and heading for the dive deck where the Aquariva had been waiting for him. He'd neither heard nor seen anything of Zolner since delivering the billionaire unceremoniously into the waiting hands of the crew back aboard the *Gemini* early yesterday morning; Zolner had been whisked away by eager hands keen to impress the boss, all under the careful direction of Zolner's wife, Kristina, the "princess" – or so the staff called her.

Morgan remembered that Kristina Zolner's reaction to the whole rescue scenario had shown a great deal more control and poise than he would have credited her with. All he knew about her was that she came from a wealthy family, was an heiress of some description, and – in Morgan's view anyway – was not exactly the type you'd expect to be so calm under pressure. Maybe he had prejudged her. She was certainly a lot calmer when Morgan had returned her husband to the *Gemini* than she had been when she'd spotted the sharks off the stern. That was fair enough. By the time they'd emerged, she'd recovered from the shock sufficiently enough to make damn sure that Hedeon Zolner was pulled from the water with kid gloves, while Alex Morgan was left to clamber aboard unaided until Norland finally managed to get past the entourage and help him. Zolner was put into the Aquariva and taken straight back to Honolulu for urgent medical attention with Kristina at his side. Morgan could have been missing a leg for all anybody knew.

Now here he was, the one being whisked back to Oahu in the lap of luxury and, as it happened, also with Kristina at his side. It was incredible how quickly everything could change.

As they sliced effortlessly across the wave tops toward the island, the skyline of the capital Honolulu, the comings and goings of the international airport and the majesty of Diamond Head all began to materialize. Kristina Zolner was giving last-minute instructions to the crewman at the wheel. She was wearing a short summer dress that showed off her legs and a pair of sunglasses that covered most of her face.

"So, what's this all about then?" Morgan asked once she'd finished issuing her orders. "Any chance of a heads up?"

"Hedeon wants to see you," she said over the noise of the engine, turning suddenly to join him on the curved bench at the back of the boat. Morgan had heard she was Eastern European, so – despite the hint of an American undercurrent – the accent made sense. She sat closer than he thought she should. He didn't mind. "He wants you to help him with something important. Why? Are you nervous?"

"Not at all," he replied. "I don't get nervous."

"That makes sense. A dangerous man like you wouldn't have much call for being scared of anything."

"What makes you think I'm dangerous?"

"We've been checking out your CV. It's all terribly exciting." Was she flirting with him? It certainly seemed that way. She held his gaze for a moment too long, smiled briefly and then turned her attention back to the coastline. Up front, the crewman answered a cellphone and then he turned briefly and held it out to her. Morgan watched as Mrs. Zolner stood to take the call.

The wind racing through the long hair of an attractive

woman certainly had a lot to answer for. That said, this was the closest he'd ever been to her. He realized that it was the impression of her that men probably found most attractive rather than the detail. The heiress tag, the tight, faultless body, the flowing auburn hair, make-up, jewelry, sunglasses, choice of clothes – everything perfectly contrived to create the brand that was Kristina Zolner. Morgan guessed she knew she had an effect on men and probably enjoyed the fact that they all knew she was way out of their league and, as Zolner's wife, completely off limits. It would give her a sense of control he suspected she'd like.

When she returned the cellphone to the crewman, any of the warmth she'd shown Morgan during their brief chat had evaporated and she was suddenly all icy efficiency. What had the call been about? They were just moments away from the island of Oahu now, following a wide curve around to starboard, heading for the Ala Wai Yacht Harbor. The twin Yanmar marine diesel engines and their 380 horses reared as the crewman reined her in and brought her alongside the marina.

"There's our transport. It'll take us out to the house at Diamond Head where Hedeon is waiting for us. Better get your gear ready."

An Agusta Westland AW-109 Grand helicopter was turning and burning at the northern end of the marina where a section of the car parking area had been closed off to make way for it. The boat bumped lightly against the jetty and a young marina attendant appeared and began tying them off.

Meanwhile, Morgan did as he was told, grabbing his duffel bags and suit carrier and slinging them up onto the jetty. The crewman had shut down the boat and was taking care of Kristina Zolner's bags. Morgan jumped ashore, turned and held out a hand for Kristina. She took it, thanked him and headed for the chopper. Morgan and the crewman followed in silence.

Within two minutes they were airborne, swinging back out over the ocean and traveling fast, southeast along the golden-edged turquoise seahorse that was the coastal strip of the Ala Wai Canal, Waikiki Beach and Diamond Head.

So, the house at Diamond Head, he thought. And then what?

One thing he'd observed about Zolner was that he was a very private person, secretive to some extent. Certainly not the high-profile billionaire of the Branson or Gates variety.

For the first time since he'd accepted the job on Zolner's security team, Alex Morgan began wondering what he'd got himself into.

Whatever it was, he was about to find out.

Chapter Four

KATAK AIRLINES FLIGHT KTA 712 - SINGAPORE TO
BEIJING, VIA KUALA LUMPUR

It was 1800 hours at Kuala Lumpur International Airport, getting close to take-off at 1910, and the crew of Flight KTA 712 were keen to get underway. It had been a long day, departing Changi Airport at 1000 with an eight-hour layover in KL. Most of the crew were changing over in Beijing but with the flight not scheduled to arrive in Beijing Capital International Airport until just after 0100, the day was definitely becoming protracted. The mood among the crew was bright and professional but subdued. Perfect.

Adnan 'Rez' Reza flew JF-17s as a squadron leader in the Pakistan Air Force. He commanded the first JF-17 squadron to see action in Operation Rah-e-Nijat in 2009, yet despite his many successes against the Taliban, his reluctant participation in the infidel-led operation to destroy his Muslim brothers confirmed emphatically where his loyalties lie. Within a year he had resigned his commission from the PAF and offered his life to jihad. His services were welcomed by his brothers, who were ready to guide his atonement for his sins. And so, he was told to establish himself as a commercial airline pilot and await activation.

Tonight, after five long years, the moment had come. Tonight he was flying not as Adnan Reza but as Captain Farooq Chaudry, the now dead man whose identity Reza had assumed and the man whose name would forever be associated with this night.

Reza sat in the left-hand seat, the captain's seat, and turned to the first officer, Safwan Khan, whom he'd met in Singapore at the commencement of the flight. Reza had kept their interaction professional but friendly enough, and avoided any unnecessary conversations during the layover in KL, choosing instead to spend his final hours in solitude and prayer. He didn't want any distractions. Thankfully Khan had taken the hint and maintained his distance.

"Are we prepared for flight, first officer?" Reza asked, preserving the formality.

"I've conducted the preflight inspection of the aircraft, captain. Everything looks good. Here is our flight plan." Khan handed him a clipboard containing the airline's predetermined flight plan for the journey to Beijing. "The aircraft has been fully fueled and I have completed the weight and balance calculations and loaded them into the computer. We have one hundred and forty-nine souls onboard."

"Excellent," Reza replied. "How are the skies ahead of us?"

"I need to draw your attention to some bad weather, captain. It's just been officially declared a cyclonic weather system, Cyclone Penciptaan, and it is currently due west of northern Malaysia. It began as a tropical depression over the Gulf of Thailand a little over a week ago and has been moving steadily west-nor-west across Thailand and

Malaysia to the Andaman Sea over the last few days. The latest report is that it has developed into a cyclonic storm and appears to be maintaining its current course toward the Bay of Bengal. Our flight plan keeps us well clear and to the east of it, but we may experience some rough weather as we approach the Gulf of Thailand."

"Very well," Reza replied. "We'll monitor the weather as we approach the coast and if necessary we'll take the aircraft further east. What are our options in the area if we have to put down?"

"As we leave Malaysia over Kelantan, we have the Sultan Ismail Petra Airport in Kota Bharu. Further north once we're over the Gulf of Thailand there's Hat Yai International or Narathiwat, domestic. Of course heading for either of those would require a change of course to the west," Khan replied, "toward the weather system. Further west, we have Langkawi or Phuket. Beyond the Gulf to the north would be Ho Chi Minh or Phnom Penh."

"Very well," said Reza. "Hopefully we won't have to consider any of them but let's ensure that we factor them into the flight plan as options. Please proceed."

Khan continued his briefing on the technical aspects of the aircraft's readiness, including some additional weather-related issues further north over China.

"Any problems with the crew? I expect they'd be reasonably well rested after a few hours off, yes?"

"Yes, captain," Khan replied. "I believe that most of them are ready to take some time off in Beijing, but they'll be fine."

"Very well, let's get underway."

With the engines already humming and the first officer beginning the radio check-in process with KL air traffic control, Reza welcomed the passengers and crew aboard over the PA, briefed them generally about the flight and, without going into any detail, mentioned the potential for some rough weather ahead. Soon, the routine of a standard take-off had passed, the landing gear was up, the flaps and slats retracted, and the passengers and crew of KTA 712 began to settle in for a long flight. Thirty minutes later, autopilot had brought the aircraft to its programed cruising altitude, the captain extinguished the FASTEN SEAT BELTS sign and the crew began to serve the evening meal. A female steward entered the cockpit, bringing in meals for the captain and first officer. Reza wondered why she was not wearing a veil. Another of the new breed. She did not linger, simply handed the meals over, exchanged some pleasantries and left, resecuring the cockpit with the help of Khan.

Khan mumbled something about the bathroom and Reza heard him close the door. Calmly Reza checked their current position. They were making good time and fast approaching the northeastern coast of Malaysia. He consulted the latest information concerning the status of Cyclone Penciptaan. Warnings to aircraft and shipping to avoid the Andaman Sea due east of Phuket were prevalent. The intensity of the storm had increased from Category 1 to Category 3.

The plan had been in train many months, only the opportunity was required. And when that opportunity presented itself in the form of the tropical depression in the Gulf of Thailand ten days earlier, the scene was set. Farooq Chaudry was finally replaced and Adnan Reza's fate was assured. Of course, nobody could ever have foreseen that the storm would intensify to such magnitude.

Khan rejoined Reza at the controls and, as they had previously agreed, began to eat his meal.

Reza heard himself making general observations about the weather system as Khan ate. He noted that his tone was relaxed yet confident, instilling in Khan an equally calm and relaxed state of mind. While the first officer had been in the bathroom, Reza had removed the fork from the cutlery pack of his dinner tray and placed it under his right thigh. During training for this mission, he'd been advised to avoid the knife. The propensity for the long blade to catch on any number of items around and upon the central control console that separated the captain and first officer, or for it to be deflected if the strike was not perfectly aligned, presented too much room for error within the confined space and range of movement that were available to him. Therefore, the fork was preferred. It enabled him to grasp and conceal the handle completely with only the four short prongs protruding beyond the soft edge of his right hand. He glanced across the controls and noted that Khan had just taken another mouthful of food and was chewing.

Reza drew the fork out from under his thigh, positioning it within his hand out of Khan's view. He took a slow, deep breath, leaned imperceptibly over to his right and then brought the weapon up above the central console. Before the movement had been noticed by the first officer, Reza struck directly at Khan's carotid artery with unrestrained force, repeating the strike three more times in quick succession.

Khan's meal fell from his retractable tray and spilled over his legs to the floor. His hands clutched uselessly at his throat as he instinctively tried to stem the flow of blood while choking on food that was only partially swallowed. The combination of hemorrhaging wounds, shattered larynx and food-jammed pharynx made any form of verbal communication impossible.

Reza stood, pulled the rapidly expiring Khan awkwardly from the first officer's seat to the floor, placed his right foot on the man's throat and rested his full weight upon it. Thirty seconds later, Khan had died of shock and suffocation.

Reza resumed the captain's seat, buckled himself back in, disengaged autopilot and reset the aircraft's flight plan for a heading west-nor-west, directly toward the Andaman Sea.

The center of Category 3 Cyclone Penciptaan.

Chapter Five

OAHU, HAWAIIAN ISLANDS

Following one of Zolner's personal assistants, a young American guy, solidly built with an immaculately trimmed beard, who'd introduced himself only as Simon, Morgan made his way from the sitting room – where he'd been cooling his heels since Kristina Zolner had dropped him there – through the twists and turns and corridors of the Zolner's palatial home. Easily in the twenty-five to thirty million range, the house was a Kahala beachfront property located on Kahala Avenue, one of the most prestigious addresses on the island of Oahu. It was an 18th-century French design nestled at the base of Diamond Head with panoramic views of the Pacific Ocean, oceanfront lawn and a hundred feet of private beach. Inside, everything was white, cream or gold, and every piece of furniture he laid eyes on complemented the French period design. For the first time in his life Morgan was up to his neck in the affluent treacle only the mega-rich could afford to immerse themselves in and he felt it with every cushioned step upon the ankle-deep plush pile carpets that carried him effort-lessly through all of it.

Morgan found himself genuinely curious about what Zolner might have to say to him. The past few months had been relatively quiet for Morgan and he had to admit that his social skills could probably do with a major overhaul. He'd been leading a solitary, bordering on reclusive, lifestyle since everything had come to a head at the end of the Night Witch operation. The trip from *Gemini* back to Oahu aboard the Aquariva, followed by the chopper flight down to Diamond Head, had unexpectedly rekindled his memory of the extraction by sea from Belize, when George Hemsworth and AJ Armstrong had returned to collect him and Jovana from the beach. They'd rendezvoused twelve miles offshore with a rigid-hulled inflatable boat from the RFA *Wave Knight*, a British fleet tanker of the Royal Fleet Auxiliary, and Morgan had bid farewell to Hemsworth and Armstrong. Then the RHIB took Morgan and Jovana out to the *Wave Knight*, the tanker steamed north toward the Florida Keys and they were eventually transferred aboard the *Wave Knight*'s AW101 Merlin, along with the prisoners who'd survived the gun battle, to the US Naval Air Station *Key West*. Everything then was pretty much a blur of handing the prisoners over to the FBI, placing Jovana into the care of the Interpol liaison officer, and then returning once again to Intrepid headquarters in London.

He shrugged away his thoughts as he followed in Simon's wake up a lavish cream marble spiral staircase that delivered them squarely into the center of Zolner's private living areas. At the top of the stairs, Simon turned and waved him on to the next stage in the conveyance process.

"Out here." Rodenko, Zolner's head of security and personal bodyguard, stood in the middle of a quarter-mile of glass doors that looked out onto a balcony the size of a football field and beyond to an unimpeded view of the ocean. Morgan didn't like Rodenko. Rodenko obviously didn't like Morgan much either. The location and views more than made up for it.

Rodenko slid the door open just as a well-dressed man, who looked to be mid-fifties, Latin American and well-groomed, was finishing up his farewells with the Zolners. He exited as Morgan was being ushered in. Morgan brushed past him, stepping over the threshold from the plush carpet and silence of the home's interior out into the sunshine. Rodenko remained inside, reluctantly it seemed, like he'd been told to "stay", and silently closed the door once Morgan was outside.

Hedeon Zolner was standing in front of a huge TV screen that appeared to be able to retract into a recess in the wall. His shoulder-length white hair was unkempt and tinged with gold in the late afternoon sun. He was in a polo shirt, shorts and bare feet. His right leg was bandaged between knee and ankle and Morgan noticed he was favoring it. Zolner's attention was glued to CNN and rolling satellite images of what looked like storms over Southeast Asia heading west across the Bay of Bengal toward the subcontinent. The weather coverage was interspersed with file images of a Katak Airlines A320 and footage of military aircraft apparently conducting search operations. Kristina Zolner was to Morgan's left, draped across a semicircular sofa that ran around the southeastern boundary of the balcony surrounding a low table covered in a variety of fresh fruits and canapés. Sipping on a cocktail, her attention was also locked onto the coverage. She saw Morgan first as he came through the door.

"Oh, hello, Morgan."

"Hello, Mrs. Zolner."

"Ah!" Zolner turned immediately from the TV screen and smiled broadly the moment he saw Morgan. He walked over awkwardly and shook Morgan's hand. "Thank you for coming." His accent was well-heeled Russian tinged with that same slight American twang many Europeans seemed to pick up when they learn English. Most likely because many would have learned it by watching American films and TV shows.

"That doesn't look good," Morgan said, glancing toward the TV. "Something recent? I haven't seen much of the news lately."

"Overnight, apparently." Yep, Russian. "It appears that the aircraft flew directly into the path of a cyclone. A hundred and fifty people on board, they say. Terrible."

"Jesus!" Morgan replied. "Any word from the cockpit before it happened?"

"Nothing. From take-off in Kuala Lumpur, everything was routine with no indication of any problems and then complete radio silence from the time they left the northeast coast of Malaysia. Malaysian air traffic control lost them until they were picked up by Thai military air traffic control well to the west of Phuket, completely off their expected course to Beijing. Extraordinary; truly, extraordinary."

"How many does that make now?" Morgan said, remembering there'd been similar occurrences in recent months. "Two or three, at least?"

"I believe this is the fourth," said Kristina.

Zolner and his wife exchanged an almost imperceptible look, but Morgan caught it and sensed some private issue between them. Then Zolner limped carefully back to the table, picked up two glasses of what Morgan presumed to be scotch, complete with bobbing ice cubes, and offered one to him.

"Anyway, enough talk about disasters," said Zolner. "I heard you like single malt?"

"I do," Morgan replied, accepting the drink.

"This one's the fifty-year-old Glenfiddich. It's my favourite; *za váše zdoróv'je!*"

"Cheers," replied Morgan, raising the glass in response before taking a brief, restrained drink. Zolner did the same. The warmth and bite of the drink instantly told Morgan it was exactly as Zolner had said.

"Good?"

"Very. Thank you. My budget only gets me as far as the eighteen-year-old," Morgan replied good-humoredly. "This is a rare treat. How's the leg?"

"I'm lucky to have a leg at all, or even a head on my shoulders. But I do, and I have you to thank for that. What you did took some real balls, my friend. I don't believe anyone else on my crew would ever have thought to do the same. Not even Rodenko," said Zolner, gesturing toward the closed door.

"I'm sure he would have. I just happened to be closest."

"Bullshit. From what I've been told, you reacted instantly. Kristina saw it all. You didn't hesitate to get in the water, even though there were all those fucking sharks swimming around out there. I mean, Jesus. You must be crazy."

Morgan took another drink. He was uncomfortable with all the praise and he couldn't tell where Zolner was going with it.

"It's what you pay us to do, isn't it? Protect you, I mean."

"Let's sit down, please," Zolner said, offering Morgan a seat on the sofa before joining his wife directly across the table. Morgan felt them both appraising him microscopically, especially Kristina.

"My husband and I are very interested in you, Alex. Can I call you Alex? It's not often we take such an interest in people who work for us. But you saved Hedeon's life without hesitation and that means a lot to us both."

Morgan remained quiet.

"So, we asked to see your resume," said Zolner. "Very impressive. Former major. Paratrooper. Won the Military Cross for gallantry in Afghanistan, the George Medal for evacuating British workers from the middle of the civil war in Malfajiri, and a string of other decorations. Now, I understand, you only work freelance? With experience like yours, you should be running your own show and living it up a little. Getting other people to do the work. You must tell me, how the hell did you end up here?"

"You really want to know?"

"Yes," said Kristina. "We really do."

"Well, it's pretty straightforward and really not all that interesting, I'm afraid. When I left the army I didn't want to be tied down anymore. I'd had enough of being told what to do, and to this day I make a point of avoiding corporate jobs. I only take things that interest me. That's why I work freelance. A friend of a friend connected me with Norland about a vacancy in your security team and I thought, why not? I was at a loose end, it was different from anything else I'd done before and you only needed someone for two months. I figured if it wasn't for me then it's only a short-term gig. So, here I am."

"That's it?" Zolner asked.

"I told you it wasn't that interesting."

"I think you get off on the rush," said Kristina. "The

idea of driving a desk would kill you. You prefer the unexpected. Am I right?"

"Pretty much."

"How long have you been with us now – six, seven weeks? When this contract is done, what then? Have you thought about that?" she asked.

"I'm happy to stay on if you still need me, but I'll understand if you don't. I knew this job wasn't forever. Besides, I'm not much of a boat kinda guy. I'm a lot more useful on land than at sea."

"All evidence to the contrary," Zolner laughed. "I like that you don't give a shit, Morgan. You're a take-it-or-leave-it guy. That's the way I am, too, and that's why I want you to keep working for me, but not as one of the troops. I have plans for you. Are you interested?"

"Sure, I suppose. It depends what you have in mind."

"I have some meetings to attend while we're here in Honolulu and sometimes in business, relationships can be tested, strained even; which is why I place a great deal of priority on our personal protection, especially when I have my Kristina with me."

"I understand," Morgan replied. "Although, at this point, I must admit that I don't have any specific knowledge about what it is you do. Apart from the publicly available stuff: oil and gas, aluminium, technology, munitions and military aircraft. That's about it."

"Very good, but we can get into all the details later. For now, suffice to say that I invest in the future and right now I'm working within a highly competitive, highly volatile operating environment. Do you understand?"

"I do," Morgan replied. "So, these meetings – you're expecting some trouble."

"Possibly. With billions of dollars at stake, it is quite normal to expect a certain type of person to react to situations or negotiations unpredictably. The people I'm currently dealing with, they are very emotional individuals, prone to sometimes violent outbursts. A man has to take precautions."

Morgan sipped the Glenfiddich. "How does this all relate to me, though?" he said. "I'm an ex-soldier, not a businessman."

"We have a meeting this afternoon with some of these people. I'd like you to come along to observe how we conduct these meetings. You won't have to do anything. Just watch, listen and then tell me what you think later. Are you interested?"

"Of course," Morgan replied. The pit of his stomach told him he was.

"Excellent. Well, we leave in an hour. You'll need to be in a suit. Rodenko will show you where to get ready."

"Very well." Morgan stood to leave.

"Oh, and Morgan," Zolner said.

"Yes."

"Observer or not, better bring a gun."

Chapter Six

An hour later, Alex Morgan was in a tropical worsted navy suit, one made for him by his tailor just off Savile Row on Conduit Street back in London, Somerville and Son. He'd matched it with a pale blue cotton shirt, black knitted tie and black brogues. He was carrying a Heckler & Koch VP9 9mm automatic in an inside-the-waistband holster on his right hip, with a couple of spare clips on his left side. He was sitting in the front passenger seat of a Cadillac Escalade SUV with another guy from Zolner's security crew he'd just met at the wheel. In the back were two more from the security crew. No one was talking. They were driving northwest along the Lunalilo Freeway, back into Honolulu, to pick up a passenger, a guy by the name of Tengku, apparently the business associate Zolner had spoken about. Meanwhile, Hedeon and Kristina Zolner had taken off in an identical car with Rodenko and their driver heading inland somewhere. Morgan's car would meet them up there once he had made the pickup.

After about twenty minutes, Morgan's SUV eventually

pulled up at an address in Bishop Street, which Morgan noted was in the center of a number of foreign consulates, and saw a man standing on the sidewalk up ahead, obviously waiting for them. Tengku. He was sharply dressed in a lightweight suit, open-neck shirt and sunglasses, late thirties, maybe early forties, and appeared to be Asian, maybe Malaysian or Indian, Morgan couldn't be sure. There was a hint of arrogance in the way he held himself, the type who was used to feeling important, although there did seem to be a level of agitation about him too, even nervousness. Morgan couldn't put his finger on it. It was just a gut feeling based on about three seconds of observation. Instinct. That same instinct followed through, running a scan of the immediate surrounds. Morgan surmised that anyone with business interests on the scale that had been suggested to him back at the house and who, on first impressions at least, appeared so concerned even at the prospect of meeting with Zolner would surely not wait alone without any form of backup or top cover of his own. Despite knowing that, Morgan couldn't see any, although that didn't mean there wasn't any. He kept his eyes open.

The Cadillac pulled up to the curb and one of the security team members in the back leaned over and opened the curbside rear door from the inside. Tengku climbed in, closed the door and before he was seated, the central locking clicked into action and the driver had them underway again.

The bang from the rear of the SUV shook them all.

Morgan's HK VP9 was instantly out of the holster and transferred across to his left hand. "Step on it!" he yelled.

The driver slammed his foot down on the accelerator and the vehicle powered away. Morgan turned in his seat to cover his side of the vehicle while the others covered the rear. Then he caught sight of the source of the noise. Down the road behind them, a cyclist was collecting himself from the tumble he'd taken when he'd run into the SUV as it pulled unexpectedly out into the traffic. He seemed dazed but physically OK. Morgan knew they wouldn't stop. That wasn't the drill. He reholstered the VP9.

"Stand down," he said, adding, "Ease off," to the driver. "We're all clear."

Now that the pickup had been done, and the minor crisis already forgotten, the security guys settled back into their positions: one sitting in a third-row fold-out seat with Tengku seated in front of him, the second beside Tengku, directly behind Morgan. It was difficult for Morgan to see Tengku and in this line of work it wasn't the done thing to turn around when you were just the hired help unless you were actually engaging someone, verbally or otherwise. Fortunately, the driver's rear-view mirror had a small fish-eye mirror attached to the right-hand side that enabled whoever was in the passenger seat to monitor what was going on in the back, too. It wasn't ideal but it was enough.

For now, Tengku was sitting quietly albeit, it seemed, expectantly.

"You know the routine," the security guy behind Morgan said. "You gotta wear this." Morgan watched through the fish-eye as a blindfold was produced and handed across. Tengku didn't protest. He simply took hold of it resignedly, then wrapped it around his head and tied it off. The security guy leaned over and verified that it was on securely. So, a familiar custom. Morgan watched for a while but nothing was happening other than the security crew both still holding their VP9s.

The driver worked the limousine around the consulate area to head southeast back along the Lunalilo Freeway and a few minutes later was turning left toward the high country of the Honolulu Forest Reserve.

Morgan was calm about it all on the basis that Tengku was clearly familiar with the routine. He so far hadn't uttered a word. The driver took the SUV up into the hills until they ran out of sealed road and the tires bit into gravel. Up here the trees grew high, right up to the edge of the road. After less than a minute they reached a wide, isolated area of the road, sheltered by the canopy of the forest, and pulled over. The security guys got out of the car with Tengku sandwiched between then. The driver indicated to Morgan to stay in the car. Outside, the blindfold remained on while the security guys conducted a body search of Tengku: one covering while the other did the scrunch and pat down. They obviously couldn't do it on the sidewalk in the center of Honolulu and Tengku still seemed indifferent to it all. More of their established routine. What the hell was Zolner into?

They were soon back on their way, continuing high into the reserve. A few minutes later the driver pulled off to the right and followed a narrow, almost overgrown, track for about 300 yards until they reached a small clearing, again sheltered by the canopy. A second SUV, Zolner's SUV, was stationary in the center. Rodenko and the driver were standing outside, one on either side. What the fuck was going on?

Morgan's SUV eased to a halt and everyone got out, including Morgan. Rodenko had already told him where to stand, so Morgan dutifully took up his position at ten o'clock in relation to Zolner's SUV. He received an acknowledging nod from Rodenko, confirming that he was where he was supposed to be. Then he watched as Tengku was walked, still in the blindfold, across to Zolner's car. The door didn't open but the rear window did, no more than four inches; just enough for a conversation to take place but not enough to see clearly inside. So, Zolner wasn't even getting out of the car for this guy, yet they went to all this trouble to bring him up here. The discussion was initially conducted in subdued tones and was barely audible from where Morgan stood. Then Morgan saw Tengku's hands go up to his face as they might if he'd received a shock or bad news of some kind. Then his knees bent, apparently at the enormity of whatever it was he'd just been told. Rodenko took a step closer, preparing to grab the man if faltering turned to falling but it wasn't necessary. This was not what Morgan expected. Some mumbled conversation followed and then Tengku, dismissed by Zolner, turned, waiting to be led back to the car that had brought him. Morgan prepared again for travel and followed the other two who returned with Tengku to the back of the SUV. Morgan climbed in next to the driver and they drove off.

For the return journey back to Honolulu, Tengku had his blindfolded face buried in his hands the entire time. Morgan couldn't be sure, but he thought he heard the man stifling tears and his body language screamed tension.

Morgan didn't like the situation one bit.

Chapter Seven

The two Cadillac Escapade SUVs drove fast in convoy along the dirt track down from the forest toward Honolulu. Morgan was keeping an eye on Tengku, whose level of agitation and general unease was worsening. Despite the blindfold, his face was turned away from the interior of the vehicle as if he was looking outside. His hands were clasped together between his thighs and his knees were rising and lowering constantly in quick succession. The two security guys in the back weren't speaking or paying any professional attention to the man, other than exchanging disparaging looks about his obvious anxiety.

The SUVs maintained a steady, well-practiced pace along the winding gravel track that led them out of the high country of the forest. They were approaching the sealed road where they would once again separate, with Zolner's SUV heading southeast back to the house and Morgan's southwest to Honolulu to discharge their passenger. Morgan noticed a Chevrolet Trailblazer pulled into a secluded clearing off to his right. It was parked far enough off the road not to be obvious, as someone might do if they wanted some peace or privacy. Initially he tagged it as a couple out for a drive and stealing a few moments together in the lush surrounds of the forest, but then something began bugging him. The same thing that had been bugging him since they'd made the pickup. What was it?

By now they'd hit the sealed road again and the convoy split as planned. All inside the SUV was still quiet and Morgan couldn't work out what it was that was bothering him so much. They were driving through a residential area; the streets were quiet and here and there people were going about their business. There wasn't much traffic and occasionally he spotted some kids on their bikes but that was about it. All completely normal. Bikes. What was it that was getting under his skin?

In answer, his subconscious flashed up an image of the cyclist who had run into the back of them when they had pulled out into the traffic on Bishop Street. In his mind's eye, Morgan could see the cyclist clearly now – even more clearly than in the instant it had happened. The bang had been completely unexpected, as if the cyclist had just appeared from nowhere because Morgan had been on constant visual as they'd approach the pickup point and had seen nothing. It was as if he'd just materialized. On purpose? Another image hit him. This one took in the cyclist again, but in the middle distance beyond the cyclist was a parked Chevrolet Trailblazer. Jesus!

"Pull over!" Morgan said. "Right now!"

The driver obviously knew that Morgan was in favor with the boss and so he wasn't about to question the request. He stood on the brakes. Morgan was out before the vehicle stopped moving, running to inspect the back bumper. He dropped to his knees and searched the area where the cyclist had impacted. He reached just under the bumper and his fingers wrapped around something that wasn't meant to be there. He dropped even lower and saw it clearly, knowing exactly what it was. He grasped it tightly and pulled. It came away easily. It was a small black plastic box about the size of a packet of matches, housed within a magnetized mounting case designed to attach quickly and easily to a flat metal surface, in this case the underside of their SUV. An electronic vehicle tracking device. Cheap, nasty, effective. Morgan popped open the mounting case, dropped the device onto the road and stamped on it until it shattered. He left it there and quickly climbed back into the car.

"Remove his blindfold," Morgan said. The lead security guy in the back immediately did as he was told. As soon as it was off Tengku was looking directly at Morgan.

"You, get out. Now!"

The man didn't need to be told twice. He fumbled with his latch until the driver released the locks again and then fell from the car into the street. Morgan looked at the driver.

"Get us back to your boss's car as fast as you fucking can!" Morgan had his cellphone in his hand and was calling Rodenko. Nothing. "Answer, for fuck's sake!"

Without hesitation the driver pulled the vehicle into a tight arc and the SUV screamed in a semicircle of burning rubber to head back in the direction they'd just come from.

"What the fuck is going on, bro?" yelled the lead security guy.

Morgan tossed the magnetic mounting case back to him; he just managed to catch it. "Get on your cell and call whoever else you can get hold of on Rodenko's team. Tell 'em they tagged us when we made the pickup. They'll be after Zolner's SUV for sure." The expression on both the guys' faces told Morgan they weren't getting it.

"That cyclist back on Bishop Street," Morgan added. "It bugged me that he didn't even seem bothered that we'd hit him. That's because he needed us to. He planted a tracking device on this car knowing we'd lead them straight to Zolner. All the routines. The familiarity. They've had their eyes on you all for ages but now they've worked it all out."

The penny finally dropped, and now they were both trying different numbers for the other team members but none of their attempts were getting through.

"Step on it, man!" Morgan yelled at the driver. "This is not sounding good to me at all."

They raced back up toward the high ground until they found the route that the driver knew was the one the other SUV would be following. He was making good time, more than once managing to keep all four wheels on the road when a lesser driver might have lost control. They were still on sealed road and hadn't reached into any residential areas yet when they spotted the tail-lights of a Chevrolet Trailblazer up ahead. The lights were flashing as the driver of the Trailblazer fishtailed recklessly, powering and braking, clearly trying to get past the car in front of him, trying to force Zolner's SUV off the road.

"Get us up there, wait till he's fishtailing again and ram him!" Morgan yelled.

The SUV surged forward. Morgan braced for impact. The others did, too. Then the unmistakable snap and crack of low velocity ammunition ricocheting off the windscreen and bodywork of their SUV told them that the two vehicles ahead were engaged in a gunfight and the wild shots from Rodenko's team were reaching them. Now all three of them had their guns drawn. Morgan yelled some quick instructions above the noise of the engine at high revs. The plan was to try to draw the occupants of the Chevrolet into having to deal with them to allow Rodenko to get the Zolners clear of the trouble. For a split second, Morgan saw a man leaning out of the Chevy with an SMG of some kind, he couldn't be sure what, firing at Zolner's SUV. There was no chance for Morgan to engage him. Christ! What a mess. They were closing fast now and as the front of their Cadillac finally leaped toward the rear of the Chevrolet, Morgan knew they were just seconds away from contact.

Ahead the Chevrolet fishtailed wildly to the left on a tight right-hand bend. Morgan's driver saw the opportunity and took it. He planted his foot down hard on the accelerator and caught the Chevy on its right rear corner. The move put the Chevy into an even worse fishtail, sending it screeching in a series of wide swerves along a narrow stretch of sealed road.

"Find a gap and get us in front of them!" Morgan told his driver. "Then we can cut them off."

Once again, the driver stayed calm and kept his focus entirely on his responsibility to drive. His face showed no sign he was in any way under stress. Morgan was impressed; the guy knew what he was doing, which he proved yet again by perfectly aligning the Cadillac within the timings of the slewing, out-of-control Chevrolet and hurling the big car through the first available gap. They were through.

"Right, now we'll block 'em," Morgan said. "Put us across the road at the next bottleneck we come to."

Sure enough, around the next bend the road narrowed, delivering a near perfect option. A creek line running under the road was deep and wide enough to be impossible to cross other than on the road itself. However, as the road was narrow and the creek line required a substantial culvert, the sealed road was bordered on both sides by a concrete siding two feet high and the same wide surmounted by steel railing that formed the boundaries of the culvert. There was no getting around it. The driver expertly turned the Cadillac hard to the right and brought the SUV to a dead stop across the road, directly in the path of the approaching Chevy.

"Everyone out!" Morgan ordered. "Port side."

Morgan and the others clambered out, weapons drawn, and took up firing positions covering the bend, keeping the broadside of the SUV between them and the approaching Chevrolet. Then they heard rather than saw the Chevy braking on approach to the bend. By the time they caught sight of it, it was at the end of a skid and the driver was crunching the gears into reverse. The Chevrolet disappeared as quickly as it had appeared, leaving Morgan bewildered. Everything was suddenly silent. Instinct told him to check back down the road in the direction they'd originally been traveling and a short sprint proved that instinct to be correct: Zolner's SUV was stationary and at an angle across the road. There were bulletholes stitched along the gleaming black panels and the front doors were open.

Morgan ran to the SUV, beckoning to his team to bring theirs down. As he got closer he could hear raised voices, muffled at first but then getting clearer. It sounded like the Zolners, both of them, agitated. Then he could hear moaning. Pain. Someone injured.

"Get us out of here!" It was Kristina.

As Morgan reached the SUV he saw the windscreen and side windows had been shot out and there was glass everywhere. Kristina Zolner was huddled over her husband on the floor in the back, protecting him. She was yelling at Rodenko through the gap between the front seats.

"Are you hit?" said Morgan through the shattered side window.

"No," she answered. "Just get us out of here!"

In the front, Rodenko, blood streaming from a gash across his forehead, was attempting to deal with bullet wounds their driver had sustained across his upper back and, possibly, his shoulder. His injuries probably weren't as bad as they looked – he wasn't coughing up any blood and he was responsive enough. Rodenko had it under control but was clearly under pressure from his employer to get going. Morgan could help with that.

The second SUV pulled up beside them. Morgan told the two security guys to help Rodenko and Zolner's driver while he quickly transferred the Zolners across to his SUV. He was in the middle of telling his driver, Muller, to get the Zolners back to their house when Hedeon Zolner himself interrupted from the back.

"No!" he said. "You drive us, Morgan. He can drive the other car."

Muller didn't question it. He got out and gave Morgan a look that said, *Just go with it. We've got this.*

"Take us straight to the marina," said Zolner. "I need to get back to the *Gemini* immediately."

Reluctantly, Morgan climbed in behind the wheel, set the GPS and drove away.

Chapter Eight

INTREPID HQ, BROADWAY, LONDON

Major General Reginald "Nobby" Davenport, CBE, DSO, MC, chief of the Intelligence, Recovery, Protection and Infiltration Division of Interpol, otherwise known as Intrepid, stood in the very center of the oak-paneled office that was his war room, the epicenter of all Intrepid operations. The jacket of his worsted navy pinstripe suit hung on the back of his chair. This was the only relaxing of his attire he ever allowed himself. The Windsor knot of his maroon tie remained squarely fixed at the collar, nine of the ten buttons of his waistcoat were fastened – the bottom button left undone, as was his custom, and the cuffed sleeves of his white fine-cotton shirt remained, very definitely, affixed by a set of aged gold and onyx cufflinks that had been, as it happened, a gift from Violet Ashcroft-James many years before.

Davenport was thinking. His hands were in his pockets and he was gazing absently at a point above the door to his office. He was considering a vast array of scenarios that lay before him, every one of them disturbing and offering only more uncertainty with little chance, it seemed, of a solution.

"So, now we have three," he said. "Correct?"

"Actually, this is the fourth, sir," came the reply from the man seated in one of the Chesterfields that sat around the old circular mahogany coffee table where the General preferred to hold his discussions. "Last year we had Patiala Airlines Flight 550 on June third, Patiala Airlines Flight 190 on August fifth, and Chimbu Airways Flight 376 on September sixteenth. So, this latest one makes four."

Davenport looked across at his chief of staff, former Green Beret Colonel Michael 'Mickey' Sheridan, a highly decorated veteran of the U.S. Army Special Operations Command. Sheridan was an expert in unconventional warfare and had led various special operations for coalition forces in Iraq and Afghanistan for almost a decade. Originally from Detroit, Michigan, Sheridan was six feet tall with the build of an athlete, honed and lean. He had light brown hair, inquiring blue eyes and, despite a youthful quality, his face wore the subtle lines and experience of a former desert warrior. After two years of searching for a new chief of staff for Intrepid, scouring select lists of recommended candidates from all over the world, Davenport had known Sheridan was the right person from the moment they first sat down together in Sheridan's office at Fort Bragg. At just forty-five years of age, he had the requisite special operations pedigree and contacts to make him more than suitable for the role, but it was his credibility in the field that made him the perfect choice.

"Four. Of course," Davenport acknowledged. "Although, as far as we know at this stage, the disappearances of three of them remain officially unexplained while one stands out for having been – to all intents and purposes – shot down. Yes?"

"Yes, sir," Sheridan replied. "We've been through every report from the authorities of all jurisdictions involved in the investigations and, while there are still some real possibilities to consider – including crew-related activity – nothing has been conclusively proven regarding how these aircraft were lost. Weather is considered a factor in at least two of them for sure, 376 and this latest one, Katak Airlines Flight 712. Officially, the jury's still out on 550."

"Another hundred and fifty people dead and still no answers. There's more to all this than we're seeing," Davenport said, returning to Sheridan. "All we have is this as yet inconclusive association between the pilot recruiter, Salazar, and Zolner – what is it that he calls himself?"

"Helldiver, sir."

"Helldiver, of course. Enjoys the notoriety, I imagine. Just like his bloody father." Davenport paused, massaged his temples for a moment. "This strategy, Michael, whatever it is they're playing at, is immense. More than just terror. Must be. I can feel it in my bones, but I'm damned if I can put my finger on it."

"While we're on the subject of the strategy behind this thing, have you had any further thoughts about the Russians? There've been literally hundreds of close encounters lately between NATO aircraft and Russian Tupolev Tu-95 bombers and Sukhoi Su-27 jet fighters."

"Don't forget their warships in the Channel, a move which just happens to coincide with NATO ships exercising in the area. And, on top of all that, we have the Syria issue and Putin's apparent support for the Assad regime."

"British RAF Tornado pilots operating in Iraq have just

been cleared to fire upon Russian aircraft if they believe they are under attack," said Sheridan. "Not good."

"It's quite clear the Kremlin has been testing reaction times and the extent to which NATO forces will be deployed in response to their infringements into NATO airspace for some time. Their sudden intense interest in Syria could be just the catalyst to take us all closer to …" Davenport paused. "It's unimaginable."

Sheridan remained silent as Davenport explored a thought.

"In addition to these deliberate infringements of sovereign airspace, Putin is clearly not afraid to test the resolve of the NATO alliance. He's rebuilding the Black Sea fleet and his occupation of Crimea ensures Russia's ongoing access to the port of Sevastopol. His influence there continues to destabilize Ukraine despite the ceasefire. We saw exactly how far the Kremlin is prepared to go to exert its position in Georgia back in 2008. It's only a matter of time before they begin to press their interest in the Baltic States, Estonia, Latvia, Lithuania. They already have Kaliningrad, of course, which maintains their warm-water port in the Baltic Sea and, as you say, there's been an encounter between the US Air Force and a Russian Su-27 over the Baltic Sea north of Poland as recently as last week."

He fell silent. Sheridan picked up the threads.

"We know Putin's objective is to re-establish Russia to the former glory days of the Soviet Union – economically, politically, geo-strategically. And his foreign policy commitment toward the integration of former Soviet territory is absolutely clear and on the record."

"And he is already setting the foreign policy agenda for the states he has successfully reintegrated without being too fussed about what they do domestically. Within reason, of course," Davenport said. "Lots of talk of Russia's national interest."

"Comply or we'll shut off the gas," added Sheridan drily. "Gunboat diplomacy at the end of a gas pipeline."

"Indeed," replied Davenport. "And beyond Eastern Europe, we now have the added dilemma of the Kremlin agreeing to supply their S-300 air defense missile system to Iran. Yet another line crossed."

"It's a return to the dark old days, that's for sure," said Sheridan.

"These kinds of operations, pushing the boundaries of the NATO defenses and so on, were routine back then. Now, countries like Germany are being forced to rethink their entire defensive strategies for the next ten to fifteen years, Britain is already being faced with the rather embarrassing realization that systematic cuts to defense spending over the past decade has been a major bloody mistake, and by successive administrations over-committing in Europe there are many influential figures in the United States who are now justifiably concerned about their capacity to defend themselves."

"The new Cold War," said Sheridan. "There's already a hashtag getting around online that the journalists are all using – *ColdWar2015*."

"This is exactly what the hardliners in Moscow have wanted since the collapse of the Soviet Union in ninety-one. And this man 'Helldiver,' his father – Zolnerowich senior – was the worst of them all," Davenport said, rubbing his brow, deep in thought, pondering a stream of long buried memories. "For our part in all this, we must find the connection between this overt shift in the Kremlin's attitude toward its neighbors and our investigations into the disappearances of these aircraft. We're missing something about this Helldiver creature, Michael. His father's blood flows through his veins. The connection must be staring us in the face."

"I agree, sir. But for my money, I'm confident we're closing in via our focus on crew-related events for Flight 712. If we can confirm that, at least with this latest one, we'll trace the line back to the source – via Salazar back to Helldiver."

"Any word from Dominique?" Davenport asked. "We must be due another situation report by now?"

"We are, in fact," replied Sheridan. "I'm expecting to hear from her controller within the next twelve hours."

"Masterson?"

"Yes, sir. He's familiar with the area she's currently operating in, fluent in a dozen relevant languages and he's also extremely experienced in post-Soviet Russia and the rise of the oligarchs under Yeltsin and Putin."

"And has the scars to prove it, I might add. Yes, Masterson's a good choice. He as good as wrote the book on counter-intelligence for field agents; still very highly sought after by governments with sensitive issues to deal with. We're lucky to have him and Dominique is lucky to have him as her lifeline back to us."

"As soon as I have anything I'll brief you."

"Very well. As things currently stand, Dominique is still our best option. She's our closest link to Salazar and the pilots and to Helldiver's involvement, but we need proof. There are so many moving parts beyond our immediate grasp. I just hope she can keep any outside interference at bay so we have time to bring all of the pieces together and form a coherent picture of exactly how and why they are creating all this bloody carnage."

"If you don't mind me saying, that's what you have me

for now, General," Sheridan replied. "I'll keep the operation in play so you can make sense of all the global factors."

"Well, you just tell me what you need and I'll throw every available resource your way. Unlike our member nations, I'm not curtailed by borders, politics or relationship sensitivities. Don't feel in any way restricted. Whatever you need, you'll have it."

"Thank you, sir," Sheridan replied. "While we're on the subject, I think it's timely that I update you on Major Morgan."

"Ah, yes. Very well. Do we know where he is?"

"Hawaii. Honolulu to be precise."

"Does he know yet?"

"No, not yet."

"How do you think he'll react?"

"Not well, initially at least. From what I've seen of him so far, I expect he'll probably kick over some furniture and want to crack a few heads." They both laughed. "But, once he's done all that, I have no doubt he'll be back on the team."

"He's going to be none too happy with me when he finds out. How do you plan to tell him?"

"Don't worry, general," said Sheridan. "I have a surprise for Morgan."

Chapter Nine

OAHU, HAWAIIAN ISLANDS

At the marina, Simon, Helldiver's personal assistant, was waiting for them. The twin screws of the Riva 33 Aquariva were already bubbling the water. Morgan was surprised; there'd been no plan for the Zolners returning to the Gemini that evening, yet Simon's unexpected presence, in Morgan's eyes at least, seemed predetermined. Morgan pulled up alongside the Aquariva and shut off the engine. Instantly the same young marina attendant appeared from nowhere and began rummaging around in the back compartment of the SUV, retrieving the luggage.

Morgan got out of the driver's seat and opened the back door for the Zolners. Kristina went straight to Simon, who had his face bent to his cellphone. Hedeon Zolner stood and faced Morgan.

"You OK?" Morgan asked. "Not an easy thing to go through."

"We're fine. Just a little shaken. As usual, Kristina handles these things much better than I."

"You've been through this kind of thing before?"

"No, I just meant she has a much greater capacity to deal with the unexpected than I do. No, this is very definitely a first for us."

"Well, whoever they are, they're not very happy about something. You've got a driver who's been shot and needs a hospital, and it's very possible that locals will be reporting they heard gunfire up there. If anyone spots the other SUV full of holes it'll only be a matter of time before the cops put two and two together. Care to bring me in on it?"

"We'll get to that. Eventually. For now, Rodenko will take care of everything. Don't you worry about it."

"So, what now?" said Morgan.

"Now I want to rest and regroup and consider my next course of action."

"And what do you want me to do?"

"Right now, all I want you to do is allow me to thank you for saving my life, twice. There's a car coming for you. Simon will take this one back to the house. You'll be taken straight to the Halekulani Hotel where you'll stay as my guest for the next few days. Once Kristina and I return we'll send for you and then we'll talk about the future. OK?"

"Well, I'm very grateful, but won't that leave you short-handed?"

"See, always the professional. Thinking of your employer's needs rather than your own. That's why I want you on my team, Morgan. Don't you concern yourself about those things. Kristina has arranged everything."

They shook hands and Helldiver walked off to join his wife at the boat. Once both the Zolners were safely onboard the *Gemini*, Simon approached Morgan.

"Here's my card," he said, sending a digital business card direct to Morgan's cell. "If you need anything, call me.

Otherwise, put your feet up for a while and I'll be in touch when they're back."

"OK," said Morgan. "Keys are in it."

"Thanks," Simon replied. "Here's your car now. Your luggage has already been delivered to the hotel. Enjoy."

A gleaming black Cadillac XTS pulled in. A chauffeur emerged and opened the nearside rear door for Morgan.

"Good afternoon, sir," he said. He was Hawaiian, mid-thirties and, judging by the embroidered crest on his jacket, was in the employ of the Halekulani Hotel. He had a cheery face and looked like he'd enjoyed a meal or two more than he should. His name tag said BILL.

"Good afternoon, Bill," Morgan replied. "I prefer to sit up front. Do you mind?"

"Whatever you say, sir," Bill replied. He closed the rear door and didn't quite make it in time to get the front door for Morgan, who was already climbing into the passenger seat.

Before they got underway, the driver made sure the temperature was to Morgan's liking and turned the techno music, evidently preferred by previous passengers, right down.

"I hope you've got more than just techno," Morgan said. "That shit makes my skin crawl."

Bill laughed. "What's your preference, sir?"

"Jazz or blues, if you've got any."

A broad smile answered him as the driver made a new selection on the Cadillac's audio system. The opening bars of "Riding with the King" through the Bose Centerpoint Surround Sound system got the intended reaction.

"Ah, B.B. King and Eric Clapton," said Morgan. "The perfect choice, my friend."

"You look like a man who's ready to relax. And there's

nothing better than some good old-fashioned blues guitar to help you with that."

"You're absolutely right," Morgan replied. "I've got this album. It's a favorite."

The Cadillac drove out of the marina and right onto Ala Moana Boulevard. High-rise hotels bordered the wide road on both sides, facing off, opposing forces in the war for the tourist dollar. The lush palm trees that lined the center islands of the boulevard marked the sanctuary of no-man's land between them.

"You drive for Mr. and Mrs. Zolner often?"

"Whenever he's here in Honolulu he asks for me," Bill replied. There was pride in his voice. "I take care of him and Mrs. Zolner and any other guests they need looked after."

"Well, he obviously holds you in high regard. That must be a good thing."

"It certainly is, sir. Mr. Zolner is a personal friend of one of the owners of the hotel," he said. "He has a big place out on Diamond Head Road; but keeps that to himself when he's here. Only he and Mrs. Zolner stay out there, it's their holiday house. His guests always stay at the Halekulani, even his special guests."

"Sometimes you just need a private sanctuary to return to where you can shut out everything and everyone else. I can relate to that." Morgan thought of the Zolners' mansion on the beach and then immediately of the modest, semi-rural retreat he called home back in Surrey and the respite he'd found there over the past few months. "I can definitely relate to that."

They turned right onto Kalia Road and got stuck for a few moments behind a Polynesian Adventure Tours bus and a private charter trolley bus before Bill managed an expertly executed maneuver to get them clear. Morgan fell silent for the rest of the drive and enjoyed the journey along the sweeping tree-lined twists and turns of the final approach until they arrived at the hotel a few minutes later.

"You know, sir, seeing as how you're into blues and jazz and all, you may wanna check out Eddie Henderson in Lewers Lounge tonight. You won't be sorry."

"I may just do that," Morgan replied, then thanked the driver, tipped him and walked into the reception area.

Before he'd had a chance to open his mouth, a young woman approached him from the concierge desk and introduced herself.

"Welcome to the Halekulani Hotel, Major Morgan. My name is Lolana and if you'd like to follow me, I'll take you up to your room. You're in the Royal Suite."

"Thank you," Morgan replied, enjoying the red carpet. Helldiver was definitely looking after him.

Morgan and Lolana took a private elevator to the third and top floor. Lolana opened the door to the suite with practiced ceremony and Morgan was instantly treated to a breathtaking view of Diamond Head and Waikiki Beach. It was late afternoon and the scene was brushed with the romanticism of impending nightfall and the promise of a totally unencumbered evening. Morgan walked straight out onto the balcony and breathed in the magnificence of the location. He could almost reach down and feel the soft sand of the beach below; instead he reached out and touched a palm that was brushing gently in the breeze across the corner of the balcony. Lolana continued to brief him on the housekeeping details of his suite and the fact that everything would be taken care of by Mr. Zolner. Morgan needed only to ask his personal butler, Makaio – who materialized behind Lolana – and everything would be arranged.

Yes, Morgan thought, the inexplicable events of the afternoon notwithstanding, he could definitely get used to this peaceful, gilt-edged lifestyle very easily.

Of course, how long it could last was a vastly different proposition. Cold fingers of suspicion had emerged from his gut and were scratching at his conscience. Who the hell was Zolner, really? And what kind of person calls himself Helldiver?

Chapter Ten

Morgan looked at his watch. It was almost 10am. He was flat on his back on Waikiki Beach, and had been dozing with a baseball cap resting on his face. Following Bill's advice, he'd spent the evening in the hotel's Lewers Lounge relaxing to the music of jazz trumpeter Eddie Henderson and shutting down the day. When he eventually returned to his suite he sat on the balcony for an hour or so, pondering the issue of the attempt on Helldiver's life while soaking up the beauty of the beach at night. Despite chasing endless theories down endless rabbit holes, his musings on the subject got him nowhere and so, after a club sandwich and a couple of Coronas, he hit the hay exhausted by 11pm.

He was ensconced on a narrow strip of beach directly in front of the hotel, soaking up the sun, alternately swimming, looking out to sea and reading Tom Clancy's *Without Remorse*, a favorite. He was actually enjoying doing nothing. There were only a few people around and they were all keeping to themselves, which suited Morgan just fine. He wasn't much for making small talk with strangers. Of course, the moment he realized that he was doing nothing and enjoying it, his mind instantly reminded him of why he was doing nothing and who was paying for him to do it. So he was mercilessly returned to his ruminations over the whole debacle of the previous day and, more importantly, the future.

He still had no idea what had gone down or who could possibly have wanted Helldiver dead so badly. They were, after all, in Honolulu, not downtown Kabul. Running gun battles between opposing SUVs weren't the norm here. Or were they? How the hell would he know? A seemingly endless stream of questions and theories that had begun last night while he was drinking beer and gazing up at the stars over Waikiki told Morgan that his naturally inquisitive mind – which he openly acknowledged was just the PC word for suspicious – was not likely to let the matter rest. He needed to know.

"Excuse me, do you mind if I lay my towel down here? Promise I won't get too close."

Morgan lifted his cap and turned his head in the direction of the voice. Bare feet very close by and half buried in the beach sand lured his gaze to a pair of perfectly toned, evenly tanned legs, then a hand clutching a rolled-up beach towel, a slender arm, an oversized faded T-shirt with a 'Hopkins 1876 Blue Jays' motif, a trail of long dark hair over one shoulder, and a face, a beautiful, familiar face, smiling down at him under a wide-brimmed straw hat.

"Jesus!" Morgan said, still flat on his back. He made a move to get up.

"Whoa, down boy. Don't jump up and hug me; especially not with that beard! Act like we just met, OK?"

Morgan did as he was told, reluctantly, sitting up

instead. "OK. But, what the hell are you doing here? It's great to see you."

"It's great to see you, too," the woman replied, meaning it. "So, can I join you or what, Morgan? Don't leave a girl hanging, here. It looks bad."

Morgan smiled and held out his hand, inviting her to the spot beside him.

Elizabeth Reigns flicked her towel expertly out in front of her and let it sail directly down alongside Morgan's, albeit with just enough space between them for it not to seem intimate or too familiar, just two strangers who were happy to enjoy each other's company for a while. A small beach bag appeared from somewhere and she dropped it beside her. She kept her T-shirt on and sat on the towel facing the sea with her arms wrapped around her knees. Morgan turned to her.

"Well, if we just met," he said, "shouldn't we at least appear to be introducing ourselves?"

She smiled. "Yeah, good call."

Morgan offered his hand. "Alex Morgan," he said. "Very pleased to meet you. And you are?"

"Elizabeth Reigns," she replied, taking his hand and holding it firmly, exactly as she'd done the first time they'd introduced themselves aboard an Intrepid Gulfstream G650 executive jet somewhere over China about a year ago. "I'm very pleased to meet you, Alex Morgan. You can call me Beth."

"And you can call me Alex Morgan." He smiled. "I like the way you say it."

"You're such an idiot, Morgan." She laughed. "And, for the record, I'm not sure about that beard. Since when?"

He laughed. "Since whenever. I almost shaved it off this morning, actually. I may just keep it now."

"We'll see about that," she said. "So anyway, it's been a while. And suddenly, here we are."

"Yes, here we are. Of all the gin joints in all the towns in all the world, you walk right into mine," said Morgan. "It must be destiny or something. Right, Reigns?"

"It's something. Not destiny. And, if you hadn't noticed, this is Honolulu not Casablanca."

"Still, you just appearing out of nowhere like this, without warning. How did you know I'd be here?" he asked, a tinge of suspicion evident in his tone. "I mean, I know it's easy to trace me to Honolulu but, Jesus! This exact spot, at this exact time and you all ready for a swim ..."

"Come on, Morgan. You know the score. You didn't expect the General to just cut you loose, did you? You and Sutherland were his A Team. He knew you needed to decompress. He just needed to be sure you were OK. You know?"

"So, he's had me under surveillance all this time, ever since he granted me a leave of absence? I was supposed to be left alone to consider my future."

Reigns remained silent, studying Morgan. "You look good," she said eventually. "Settled and healthy, I mean."

"I'm better, that's for sure. I've been setting my own agenda and it feels pretty damn good after years of being told what to do."

"I'm glad, Morgan. Really. It's good to see you this way. Hell knows you were pretty intolerable back there for a while. Remember?"

"Yeah, I remember." He looked at her. Memories, lots of them, swirled in his head. Good memories. Memories dominated by her. The relationship they'd kept secret from Intrepid. Her patience with him and her support as he struggled to deal with mission fatigue and a textbook case of burnout. He owed her so much. "Beth, there's—"

"No, Morgan. Not now. Not here. There are things I have to tell you first. Things we have to discuss. The personal stuff will wait."

Morgan bristled but fell silent. The sounds of the ocean and the people around them enjoying it filled their world for a while, neither prepared nor able to speak. Clearly they were entering territory that was going to be difficult to navigate and Reigns was taking her time, making up her mind how she was going to kick off.

"I can't help but think you're an olive branch, Beth," Morgan said. "Otherwise, why else would you just turn up here out of the blue like this? Why else would they have sent you? And don't tell me Davenport is just getting himself a whisky from the bar and is heading over here with his towel and trunks."

Reigns laughed out loud. "I can't even imagine him like that. Maybe he has a suit made especially for the beach."

"I wouldn't put it past him," Morgan said. "But seriously, I have a bad feeling that this unexpected reunion is about to get ruined by whatever it is you're actually here to tell me. So why don't we get that out of the way first?"

"Why does it have to ruin everything?"

"I don't know," he said. He was enjoying just looking at her and didn't want anything to taint the moment. "It's great to see you."

"Yeah, you too," she said.

After a while, Morgan sighed. "So, what's going on, Reigns?"

She looked away from him and back out to sea, clearly conflicted. "You should know, when they asked me, I agreed to come here for two reasons. Well, three really. One, it's

Hawaii, right? Two, I wanted to see you. I had to see you." Morgan tried to speak but she wasn't about to let him. "Shut up, OK, and just listen. Three, I knew if you heard this from anyone else we'd probably lose you for good."

"Jesus. What the hell is it?"

The two of them were looking directly into each other's eyes, gauging, wanting to just forget all of the baggage and enjoy the moment but struggling with the context of their meeting.

"I've been leaving you alone, remember? Because you asked me to. So, it took a lot for me to accept this job, knowing what it could do to us."

Now Morgan looked away. "Unless we're faced with some real-time, global-level event that I don't know about, then I'm going to need some serious convincing if this is about getting me to come back. Because, I've gotta tell you, all this freedom has been good for me."

It was Reign's turn to bristle. Morgan saw it.

"I didn't mean it like that. I meant ..."

"The truth is, Morgan, you never really left."

"What the hell does that mean?"

"What it means is that every move you think you've made of your own free will over the past six months has been carefully choreographed in accordance with a very detailed strategy."

"What fucking strategy? Wait, don't tell me – this is some psychological profile assessment. He's trying to work out if I've lost it. Is that what this is? Jesus!"

"Would you shut up! It's nothing like that. The General knew you'd be fine. He has more faith in you than you give him credit for. So does Sheridan, by the way. He's been in your corner the whole time."

Morgan stood and wandered down to the water with his

hands clasped behind his neck. Reigns dropped her hat, peeled off her T-shirt and followed him.

By the time she reached him, Morgan was waist deep in the ocean, standing quietly. He turned when he heard her splashing up to him. He couldn't help but check her out despite his frame of mind. In nothing but a brightly patterned bikini, she looked spectacular, her honed body just as he remembered: absolutely perfect.

"Jesus! That's not fair, Reigns," he said. "Getting around looking like that, you've got to be in breach of the Geneva Convention, or something. There are strict rules about torture, you know."

"All's fair in love and war, Morgan. You know that. Besides, pain is gain, remember?"

He smiled at a memory they shared and kept his eyes on her until she was finally close to him.

"OK, so you've completely disarmed me and I'm fighting every natural impulse to grab you just in case we're still being watched, so now's probably your best shot at giving me all the gruesome details. Just say it, Beth. Whatever it is, just spit it out."

"You're really ready for this now?"

He nodded. "As ready as I'll ever be."

"OK, Morgan," she replied. She took a deep breath and looked out to sea, standing closer than Morgan could reasonably cope with. "You've been infiltrated into the center of a major investigation into Hedeon Zolner – aka Helldiver – his wife Kristina and their entire global empire. Helldiver is believed to be behind the disappearances of the commercial airliners – Patiala Airlines flights 550 and 190, Chimbu Airways flight 376, and most recently Katak Airlines 712."

Morgan's eyes locked onto hers, his attention so focused

on what she was saying that he had subconsciously shut out the interference of everything else around them. A knot was forming in the pit of his stomach as though he was being punched, blow by blow, until his solar plexus had fully constricted and all the air had been forced from his body. Suddenly all those suspicions he'd been harboring about the Zolners were lining up one by one. Reigns kept going.

"We believe their actions so far have been directed at Islamic countries in Southeast Asia, targeting their national carriers. Global enough for you? We're reasonably confident that these aircraft have all been deliberately brought down following failure by the targeted countries to meet certain demands within stipulated time frames. To what end we're not yet sure, although I know that the General and Sheridan are working on a theory involving deliberate action by crew members. And that's where you come in."

Morgan didn't speak. He couldn't. To any onlooker he and Reigns would appear to be just two people chatting, enjoying the sea and each other. Now his thoughts had shifted away from annoyance at having been monitored by Intrepid and back to his old self, the secret agent, recalibrating to tradecraft and the need to maintain the facade of two strangers engaging in full public view. It all returned to him instinctively.

"We believe the incident you were involved in yesterday was an attempt by one of the targeted countries to take Helldiver out. Obviously, probably thanks to you, it failed."

Morgan suddenly remembered his observation about the pickup of Tengku occurring in the center of a number of foreign consulates. "The consular area downtown…"

"I said 'thanks to you,' Morgan, so don't beat yourself up about it. We don't want Zolner dead. Not yet anyway. We need him alive because we still don't know what his next move is or even why he's doing it. Like I said, we have some theories but we're light on detail. I'm authorized tell you more but before I do, there's something I need to ask you."

"What? Ask me anything."

"Are you ready to come back?"

"You mean, am I ready to come back in from the cold?"

"Yeah, something like that. Unless you prefer all this freedom you've been telling me about."

Chapter Eleven

CAP D'ANTIBES, CÔTE D'AZUR, RÉPUBLIQUE
FRANÇAISE

Masterson enjoyed the trip along the Côte d'Azur from Aéroport Nice to Antibes. He'd done it over a dozen times now and each time he found himself enjoying it more. It was a welcome change from the complexities of his clandestine life and a million light years removed from the warzones and dark allies that represented the traditional tapestry of his personal history. The drive was quick, about thirty minutes, give or take, and always agreeable, especially once you were past the Marina Baie Des Anges and heading south, treated to the spectacle of the bay itself with its golden sands paralleling the Route du bord de mur and nothing but clear blue skies and a turquoise sea for company. In the far distance, Pointe Bacon reached out into the bay and the resort town of Antibes itself began to emerge. The rendezvous point always changed but still it needed to be within a certain general radius; his contact didn't always have a great deal of time to disappear from her duties at the château. Fortunately Masterson had a healthy acquaintance with this corner of France now – he'd rented a villa in St. Maximin-la-Sainte-Baume, a small country town about an hour and a half drive to the west – so he knew the general layout of not only Antibes, but all the key features of the nearby towns, surrounding country-side and main approaches; a force of habit from a lifetime of having to become rapidly familiar with places he'd never heard of, been before and thankfully, in many cases, never would again. Today, however, he'd flown in from Paris on another task. The US State Department had requested his help with a politically sensitive issue involving one of their embassy staff. Masterson knew a few of the right people. It wouldn't take too long to sort it out.

The cab driver eventually took him along the Boulevard President Wilson where he saw the sign above the red awning of the art deco entrance that read LE CRYSTAL, his destination. He told the driver to stop about fifty yards short of the place, got out, paid the fare and then spent the next thirty minutes to all intents and purposes meandering around the general area of the pentagon formed by Boule-vard President Wilson, Boulevard Edouard Baudoin, Avenue Maréchal Joffre and Avenue G. de Maupassant. He still had plenty of time up his sleeve, so to give his counter-surveillance measures the look and feel of those of a genuine tourist, he took a brief stroll along the promenade of Boulevard Edouard Baudoin. He stopped for coffee to enjoy the views of Golfe Juan, the site of Napoleon's return from exile and the commencement of the infamous 'Hun-dred Days' before his defeat at Waterloo, and then worked his way back via Avenue G. de Maupassant toward the RV.

Inside LE CRYSTAL, Masterson asked for a table on the outdoor terrace so he could maintain a view of the approaches to the restaurant and not be easily overheard and, as a bonus, he could enjoy the sunshine. Satisfied with the table, he ordered a bottle of rosé as he perused the menu. Traveling as much as he did and living out of a suitcase far too often, Masterson always made a point of enjoying his meals. It was one of the few luxuries he could enjoy when his profession required him to be constantly on the move. Feeling like something substantial, he liked the look of the *filet de bœuf grillé, croustillant de pommes de terre truffé* and decided that he'd order that when she arrived. Based on past experience, he expected she'd probably opt for seafood, which he generally considered to be cat food and avoided like the plague. By the time the waiter returned with the wine, Masterson saw his contact emerge from a store named RIVALE and then unhurriedly cross the street at the pedestrian crossing. She was wearing a white T-shirt under a loose-fitting patterned blouse with tight white jeans and ankle-strapped sandals. She was about five feet eight, tanned and toned, and moved with grace and confidence. Her hair was dark brown and cut in a messy bob, which he guessed was popular for young women. Whatever, it all worked.

"Uncle!" she said in perfect educated French, which was no surprise because she was, according to Mickey Sheridan, French. Although Masterson often thought he heard traces of an English background in there somewhere, along with an occasional slice of America. They'd kept French as their default language during all their meetings. Masterson stood and they embraced briefly, kissing on each cheek as they established the pretence of close familial connection.

"How lovely to see you again," she said.

"Hello, my darling." Despite himself and his habitually strict adherence to the stoic detachment demanded of his profession, he still found her bright blue eyes mesmerizing. "I couldn't miss the opportunity to come and see you. You look as beautiful as ever."

He remained standing as she sat down and then followed suit, both of them smiling amiably and falling into general chatter about family, weather and what she'd been up to. They maintained it for some time while the wait staff saw to their orders. He went with the beef while she, as expected, ordered the *filet de daurade grillé, ratatouille à l'ancienne*. She was happy to start with a glass of the rosé he'd recommended. When they were finally settled and their conversation had run the gamut of innocuous pleasantries, purely for the benefit of any inquisitive ears, they got down to business.

"OK, Dominique," he said. "What's the latest? The General is eager for progress."

"There's been a lot of activity since the last one went down."

"You mean 712?"

"Yes," she said. "Helldiver is still in Hawaii, which I'm sure you already know, but we received word late yesterday that he's returning here soon."

"How soon?"

"Can't be sure. Apparently they're going to spend some time aboard the *Gemini* before heading back here. I expect they want to lie low after the attempt on their lives. Do we know who it was yet?"

"Headquarters say Malaysians, most likely," he replied. "Whoever it was, they didn't really think it through. What about the recruiter, Salazar – any news on him?"

"Only that he is meeting Helldiver in Hawaii and –

don't quote me on this bit – I believe he may have a couple of recently recruited pilots in tow. Based on the last occurrence, before we knew what they were doing I mean, I wouldn't be surprised if this latest trip to Hawaii doesn't turn out to be a rerun of the last time they hosted pilots – ahead of 712, where Helldiver and his wife wine and dine their latest kamikazes before sending them off to their great sacrifice in the name of you know who."

"Which means we have even less time than we thought. If the last one is anything to go by, we could be looking at just a couple of weeks before they bring down another."

"Exactly. That's what unsettles me most of all about this. I'm constantly asking myself: Am I missing anything? Can I do more?"

"You've been doing everything you can, Dominique, and more; but I must say, on the basis of this latest information and the high probability of an attack occurring much earlier than anticipated, we need to ramp things up a few notches ASAP. That means you'll need to be more aggressive in terms of fighting for information, which inherently involves a much greater risk potential for you actually being caught. Are you up for it?"

"Of course. I've not come this far to let things fall over now. I'll do whatever needs to be done."

"I don't doubt that for a moment," he said. "From here on the critical element is information, and we'll need it fast, like as soon as you have it. Meanwhile, right now, if there's anything, even the slightest whisper of an idea or a conversation you've overheard that you think might be valuable, let's have it."

"There's a new face at the château. An older man, maybe late sixties, possibly even older. Eastern European. He visited recently before Helldiver left for Hawaii and returned again two days ago. I've only been privy to snippets of conversations between Helldiver and this guy on the last visit, but my take on his accent is that he's most likely another Russian. Physically he looks quite good for his age, although the face definitely shows the years. Hard life, you know. And there's a military kind of bearing to him. Formal. Upright. Powerful even. He was welcomed to the inner circle immediately, almost reverently, and I've never seen Helldiver embrace anyone before, but he definitely embraced this guy. I got the impression he was family."

"But from what we know about Zolner, his father, General Igor Zolnerowich – a former KGB operative – was killed about ten years back. Shot in the head in some sort of interagency reprisal. Rumor had it that it was done by the Russian Security Service on the orders of someone in the hierarchy settling old scores. Zolnerowich was one of the old school Communists who didn't like it when the wall came down and everything changed."

"Well, if it isn't a family thing there is definitely the business end," she said. "Because the old Russian is involved in something big with Helldiver. On this visit he's pretty much kept to himself in the suite of rooms prepared for him. Unfortunately my duties as Helldiver's executive officer restrict me to only their legitimate, public business interests. Getting access to their closed-door meetings, even their private rooms at the château, is still proving impossible."

"Maybe we should kit you out to bug the place?"

"It's a possibility. They sweep the place for tech pretty regularly but not routinely. Rodenko, the head of security, sees to it. They'd pick up a bug in a flash if the timing was out."

"Well, we may have to risk it. I'll see what I can arrange and you'll have to find a way of getting access to those closed-door sessions, at least to the rooms ahead of the sessions, and you have to do it soon. You need to be at the table, remotely or otherwise, especially with this new player, the old Russian, on the scene and Helldiver potentially getting ready for another attack."

They chatted with the wait staff as their meals were laid out before them and their wine glasses were refilled. Masterson felt they were getting somewhere, he just had to let Dominique explore her thoughts some more, away from the pressure of being undercover in the château. He wanted to keep the meeting relaxed and conversational so she could guide herself through her observations without feeling she had to deliver. It was the best way to handle an agent like her. She'd been under for almost a year, working her way in from the outer layers of the Zolner empire, and until recently she had been Intrepid's only asset on the ground. Every time he met with her, Masterson was even more impressed. Apart from being one of the smartest women he'd ever known, she had guts, there was no doubting that, and in this game you needed them. The General had chosen well when he'd picked her for this job.

"What about the wife," Masterson began when they were alone again. "What's her level of involvement like? Last time you mentioned she'd started off slow in the early days but over time she's become very hands-on in terms of his business dealings. That still the case?"

"Oh, yeah," she said. "She is definitely the Hillary Clinton in their relationship. If anything, over the past six months she has exerted even more influence over him. She chairs some of those closed-door meetings when he's not around and, when he is, she's still in on all of them. It's interesting given they've only been married a year or so. She's very much a part of his decision-making apparatus."

The wife was definitely worth a lot more attention. Masterson's thoughts instinctively returned to the old Russian. There was something there. The military bearing. Powerful. Another old school Communist? On the basis of his age it was a serious possibility, but what was the connection between the old guard and a Russian oligarch like Helldiver? Strategy. Motive. He thought of Russia's recent attempts to so publicly unnerve NATO, putting a shiver across Europe.

"What's the relationship like between Kristina Zolner and your old Russian? Noticed anything? Could that be the family connection?"

"I wondered about that initially, but the more I saw of her interaction with him on the most recent visit, I got the impression she was almost deferential, which, trust me, is not like her at all. She's a formidable woman. But this guy brings out a submissive side that I've not seen in her around anyone else."

"Remind me – her nationality; didn't we have her pegged as Eastern European, too?"

"Originally the popular view was that she was Turkish, mainly because that's what the Zolners have suggested in the media, along with a history connecting her with one of the wealthiest families in Turkey, and that she is an heiress of some description. Very clever manipulation of a very distant ancestry as it turns out. Anyway, I handle their passports with reasonable regularity these days because I'm now responsible for arranging their international travel and so on. She was back here about a week ago before she joined her husband in Hawaii. She often comes and goes while he's away. When she asked me to arrange her flights to Oahu, she mistakenly took a blue passport from the drawer of her desk, but then realized she had as she handed it across to me and snatched it back, replacing it with a red one, the Turkish one that she usually uses. Yesterday I finally managed to get clear of the other household staff and accessed Kristina's private office. I picked the lock on her desk and found the passport. She's actually Armenian. Her full name is Khrystya Elena Bedrosian. Date of birth: twenty-three April, 1978. Place of birth: Yerevan, Armenia. Perhaps that might assist in tracing her background a little more accurately than what's on offer in *HELLO* magazine or *Harper's Bazaar*."

"You're right. That'll be extremely helpful," he replied, memorizing all of it. "Who knows, that connection to the Russian may just be staring us right in the face."

"You got one of those famous hunches of yours?" she asked with a smile.

"I prefer to consider them informed intuition," he replied. "Playing a hunch is far too Raymond Chandler for me. Hell, you're probably too young to even know who Raymond Chandler is!"

"I know who Raymond Chandler is," replied Dominique. "He wrote all those detective books my granddad used to read when he was a young man. Older men still like to read them, right?"

"Whoa! I guess I had that one coming!" Masterson laughed. "But seriously, this deferential thing you mentioned about her attitude toward the old Russian – could be something there, especially given the timeframe of their respective appearances on the scene. Keep an eye out for any angles that may connect them. And if you can, try to get a picture of him, ASAP. Meanwhile, I'll feed this info about her back to London and they can get their people working on it. You got anything else?"

"No, that's it. If anything changes I'll let you know."

"OK. If a person like Helldiver can maintain such a positive public profile while still covering his tracks so effectively on the non-public side … well, we all know he doesn't deal in small change. So, proceed with caution. If he's into what we all think he's into, then he'll be prepared to do just about anything to make sure it stays under the radar."

"You think I should be worried? More than usual, I mean?"

"No, not worried. You can't afford to worry in this business. Just be cautious, particularly if you're going to get in on those meetings. And while we're on that subject, I have some of my own news for you."

"Out with it then."

"Well, if all goes to plan, you should be getting backup around the time that Helldiver arrives from Hawaii."

"Backup? What do you mean?"

"That's as much as I know and as much as I'm allowed to tell you. They've infiltrated another agent into the Hawaiian end of this thing and it's very possible he'll be returning here with the Zolners. So, keep your ear to the ground and your eyes peeled."

"Will my orders change once this new person arrives?"

"A fair question. From my viewpoint, no. I expect they'll keep you doing what you're doing, and the new guy will be their person to shake things up a bit on the operational side. Coming at it from two angles. Whoever it is, I'm sure they'll make contact with you when they hit the ground. After all, there's no point in us having the two of you spying on each other, now, is there?"

"OK, if they must. I just hope whoever it is knows what they're doing when it comes to dealing with people who operate at this level; you know, when money is no object. They're very different from us mere mortals. In every way."

"Don't worry," he said. "I'm sure the General wouldn't be sending in some wet-behind-the-ears rookie. He'll send someone with experience who's not afraid to take them on. Until then, all I need you to do is take care of yourself. You got that?"

She nodded and smiled bravely back at him, but Masterson wasn't buying it. He felt there was something about the introduction of another agent that had her spooked.

And for the life of him he couldn't work out why.

Chapter Twelve

"After 9/11," Reigns began, "anyone with even the slightest leanings toward extremist Islam who was either already a pilot or in the process of becoming one, came onto the radar of international authorities. One of these guys was a former Skyhawk pilot of the *Fuerza Aérea Argentina* by the name of Carlo Alfredo Salazar. He flew missions against the British during the Falklands War in '82 and, notwithstanding the fact that he is one of only one percent of the Argentine population who practice Islam, he was identified as being supportive of extremist action against the US in 2001 and was subsequently flagged when it became known that he was working as a pilot-recruitment consultant to a number of major international airlines around the time of the US invasion of Iraq in 2003."

"Jesus. I reckon this is the guy I saw leaving Helldiver just as I was being ushered in," said Morgan.

"When was this?"

"Yesterday. They'd been watching the CNN coverage

reporting on the missing plane and the cyclone just as I arrived."

"Makes sense," Reigns said. "Our team has been monitoring Salazar here in Hawaii, too. He was followed to the Zolners' house out at Diamond Head yesterday. No doubt he and Helldiver were checking in after 712."

Morgan shook his head in disbelief and took a swig from his Corona. He and Reigns were sitting in the Kuhio Beach Grill at the Waikiki Beach Marriott where Reigns was staying. They'd parted company earlier and spent the rest of the day separately. It was important to maintain the appearance of two people who'd just met and who had decided they'd liked each other enough to follow up with dinner. It also gave Morgan time to digest the fact that he'd been on the Intrepid books the whole time he'd thought he was unwinding and trying out a new life. He'd taken the opportunity to process the full extent of the anger, frustration and utter powerlessness he felt at having been manipulated so systematically. However, when all was said and done, he knew that the General – and Sheridan for that matter – had little choice: they had to get someone on the inside. If Morgan had had even a whisper of the truth about Helldiver, he knew that Rodenko and his team would have eventually smelled a rat. They needed to get Morgan in with a completely clean slate as far as Helldiver was concerned. They'd had no choice.

Morgan worked his conflicting emotions out in the gym for a solid two hours in the afternoon before taking a swim in the hotel pool and getting ready to meet Reigns, which included his first shave in well over a month. Now that he was with her and taking in the details of a new mission, that one elusive element that had been bugging him over the months of his self-imposed exile from Intrepid had finally fallen in his lap: more than anything else in his life Morgan knew that he needed a purpose, a reason to do the things he did; something bigger and more important than himself. Being a soldier and an Intrepid agent gave him that purpose.

"Salazar's background initially got him on an Interpol watch list," Reigns continued, "particularly because of his role in identifying and recruiting commercial pilots at that time. However, despite a lot of covert attention being directed toward him and his associates, he was squeaky clean. Interpol and the FBI found nothing to indicate that he was doing anything other than legitimately working with the airlines to recruit their pilots. So, with worldwide law enforcement resources already stretched to the limit, attention was directed elsewhere and he fell off the radar and into the background."

"When was that?"

"About 2005."

"And so what got everyone interested in him again?"

"All these recent air disasters, for one. Fresh eyes started looking at the major players operating in that space and, lo and behold, Salazar's name cropped up. This time he was connected to a number of pilots who had been crew members on the planes that went down. He was immediately back to being a prioritized person of interest and returned to the top of the watch lists. His travel going back over the past five years was scrutinized and it was confirmed that during the past two years he'd been traveling back and forth between his home in Spain, Oahu and Antibes in the south of France."

"What's in Antibes?" Morgan said, although the answer came to him just as Reigns was answering.

"That's where your man, Helldiver, has his main residence. Hiding right out in the open in a château located in the heart of billionaire and movie star territory."

"Château de la Lavande," Morgan replied. "I've heard it mentioned. I see the circumstantial connection but I'm guessing we have more than that, right?"

"Correct. Salazar was placed under surveillance by our people. Therese St. Marie has been leading the teams for well over a year; you remember her?"

"For sure. Therese had my back in Albania when we were after the Serbs. I still call her Aunty." He smiled. "She's great."

"Well, she coordinated a protracted, round-the-clock global surveillance operation with the objective of proving unequivocally that contact between Salazar and Zolner was occurring. About a year ago, they hit pay dirt. Not only was Salazar identified visiting Zolner's residence in France, but he was also a regular on Zolner's yacht, the *Gemini*, operating out of Oahu. So—"

"With the connection established, the boss infiltrates me into the Zolner security machinery."

"Correct, but not before infiltrating another agent into the center of the Zolner empire at the main residence in France."

"Another agent? Who?"

"A woman named Dominique. She's a shared asset, not just one of us. Sheridan's keen to keep each component of this one very much compartmentalized to avoid the risk of any operational cross-contamination, so all I know is that she's Europol but being run by Intrepid. You're to make contact with her if you get to the residence with Helldiver."

"OK, so where are we at right now? Anything from this Dominique?"

"Yes, and that's exactly why I was sent out here to activate you," she replied. "We believe Helldiver is preparing another attack. Salazar is the key. As far as we know, and his actions support this view, Salazar is not aware that he's under any kind of scrutiny, which makes him easier to follow and therefore the weak link in Helldiver's personal security arrangements. We know that Salazar has already been actively on the lookout for a new pilot in readiness for the next attack. He's based out of Singapore and has been observed meeting with a number of possible candidates, all of whom we've identified as being in some way sympathetic to the extremist philosophy."

"Yeah, the scorched earth philosophy," Morgan said, the bitterness evident in his tone.

"Exactly. Latest information from Dominique suggests that Helldiver and his people are already in the advanced stages of planning. We – and when I say we I mean you, too, Morgan – have to find out the who-when-where and, whatever it is that they're doing, stop it before they bring down another plane."

"Jesus," he whispered, half to himself. "I still can't quite get my head around the 'why.' Why is a person like Zolner behind all this, and what is the objective? I mean, it's got to be more than just straightforward extortion. Threatening these targeted countries – all of which are Islamic states – through their national airlines just seems pointless. It has to be something much more significant."

"That's our biggest dilemma. The motivation for the attacks isn't apparent, yet. What I do know is that we have to stop the next one. The agent in France has been tasked to find out why they're doing it. They're throwing everything at this, Morgan. The General's final words to me before I left London were that we were leaving no stone unturned."

"So, what's next for you, Reigns? I don't expect they'll let you swan around Hawaii in that bikini of yours for too much longer." He smiled.

She smiled back. "Singapore is next. I'm following up on Salazar, starting with the crew of 712. Apparently Singapore cops have turned up something so I'm going in as Interpol liaison to check it out. I may find something that'll help you."

A few moments of silence fell as they finished their meals and drinks, each contemplating the tasks ahead. Reigns spoke first.

"And so here we are, Morgan; you and me in Hawaii, and a set of new mission objectives currently sitting on Sheridan's desk back in London with your name all over them. People are relying on you. Not just back in HQ but also the agent, whoever she is, currently operating within the French end of Helldiver's operation. And, if you think about it, potentially hundreds more innocent people who may still fall victim to these assholes unless they're stopped."

"I guess I can't refuse then, can I?"

"Not really," she replied, sipping her Corona. "And, if I remember correctly, you never were any good at saying no to me. P.S. I'm glad you shaved." There was that look, the one with which she had so easily wrapped him around her little finger not so long ago.

"I'm glad you noticed," he replied. "So, are we still under surveillance or have you called off your dogs?"

"I called them off hours ago. It's just you and me, Morgan; right here, right now."

"Then, what about you and me getting out of here, right now?"

Reigns stood and signed the docket to put their meals on

her room account, then she walked around to Morgan and whispered in his ear.

Morgan stood immediately and said, "OK, but only if you promise to be gentle with me."

"Don't worry," she replied. "I won't hurt you...too much."

Chapter Thirteen

OAHU, HAWAII

Rodenko sat in the passenger seat of the SUV. It was a new one, a gray Toyota. The cops, if they'd been tipped off, would be looking for the Cadillacs. Beside him at the wheel was Muller, their best driver, and in the back were Kazloŭ and Delemović, two of his biggest guys, who weren't averse to getting their hands dirty. And this was going to get dirty.

They'd been parked in the shadows about a mile away from the apartment block where the Malaysian, Tengku, lived. Tengku was a mid-ranking diplomat in the Malaysian consulate and had been the appointed emissary between the Malaysians and Zolner. Of course, the Malaysians had absolutely no idea who they were dealing with. Their attempt to take Helldiver out was a line they should never have crossed.

They moved closer to the apartment block, parking in a side street that was well covered by a surrounding garden area with plenty of trees and plenty of darkness. Rodenko, Kazloŭ and Delemović were all dressed differently but practically; the only thing they had in common was that they were all wearing baseball caps, innocent enough at first glance, but the brims would shadow their faces and obscure their features on any of the apartment block's CCTV cameras.

They entered separately spread over a fifteen-minute period. Rodenko was first through the main foyer and Kazloŭ and Delemović followed, accessing the building via the underground carpark, using codes that had been identified during previous surveillance of the premises. Muller stayed in the SUV. In the foyer, Rodenko took the elevator to the fifteenth floor and then, using the fire stairs, made his way back down to the fourteenth. Kazloŭ and Delemović would do the same. Kazloŭ had a trolley and Delemović was carrying a large, flat, rectangular bag. When they had all arrived on fourteen, Kazloŭ and Delemović hung back a little farther along the corridor while Rodenko approached the door. He removed his baseball cap and then the spray jacket he'd been wearing, revealing a navy blue open collar shirt, which, on a cursory check through the fish-eye lens in the door, was designed to suggest that he was something he was not. He took a quick final look along the corridor in both directions, nodded to the others, who were poised just six feet to his right, then gave two sharp raps on the door. A few seconds elapsed and then he heard movement just inside.

"Yes, who is it?"

"Mr. Tengku, I'm Officer O'Loughlin from HPD, sir. I've been tasked to check in with you following an incident that occurred yesterday."

There was a momentary pause followed by a rattling chain and a latch being turned. The door opened.

"Yes," said Tengku from the open door. "How can I help you?"

Tengku cast a wary eye over Rodenko's clothes, quizzically noting the trainers, jeans and spray jacket and cap.

"Oh, yeah. Sorry, sir," said Rodenko. "No need to be alarmed, I'm off-duty. I live nearby, so dispatch asked me to check in on you when I finished my shift. You can call my precinct if you'd like; I can wait here. Just seeing if you're OK, is all, and if there's anything you need."

Tengku visibly relaxed. "That's very kind of you, officer. As you can see I am completely fine. In fact I'm very tired, so I was planning on turning in."

"Well, that's great, sir," Rodenko replied amiably. "Just one thing. You may not be aware, but we have an unmarked squad car downstairs in the street. So if you need anything at all, there are cops within reach. I can point out the car if you like. You'll be able to see it from your balcony."

Tengku paused for a moment, clearly uneasy, but Rodenko's easy, unthreatening manner had the desired effect – the man relented and stood aside for Rodenko to enter, then led him through the apartment. Rodenko allowed the door to hang ajar behind them. By the time they'd reached the center of the living area, Kazloŭ and Delemović had entered. Kazloŭ's trolley bumped the door, the unexpected noise causing Tengku to turn. The sight of not one but three men now inside the apartment startled him. He opened his mouth to protest. Rodenko struck with the side of his right hand directly at Tengku's throat, stifling the sound and inducing a choking sensation as his vocal cords went into trauma, restricting the airway. But Rodenko had pulled the strike just enough to stop Tengku attempting to yell for help while giving them the seconds they needed to bring him under their control as they prepared to remove him from his apartment.

Kazloŭ closed the front door. Delemović laid the

rectangular bag on the floor and loosened a series of ties that had bound it together. The bag was actually a large sheet of heavy-duty plastic and concealed a cardboard box, which he began to fold out. It was low and squat, but big and durable enough to contain a washing machine. Which is exactly what it had been made for.

Rodenko ensured that the semi-conscious Tengku was still breathing, then bound and gagged him. With the help of the others, Rodenko prepared Tengku for the box, wrapping him tightly within the black plastic sheet, allowing only his head to remain free. Then they lifted him into the box, closed it, positioned the tongue of the trolley under it and, using a number of long canvas belt ties, secured the box to the trolley.

Less than five minutes later they were back in the SUV and driving out of the underground carpark, the washing machine box shoved into the back.

They drove back to the house at Diamond Head and straight into the multi-vehicle garage that was attached to it. Once the roller door had shut again they opened the back of the Toyota. By now Tengku had come to and was wriggling around and moaning inside the box. Rodenko and the others dragged the box from the vehicle, allowing it to topple and fall hard onto its side on the concrete floor. Tengku let out a groan, shuffled some more but then settled. Delemović opened the box and Tengku's face appeared, his nostrils flared and whistling as he desperately drew in fresh air. Delemović tore away the gag. Vomit and bile instantly streamed across the black plastic that was wrapped around the prisoner.

"What are you doing to me? My government will not stand for this."

Rodenko and the others didn't say a word, not even to

each other. Instead they dragged Tengku from the box, cut him out of the plastic sheet and removed the bindings around his ankles, then got him to his feet and shoved him, stumbling, out of the garage down the stairs to the basement, where an area had already been prepared. The far corner of the basement was empty but for another large sheet of black plastic, a heavy wooden chair, a large black flag embossed with white Arabic characters fixed to the wall directly behind the chair, and a small digital camera on a tripod angled toward the chair. The scene was lit by the stark, impersonal glow of the fluorescent tubes set into the ceiling above. Tengku was coherent enough to see it and know exactly what it represented.

"No! No! No!" he screamed, trying to push uselessly against Kazloŭ and Delemović, his shoes slipping upon the polished concrete floor. "No, I am a Muslim! I am a Muslim. You cannot do this to me. It is against God's law!"

Still Rodenko, Muller, Kazloŭ and Delemović said nothing. None of them were Muslims. Tengku was thrust down upon the chair and tethered to it. Another gag was produced, shoved into his mouth and the ends were tied behind his neck. Once he was fastened to the chair and groaning through the gag, eyes full of terror, Kazloŭ and Delemović looked at Rodenko. This was where the dirty work started. Rodenko nodded and the two men gave Tengku the beating of his life. The chair rocked and blood gushed, with barely a sound to be heard but for grunts of exertion from Kazloŭ and Delemović and the occasional groan from Tengku.

After about a minute, Rodenko indicated that Tengku had had enough. Tengku's head fell forward onto his chest.

Kazloŭ and Delemović crossed the room, clambering out of their overalls, then changed into black clothes that had been carefully selected to convey a very specific message. They pulled balaclavas down over their faces. Kazloŭ slung a Kalashnikov around his neck and Dele-mović picked up a Makarov pistol. When they were ready they presented in front of Rodenko, who checked them down to the finest detail. Satisfied, the two of them took up their designated positions either side of the barely conscious Tengku, the flag suspended behind them. Muller took up his position behind the camera.

"OK," said Rodenko, finally breaking the silence. "Let's get this done."

Chapter Fourteen

THE RED LION, WHITEHALL, LONDON

"Dominique is working as fast as she can, Mickey, and I think she's done pretty well for us so far," said Masterson. "She knows the stakes."

"I know, but we need more. If she's right and they are close to initiating another attack then we must get ahead of their game. If we don't, hundreds more people will die and we'll be no better off than we are right now."

Masterson and Sheridan had found a quiet slice of the bar, sitting at a window on the Derby Gate side. Masterson had just arrived from Paris. It was late afternoon, the peak hour hadn't quite set in on Whitehall yet and they were halfway through their first round of scotch.

"So, how did you go with that name I sent through?" Masterson asked.

"Actually, that's the only gem in all this whole mess," replied Sheridan. "Dominique hit the goddamn jackpot uncovering that name. Khristya Elena Bedrosian, aka Kristina Zolner, is much more than just some heiress and wife of a billionaire."

"Let's have it then," said Masterson. He took a long pull of his scotch.

"Khristya Bedrosian is a former officer of Russia's Foreign Intelligence Service, the SVR."

"*Sluzhba Vneshney Razvedki*," Masterson said in perfect Russian. "The successor to the KGB. Changing the name hasn't changed anything. Still the same machine."

"You got that right. Bedrosian was recruited from university in the late nineties and by 2002 was operating within their counter-espionage directorate. From what we've gathered so far, she was eventually selected for covert operations and we understand she was specifically involved in a program which involved the targeting and deliberate blackmail of foreign diplomats and businessmen operating in Russia around the time that the Putin administration started turning on their oligarchs and jailing people like Mikhail Khodorkovsky."

"A honey trap," said Masterson. "Why am I not surprised?"

"Because when you've been in this game as long as we have, nothing surprises you," said Sheridan. "The only thing is, around 2010 we hit a dead end. The trail runs stone cold and we can't find a thing on her from then onwards until around 2013–14, when she suddenly re-emerged as Zolner's fiancée, a woman allegedly of Turkish origin and heiress to a huge fortune.

"But it doesn't stop there. In her SVR days, she was the protégé of Vasily Latushkin, now General Vasily Latushkin – current director of the SVR, a position which is personally appointed by the Russian president. He's an identified hardliner with loyalties to some seriously old-guard Communist Party types – which fits right in with Putin's Russia – not the least of whom was one of General

Davenport's old foes, a general by the name of Zolnerowich."

"Well, sure, I know Zolnerowich," said Masterson. "Our guy Helldiver's old man. Former assassin for the KGB and an all-round evil son-of-a-bitch. Copped a bullet in the back of the head about ten years ago. I was just recapping on him with Dominique yesterday."

"Well, you can imagine, just the hint of this connection between Zolner – aka Helldiver – and an old-guard Communist like Latushkin – especially as he was one of dear old Dad's closest friends – has got General Davenport champing at the bit to get to the bottom of this. When Latushkin was just a major in the KGB, he was allegedly involved in the 1991 coup attempt to oust Gorbachev, but miraculously survived the aftermath, including the disman-tling of the KGB and the purge of the security services that followed. Clearly, he had some very influential people in his corner. His mentor, the late General Zolnerowich, to name one."

"And a former KGB alumni called Vladimir Putin, to name another," added Masterson.

"Exactly. And now, he's the head of Putin's intelligence apparatus." Sheridan paused for a moment, thinking. Both men settled into their Scotches. Masterson started checking the menu.

"Davenport's theories on the global significance of whatever it is that Helldiver is up to – destroying all these aircraft and so on – are finally starting to take shape with this Russian angle. But I gotta admit, man, this Russian–Islamist thread – this thing between Helldiver, Salazar and these extremist pilots – has got me second-guessing every theory I can come up with."

"What does your gut tell you, Mickey?" asked Masterson. "I've known you a long time and nothing gets past you. So, whatever it is that's bugging you, explore it. Don't dismiss it."

"You got a theory?" said Sheridan; he knew Masterson equally well and the tone told him as much.

Masterson took another drink. "Well, since you asked … It suddenly occurs to me that this SVR element is the key."

"OK, go on."

"We now know that Helldiver's wife, Ms Bedrosian, is a former SVR agent. Not only that, she was Latushkin's protégé. We also know that she specialized in targeting foreign businessmen and diplomats operating in Russia. Now, you mention that the Russian–Islamist thread is bugging you. So let's consider that. Over the past few years SVR has been criticized for not doing enough to combat the Islamic extremists in Russia. Right?"

Sheridan nodded. A smile formed as he listened to his old friend piecing together the strands of information that Sheridan and Davenport had been grappling with. The benefit of an experienced and fresh set of eyes.

"One of the principal responsibilities of the SVR," Masterson continued, "is destabilizing foreign governments and, if recent history tells us anything about them, they're not averse to creating instability internally as well – when it suits them. Think of the apartment block bombings in 1999. Nearly three hundred dead, over six hundred injured. These were their own people. It secured Putin's path to the presidency and got them back into Chechnya. That operation had General Zolnerowich's name all over it."

"So what's the big deal about a couple of crashed planes and a few hundred dead foreigners?"

"Exactly," replied Masterson.

"And who's to say that Khristya Bedrosian isn't still on

the SVR payroll and that her marriage to Zolnerowich's son, Helldiver – who by the way just happens to be a favored Russian oligarch who was spared during Putin's purge of the oligarchs in the nineties – isn't just a cover?"

"Now you've got it," said Masterson. "That's the way I see it, for what it's worth."

"Then this whole goddamn thing is a classic destabilization operation," said Sheridan, following his train of thought. "Damn! I knew it. The General and I have been circling this issue for ages, but this latest development – the Khristya Bedrosian angle – makes it all fall into place."

"Behind every great man ..." Masterson said. "These guys don't do anything unless it has a purpose. They don't just happen to put one of their best agents on the arm of one of their favorite sons because it's a nice thing to do. Dominique is absolutely sure that Khristya Bedrosian is playing a significant part in the organizing of their closed-door sessions. She's not just 'the wife;' this has all the hallmarks of old-school Soviet global destabilization. It has to be part of a much bigger deal."

"Now all we need to do is prove it," replied Sheridan. "We need information and we need it fast."

Masterson's phone buzzed with a text. It was the phone he used specifically for Dominique. He unlocked the phone and tapped the screen. An image appeared: a hastily taken snapshot. Masterson could scarcely believe what he was seeing.

"Jesus Christ," he whispered. Without another word he handed the phone across to Sheridan.

Chapter Fifteen

OAHU, HAWAIIAN ISLANDS

Alex Morgan slid his feet into a pair of well worn brown leather R.M. Williams boots, stood and wandered over to the balcony doors tucking his shirt into his chinos. He slid the doors back and was greeted instantly by the smell of the ocean and a strong breeze that filled the curtains like sails pushing them high toward the ceiling. He noticed that out past Diamond Head the sky was looking decidedly overcast and he thought there may even be a chance of rain later in the day. Great. A good day to leave, he supposed. As if there was ever a good day to leave Hawaii.

Back inside he saw that his butler, Makaio, had been in and set a pot of tea down on the coffee table. He sauntered across the room and poured himself a cup. It was exactly the way he liked it: strong and hot with a good dose of milk, no sugar. He took the tea back outside and pulled up a chair on the balcony, enjoying the view, the tea and thinking about Elizabeth Reigns and the message she'd been sent to deliver. After all the self-righteous soul-searching he'd demanded time for, he now had to suffer the ignominy of having been on the books the whole time, without even knowing. He had to hand it to the old man, he knew how to get what he needed out of his agents. Who else but Davenport and Sheridan could have an agent deep undercover for months without the agent himself even realizing? He laughed to himself at the deviousness of it. Clever bastards. He hadn't been quite that forgiving when he'd first received the news but Reigns had talked him off that particular ledge.

Reigns. He'd missed her most of all over the past months and while he'd been in self-imposed exile he'd fought the temptation to reach out to her too many times to remember. But from the outset they'd both agreed that time apart was for the best. He'd go and get his head straight and then they'd see. She wasn't going anywhere, she'd said. She was amazing. He closed his eyes and remembered everything he could about her face, her voice, the way she smelled, walked, kissed. Jesus. He was obsessed. He knew she'd laugh at him if he ever owned up to thinking about her like that. And that's what made her so incredible – the freedom and unabashed confidence of her spirit. And she didn't take any shit.

There was a shuffle of activity from the kitchen and Makaio entered with breakfast. He called out a warm "Good morning, sir," to Morgan, who waved in reply from the balcony, and then he set to work arranging Morgan's breakfast on the suite's circular dining table.

"Did you sleep well, sir?" Makaio asked, casting his gaze across to the bedroom where the sheets and covers had been tossed onto the floor. His big face split into a broad, conspiratorial smile. "You look a little tired."

Morgan read the intended suggestion and laughed. He walked back into the suite and sat down at the table.

"I actually did sleep well, Makaio; thank you. And, I am feeling very well rested, too. This tea is great, by the way. Thanks very much."

Makaio withdrew quietly from the suite still smiling and left Morgan to his breakfast.

Morgan turned his mind away from the distraction of Reigns and the machinations of Davenport and Sheridan's strategy to infiltrate him. For the first time in a very long while, Alex Morgan had a purpose again. He was an Intrepid agent and there was a job to be done. A Russian oligarch, the son of an old hardline Communist, who lived in the lap of luxury day and night, and indulged any and every pathetic little whim and fancy that came to his mind, was bringing down commercial airliners and killing hundreds of innocent people at a time to break the resolve of nation states into doing his personal bidding. Intrepid was tackling the mission from multiple angles: an agent infiltrated into Helldiver's headquarters in France and Reigns on her way to Singapore to pick up the trail of the pilot recruiter, Salazer, and, hopefully, follow it all the way to the latest recruits for aerial jihad. And then there was Morgan. All he had to do was stay as close as possible to Helldiver, find out whatever the fuck he was up to and stop him. Simple.

He walked back into the bedroom and took the Heckler and Koch VP9, spare magazines and extra ammo from his suitcase and brought them back to the table. He laid them out and mechanically went through a basic strip-and-assemble routine, including emptying and reloading the magazines, all to make sure that everything was working as it should.

Satisfied, he fitted the gun and mags back into the BlackHawk Tactical Pistol Case Rodenko had given him and then put it down. That would stay with him until he worked out what was going on. His cellphone buzzed. It was a text from Simon, Helldiver's personal assistant.

Wheels up in an hour. Car downstairs in fifteen. Destination to be advised once airborne.

Acknowledged, he replied. No heads up on where they were going. Morgan felt the familiar tension of pre-mission anticipation building. It was a good feeling to be back in the game properly now. He topped up his tea and returned to the balcony, deciding it was time to take a private moment to enjoy the cool breeze and a few minutes of nothing. Who knew where the day would take him?

Morgan put on his lightweight navy sports coat, checked his watch, and went downstairs. In the hotel reception area, Makaio and the duty manager were waiting for him. Makaio had already taken care of Morgan's luggage. Morgan attempted to tip him but his butler politely declined; Mr. Zolner had apparently been more than generous already. Morgan thanked him and walked outside.

The car was waiting and his luggage had been loaded. Unfortunately the driver wasn't Bill; Morgan recognized him as being one of the security guys on Helldiver's payroll, so he got in the back and they drove in silence all the way to Honolulu International Airport. Morgan was pleased to avoid small talk. The car took him straight to a private hangar where he saw Simon with a couple of US Customs and Border Protection officers in their navy blue uniforms standing in front of a gleaming fire engine red Gulfstream IV with a large white Z emblazoned upon the tail fin. Morgan decided to leave the HK VP9 with the driver.

He walked over to Simon, who was in the midst of discussing the arrangements for the flight. As had previously been Morgan's experience, the CBP officers were being friendly but professional. They engaged immediately with Morgan, who handed over his passport and, with a discreet nod from Simon, went with the flow of the conversation regarding his impending departure for France. He was on his way, although there was no sign of the Zolners or any of the other crew, for that matter. Morgan's luggage was being unloaded by the driver and presented for inspection to the CBP officers. For a few moments, Morgan found himself alone with Simon and out of earshot of the others.

"So," he said, "care to enlighten me?"

"You're off to France," Simon replied. "Nice, to be precise. I'm staying here."

"And what about the Zolners; are they onboard already?"

"No, they flew out last night. Rodenko and the others flew with them. Mr. Zolner thought you'd enjoy some more time to yourself before he gets you working, so he arranged this plane just for you. He has three of them."

"Very kind of him," replied Morgan. On the surface the gesture appeared generous although from what Morgan knew of Helldiver now, it was apparent that he was to be kept on the outer edges of Helldiver's circle for a little longer yet. "What happens when I arrive?"

"You'll need to refuel en route, the pilot will advise you of that in flight. When you arrive in Nice you'll be met at the airport and taken to Mr. Zolner's private residence in Antibes, Le Château de la Lavande. Mr. Zolner will see you there."

Morgan watched as the CBP officers finalized their inspection of his gear. They returned to ask him a few questions and he completed and signed some exit declaration forms. He got the all clear, his passport was stamped and returned to him and his luggage was loaded into the Gulfstream by the ground staff. Finally he was being ushered aboard by a beautiful young stewardess, who introduced herself as Famke.

Famke familiarized him with the aircraft, including his sleeping quarters, bathroom, film, audio and computer facilities and then settled Morgan into his seat. She gave him the standard safety brief for the flight and offered to get him a drink for take-off. Morgan chose scotch. As she disappeared in the direction of the galley, the pilot appeared, introduced himself as Thomas and talked Morgan through the flight plan, including a refueling stop in New York, and then left him to his scotch.

Within fifteen minutes they were airborne. Morgan figured there wasn't anything he could do in flight so he'd just go with the flow until they arrived in France, and then he would see what he would see. He rummaged around in his carry-on daysack, found his copy of *The Count of Monte Cristo* by Alexandre Dumas and got comfortable.

The mission was unfolding faster than even he'd anticipated.

Chapter Sixteen

Elizabeth Reigns waved off another wave of advances from the detective who was her appointed contact in the investigation to track down Salazar. Detective Leong of the Singapore Police Force had been unrelenting in his campaign to convince her that dinner would be a great idea and she had been equally resolute in conveying her disinterest. She was there for one reason and one reason only, and Detective Leong was not it. Apart from anything else, he was short, twice her age, she could see that he'd removed his wedding ring, and he stank of cigarette smoke and body odor. Not a winning combination.

Reigns' mission was to trace the connection between a body discovered by garbage collectors three days earlier and Carlo Alfredo Salazar, the former Argentine Air Force pilot turned commercial-pilot recruiter who was squarely in Intrepid's sights. Detective Leong wasn't aware of Intrepid's interest in Salazar, he was simply the appointed contact from SPF's International Cooperation Department, the ICD. As far as he knew, Reigns was the Interpol liaison between the FBI and SPF regarding the body. That was all. Leong's job was to make sure that she got the access she needed to get her job done. She wished he would just stay focused on doing that. Between picking her up at Changi Airport and escorting her to meetings at SPF Headquarters, they'd been together for almost six full hours. It had been painful. The police officers who were actually responsible for investigating the murder had all been absolutely professional and courteous and she wished she'd been allowed to deal directly with them, unescorted, but in international circles certain protocols needed to be followed. In this case, she had to be hosted, which Leong interpreted as escorted at all times. His presence was supposed to be simple professional courtesy but his constant attention was verging on plain creepy.

Reigns sighed and turned her mind back to the case. Workers from Veolia Environmental Services, one of Singapore's contracted public waste collectors, had found the body when they'd returned to the waste-to-energy incineration plant at Tuas to unload. The police were called, SPF forensics subsequently confirmed the identity of the body and, armed with that information, were able to confirm his next-of-kin details and importantly his previous employment status. The dead body belonged to Captain Farooq Chaudry. Chaudry had been a pilot for Katak Airlines. More specifically, according to airline records, he had been the pilot at the controls of Katak Airlines 712 when it had disappeared from Malaysian civil aviation radar only to reemerge on Thai military radar flying directly into the path of Cyclone Penciptaan over the Andaman Sea a week ago. Despite the assurances of the airline that Captain Chaudry was confirmed as taking command of the aircraft from the origin point, Singapore, and was again in command from

Kuala Lumpur, following an extended layover, clearly the actual Captain Chaudry had not been the man at the controls of flight 712 at all. Working back from the last known sighting of Chaudry, SPF traced his final movements to the Holiday Inn on Outram Road. The discovery in Singapore of a body that technically should have been in the cockpit of flight 712 when it flew into a cyclone enroute to the Bay of Bengal had prompted Reigns' redeployment to Singapore and away from Alex Morgan in Hawaii.

For most of the day, Reigns had been receiving a string of detailed briefings covering everything SPF homicide investigators had found out about the deceased since they'd confirmed his identity. The body of Captain Chaudry had been wrapped in bed sheets, stuffed in a dumpster and dropped into a waste collection truck, destined to rot among the garbage until incinerated at the Tuas plant, never to be seen again. The coroner reported that a hypodermic needle had punctured the skin on the left-hand side of the neck and blood results indicated it had contained a concoction designed to immediately render an adult unconscious. The two bullet wounds in the back of the head from a .22 pistol had happened some time later.

Now, as she'd requested, they were at the hotel with the Holiday Inn security team, reviewing CCTV footage.

"So, this is the last day he was here, correct?"

"Yes, ma'am," replied the security operator. They were in front of the hotel's security monitors. "This footage was captured in the late afternoon of last Saturday, just as Mr. Chaudry checked in."

The capture was good, from a camera facing across the reception area. It had been well placed to cover the lobby and entrance, with the added benefit of filming people signing in and out. Reigns' eyes were glued to the screen.

She studied the occasional glimpses of the face on the screen, comparing it with the airline ID photo provided to the police by Katak Airlines. It easily could be the same man, but she couldn't swear on it. She had to rely on the cross-correlation of the date-time stamp on the CCTV footage, along with the entry in the hotel's register recording the time the man checked in and had his credit card swiped by hotel staff as his account was established and his room booking confirmed.

"I heard mention earlier of a young woman who came to the lobby a little while later, asking for Mr. Chaudry. Do we have any footage of her?" Reigns asked.

"Yes, we do. She came in about an hour after he did. I'll bring it up for you." He tapped some commands and a screen to the left showed new footage. There was a young woman with a small overnight bag, blond, attractive, dressed provocatively in a tight dress and high heels, getting out of a cab at the main entrance and then from another camera was seen speaking with hotel concierge staff. Reigns could almost hear the exchange between the young woman and the staff: "Of course, madam. Just one moment please." The phone was lifted. There was some nodding of the head. The all clear was given. "He is in room …" And up she went.

Reigns was impressed by the manner in which the security operator followed her train of thought so seamlessly as she suggested some possible alternatives to track the young woman's movements through the hotel, which led her eventually to Chaudry's room. Reigns was collecting data that gave her a clear image of the young woman, as clear as if she was standing there beside her. She knew the way she walked, her height – give or take, the confident upward tilt of her chin, a brazenness in her demeanor. It was all there and it was all Reigns needed to recognize the woman should she encounter her again.

Reigns and the police discussed general timings surrounding Chaudry's movements, phone calls from the room, any other visitors – there were none. Only the young woman. The next sighting of Chaudry and the young woman was almost two hours later when they appeared in the lobby with another man and then left the hotel. Chaudry and the girl had changed their clothes.

Reigns asked to see any more captured footage of Chaudry's movements and when she had, she was certain that the other man was the pilot recruiter, Carlo Salazar. While Reigns and the police were conferring, the security operator who'd been pulling out the footage for them looked like he wanted to say something.

"Go ahead," said Reigns.

The security operator cleared his throat. "When I was downloading all the footage of these people I found something I hadn't noticed before."

"OK," Reigns said. "Let's have it."

The man tapped the keyboard and soon a number of the screens showed different locations within the hotel.

"When we were looking for the others I remembered that I'd seen something unusual on the same floor as Mr. Chaudry's room around the time, actually just before they all left the hotel." He drew their attention to the first screen. "Here's the other man getting out of the elevator on Chaudry's floor, but it appears that Chaudry is already with him."

The operator was right – Salazar could be seen leaving the elevator with a man who appeared to be Chaudry, then they walked out of shot in the direction of Chaudry's room.

"Then this happens," the operator said, tapping keys.

"If you look at that same screen you'll see a man leave the service elevator pushing a laundry trolley; the ones our cleaning staff use to collect dirty linen from the rooms. Two things struck me about this. Firstly, it's very unusual for linen to be collected at that time in the evening, unless a guest has actually requested it. So, I checked with the night staff who were on that evening and the laundry staff, but there had been no requests from guests to change linen that night.

"The second thing that struck me was the man himself." He tapped a few keys and two other screens showed the same man again pushing the trolley. Nothing necessarily out of the ordinary. There were a couple of moments when his face became visible. He was young, solidly built with dark hair. Reigns and the police looked at the operator expectantly.

"He's not Asian," he said. "This guy is a Caucasian, possibly even Slavic. But he is definitely not Asian and I've worked here a few years now, so I know that we only have locals working laundry. And, yes, I double checked." He smiled.

"OK. I see where you're going," said Reigns, impressed by the man's thoroughness. "You have more?"

"Of course," he replied. "There's more footage of him moving not only toward Mr. Chaudry's room but about twenty minutes later he appears again, leaving that floor. He gets back into the service elevator and ends up in the basement but then I lose him. Look, whatever happened in the room we can't say for sure but either way, I reckon this guy's job was to get Mr. Chaudry out of the hotel after they'd drugged him. He could even be the trigger puller. I've grabbed some footage of routine vehicles leaving the loading dock area throughout that night – deliveries, some staff, garbage, laundry – I can't guarantee anything. I've put all this onto a couple of flash drives for you guys, including as many clear snapshots of faces as I could get on each of them; should help with IDing them, at least." He smiled and handed over the drives.

Reigns patted the operator on the shoulder. "You should speak to these SPF guys about a job," she said.

"Been there, done that, ma'am," he replied jovially. "Ten years on the job. I came off a motorcycle during a pursuit. We got the guys but I ended up medically retired. These days, I'm happy right here."

"Well, you've been of immeasurable assistance to us. Thank you so much."

Reigns and the SPF officers left the security control room and headed for the lobby. A sullen Detective Leong followed. It seemed that he'd finally got the message. On the drive back to SPF headquarters, Reigns continued to discuss the issues, as much as she could, surrounding the murder of Captain Farooq and, as the evidence was suggesting, his subsequent replacement by a lookalike. She received an undertaking by the investigators that they would continue to work on identifying the young woman, the young Slavic guy with the trolley and, if possible, Chaudry's lookalike via their own records and those of Singapore's Immigration and Checkpoints Authority. Reigns committed to working on confirming the identities as well, via the Interpol network.

When they all arrived back at SPF HQ, Reigns made her way straight for Interpol's National Central Bureau office, which was co-located with the International Cooperation Department. Thankfully, despite the ICD being the department Detective Leong was assigned to, he had apparently given up on his quest to wear her down and had left for the day. A middle-aged woman from the National Central Bureau's administrative staff greeted Reigns at the bureau's reception desk and showed her to the office that had been prepared for her. She gave Reigns the rundown on where everything and everyone was, and if she needed anything at all, she just had to ask. Reigns thanked her and then, for the first time since she'd arrived, was finally alone – blissfully unescorted. She got straight to work, logging into Intrepid's secure network. She took the flash drive containing the surveillance footage she'd been given at the Holiday Inn and began uploading the files to Intrepid's intelligence team back in London. She wrote some emails, including a status report for Sheridan, cleared a few others and decided it was time to return to her hotel and get some rest. It would be up to the intelligence team to make sense of the images she'd sent, along with the information and statements she'd gathered from the SPF investigators. She'd had the foresight to drop her bags off at the hotel when Leong and his driver had picked her up, so all she had with her now was her satchel. Alex Morgan called it her manbag. She laughed to herself as she gathered up her things and tossed them into it. Morgan. If only he were around for dinner. She wondered where he was right now and if he was OK. She hoped he was.

Reigns walked out of the headquarters building and onto Irrawaddy Road. It was 8pm, dark, and the surrounding streets were busy. She needed a cab but it didn't take long for her to realize that they were in short supply. Great! She wanted a bath and she needed bed. She looked back to the foyer of the headquarters and was contemplating asking for a lift back to her hotel when she saw Detective Leong emerging from one of the elevators and, it appeared, heading straight for her. Oh, God. No.

Where are the taxis? She was sure that if she turned around and walked back inside then she'd get stuck with Leong and it would be one of those moments when a dozen cabs would instantly stream past. She decided the best way to avoid any more awkwardness with him and quell her general annoyance at the situation was to bite the bullet and walk back to the hotel. It was close enough, a little over two miles. Besides, the walk would do her good.

She thought she heard Leong call out to her but she walked off anyway, making her way south-west along Irrawaddy Road leaving the SPF Headquarters at New Phoenix Park behind her, eventually turning left down Thomson Road heading in the general direction of the InterContinental Hotel. She hazarded a quick glance back and thought she could still see Leong standing out front of the headquarters. It looked like he was holding a cellphone to his ear. She picked up her pace.

For the first fifteen minutes the streets were busy and well lit, which was always a bonus when walking alone at night, and before long she'd worked her way further along Thomson Road, passing under the Kampong Java Flyover, continuing southeasterly along Keng Lee Road. As she reached the intersection of Keng Lee and Dorset Road she registered that a dark sedan was slowly edging up to the corner close to the curb but then it stopped short, staying back just far enough from the intersection to not be easily seen by traffic traveling around the sweeping bend in the road. She could see the Farrer Park Swimming Complex coming up on her left. Farther along, she noted that the road and the path she was walking along passed over the Rochor River aqueduct. The path veered around the bend along the edge of a small triangular park. The park was black as pitch in places where light from the surrounding area was blocked by a small enclave of trees.

In the moment that the penny dropped about the car she realized that a man was getting out of it, and in the same instant, another man emerged just ahead of her from the darkness of the trees in the park. Both of them began closing on her, unhurriedly, confidently, as though this was just routine for them. Was it intimidation, or was it going to be more than that?

Reigns slowed her pace, not overtly, just enough to buy some time to evaluate and prepare. She was scanning for escape routes and, if necessary, places she could stand and fight. *Where is everyone? And why the hell am I suddenly the only one out here?* While her subconscious was flagging the danger areas, the dark corners and obstacles that could force her toward a potentially indefensible position, her radar was already telling her that the location had been well chosen: it was the perfect place to ambush a defenseless female while remaining essentially in full view of passing traffic. She heard another car door open and registered a third man now on the pavement and closing in from behind her. Two behind and one in front. She began tightening and releasing her fists and filling her lungs with deep breaths to get the blood flowing and her body ready. She was still only about halfway to her hotel and too far from the next major inter-section to draw anyone's attention. It was pitch dark up ahead where the cut-off man was standing among the trees. The two coming up behind her had closed the gap now and were almost within reach. She'd been deliberately corraled and she knew it. She needed a plan.

She could now see the area to her left where they obvi-ously planned to drag her in order to have her in complete darkness. Option one was to allow them to do that. Option two was to her right, the only obvious escape route, straight into the oncoming traffic in order to be seen and hail for help. Option three, her preferred option, was the one thing they wouldn't expect her to do – a frontal assault on the man ahead, if possible, drawing them back to the safety railings designed to prevent anyone falling twenty feet onto the uncompromising concrete of the aqueduct below. She would have the element of surprise. Her fists were clenched, her breathing was now deep and steady, and Elizabeth Reigns prepared for action.

With a silent count of three she burst out of the blocks, running directly at the man in front of her and closing the space between them in four paces. The move caught him off-guard. His body lurched toward the road, the direction he'd expected Reigns to take. He was wrong. She went straight at him then dropped into a roll. There was a blaze of headlights from a passing car and she took advantage of the man's disorientation to launch up from the ground directly in front of him. She drove an unrestrained right fist into his crotch and as he bent forward in waves of agony she followed through with a flat-edged left-hand strike across his throat. He went down, in pain, struggling to breathe.

The other two men dived on her, grappling to restrain her legs. It was all too sudden and clumsy – they weren't expecting this to be arduous. Reigns got a leg free and kicked with everything she had at the first face she saw. The heel of her boot made contact with a crunch. The man let go and fell onto his side, clutching his jaw, wailing. By now the third man was on top of her legs and his rough-skinned hands were around her throat, squeezing. She began to gag. She needed oxygen. He crawled on top of her, trying to get his knees onto her chest to force the remaining air out of her while cutting off the chance of her breathing in any more.

Reigns' lungs were bursting. She knew she was in trouble. Even though she was clawing at his hands, she knew there was no point in trying to pull them away – he was too strong. Her only choice was to damage him. She had to make damn sure that he was the one in serious trouble, not her. Damage. Damage. Damage. Training came flooding back. She could see Tom Rodgers, Intrepid's chief instructor and unarmed combat guru, as clearly as if he was flat on his belly beside her yelling directions: *"He may be stronger but this guy's shorter than you, Reigns. You've got the reach on him. Go for his eyes! The eyes, Reigns!"*

The eyes were just a foot above hers. There was a flash of light from another passing car then darkness. Someone familiar? Impossible. *"You've got the reach on him, Reigns!"* She let go of his wrists and drove her thumbs straight into both eye sockets and clamped her long fingers tightly around his head. She squeezed. The man tried to clamp down but he was too late. Her thumbs were buried in his sockets and the pressure was building by the microsecond. It was only a matter of time before the eyes were destroyed. Reigns clamped down even harder and her manicured fingernails began to burrow into his scalp. He tried to shake her off but she wasn't letting go. His hands around her throat loosened, but she didn't let go. Then he did. He had no choice. He let her go and withdrew with a howl, his hands coming up to his bleeding eyes. Then he toppled to the ground in the fetal position, whimpering. Reigns was back on her feet, coughing and gasping for air. It had all happened so quickly that the first guy, groaning, was just recovering, still holding his balls. The second guy was on his back, cradling a broken or at least dislocated jaw. The last guy was in a bad way.

Reigns took her phone from her pocket and standing over each of them in turn, snapped a series of shots. Then she retrieved her satchel and walked back out to the road to hail a cab. This time one came along. She stepped over the safety rail that divided the path from the road, and got in.

"Intercontinental," she said.

Chapter Seventeen

CAP D'ANTIBES, CÔTE D'AZUR

The Rolls Royce Phantom entered the property via an ornate gateway of stone and iron and Helldiver's castle appeared in the distance. Morgan's immediate impression of the Château de la Lavande – via some vague recollections from his history studies at university – was that it was most probably Baroque. The château was situated on high ground and so appeared to ascend, supported by cupped hands as you got closer to it; the cleverly crafted illusion was designed to draw the eye to two enormous semicircular hedges – the hands – that held a lush garden of lavender at the end of the long avenue of holly oaks. Dozens upon dozens of classical colonnades framed the château's windows and doors to create a formal symmetry providing the only indication of the three-story arrangement. The structure was surmounted by a mansard roof of immense complexity, sitting as a crown that disappeared behind the façade as you approached. Baroque architecture was rare in this part of France which explained the turret just visible over the north-eastern corner, designed to protect by providing observation far out to sea in the days when that was necessary. The house was most likely built upon the remnants of a twelfth-century home that would have originally stood there. As the Phantom drew closer and broke free of the columns of holly oak, on either side of the central garden directly in front of the house oases of lavender dominated among broad-leafed evergreen shrubs, arbutus and stone pines within flawlessly landscaped grounds.

The car drove to the right around the hands of the lavender garden and pulled up at the bottom of a dramatic staircase, which led up to a podium that ran across the front of the building. The openness of the podium suggested a middle ground, a no man's land, mediating between the formality of the house and the beauty of the gardens. It was breathtaking. The car rolled gently to a stop, the tires crunching on the pebbled driveway. The driver got out and opened Morgan's door for him.

"Pour vous, monsieur, je vais veiller à ce que les bagages est transféré à votre chambre immédiatement," he said, reassuring Morgan that his bags would be taken care of.

"Merci bien."

Morgan approached the entrance of double oak doors that were at least fifteen feet high. Before he had a chance to knock, one of the doors was opened and a young woman appeared dressed in what Morgan recognized as traditional wear for a butler – pinstripe gray flannel trousers, gray vest, black morning-coat, white wing-collared shirt, black tie, white gloves and high-sheen black shoes. She greeted him familiarly as "Major Morgan," introduced herself as Micheline and told him that Mr. Zolner was expecting him, but first she would show him to his room so he could freshen up after his long trip from the Unites States.

Micheline led Morgan through the grand entrance hall of the residence and, despite two separate visits to Buckingham Palace in the past to receive the Military Cross and, later, the George Medal, Morgan had never seen anything like it – he was staggered by the overwhelming opulence of the interior space, matching in every way the scale and grandeur of the exterior. Everything around him was larger than life, from the artwork to the statues to the huge spiral staircase that rose through the center of the house for three floors. But most captivating of all was the open design of the foyer, a contemporary refurbishment that split the house in two – northern wing to the left and southern wing to the right – with floor-to-ceiling windows three stories high at the rear of the house, looking out across the gardens and on to the sea. After a general explanation about how the house ran and a couple of detours to assist him in understanding the general layout of the place, Morgan and Micheline arrived at the room that had been prepared for him. His luggage had also arrived. The room was larger than his modest semirural home in Farnham back in England, and located at the rear of the house on the second floor, it afforded Morgan unimpeded views out to sea. Micheline told him she'd return for him in an hour.

As the door clicked behind her, Morgan dropped onto the bed, staring up at the ceiling, which he saw was painted with a montage of religious iconography. Jesus! He had to sleep under that? He closed his eyes for a moment and decided he had to shut down the distraction and irrelevance of trying to comprehend the scale of Helldiver's wealth, including the travel brochure explosion of lavishness he was in danger of being consumed by. He had to recalibrate mentally to the job at hand. He was, after all, an Intrepid agent, not some flake salivating over the lifestyles of the rich and famous.

Most importantly, he had to remember where he was and to see it for what it really was: the center of an empire intent on causing global instability, killing hundreds if not thousands of people, all for what? Of course, there would no doubt be the ancillary benefits of even more power and wealth to be derived for Helldiver personally. Morgan remembered Reigns' simple but nonetheless effective mission brief back in Hawaii: "… *find out the who-when-where and -how, and, whatever it is they're doing, stop it before they bring down another plane.*"

Morgan showered for about fifteen minutes, allowing the hot water to relax him while purging any underlying stress and tension that were building in anticipation of his mission. He dressed in a light gray, tropical worsted suit with a pale-blue shirt and patterned maroon tie, keeping it simple with black shoes and belt. He clipped on the new metal strap he'd had fitted to his favorite old Tag Heuer watch, which he'd managed to rescue after it had been damaged by the Night Witch's crew back in Belize. Although, that had been such a close call he'd considered retiring it. Morgan wasn't sentimental about many things but he'd formed an unusual attachment to the watch. The possibility of ever losing it hadn't ever occurred to him until Belize. He checked the time. There was a tap at the door.

When Morgan opened it, he could scarcely believe who was standing in front of him.

Chapter Eighteen

SINGAPORE

All it took was that passing car and an infinitesimal flash of light. It was just enough for her subconscious to register that the face of the man on top of her, the one whose fingers were clasped around her neck trying to choke the life from her, the one whose knees were bearing his full weight down upon her chest trying to force the last remaining breath from her body, was someone familiar to her. Someone she knew, but not someone she knew well. Someone recent. Someone from today. Someone who had annoyed her.

Detective Leong.

All of this had occurred to her during the taxi ride on the way to her hotel. It had taken only a matter of minutes as she sat quietly, recovering in the back of the taxi from the ambush-cum-attack Leong and two of his accomplices had unleashed upon her. As soon as she'd realized it had been him, she was on the phone to Sheridan back at Intrepid HQ in London. By the time she'd returned to her hotel, showered, changed and regrouped, officers from the SPF Internal Affairs division were waiting for her in the foyer of the Intercontinental, while outside a team from the police Special Tactics and Rescue unit were waiting in two black four-wheel drives with the engines running.

With the impetus of 'special interest' directed via Interpol Headquarters in Lyon, France, SPF immediately swung into action. A car fitting the description Reigns had provided had been traced – via traffic management cameras located in the area she was attacked – back to Leong's apartment. It was anticipated that Leong and his accomplices had gone there on the basis that their plan to overwhelm Reigns had gone so wrong they wouldn't risk exposure by going straight to a hospital emergency room. When Internal Affairs officers confirmed Leong's location, STAR was activated to make the arrest.

In the corridor outside Leong's apartment, Reigns was kitted up with police issue overalls, a balaclava and a Sphinx Alpha 9mm automatic she'd borrowed from the STAR team. There'd be no knocking. The first STAR officer in the line pressed his ear to the door and after a few moments held up three fingers. Each officer in turn down the line held up three fingers. Then the biggest guy in the team was called forward. He stepped out from behind Reigns carrying the thirty-pound battering ram. Reigns tightened her grip around the Sphinx. They'd be in the door in three, two, one …

The big guy swung at the door lock. They'd decided the door was light enough and the lock uncomplicated enough to be taken out easier than an assault on the hinges. It was the right call. The silent corridor exploded with the boom of the impact followed by the chorus of officers calling, "Go! Go! Go!" as they erupted into action, pouring into Leong's apartment. As the door opened, everything Reigns saw confirmed everything she'd thought. She followed the

STAR team in. Leong was standing dumbfounded in the center of the room clutching a bloodied towel over one eye with blood streaming down his face from the other, knees buckling under him as he was being forced to the ground. To the left was a guy holding a bag of frozen peas around his jaw. He was on the floor, evidently dragged from the sofa he'd been resting on moments earlier. To her right she saw an officer disappearing into a room, chasing the third man. A torrent of bellowed commands followed, then the distinctive *boom-boom* of a weapon being fired in a confined space. The officer reemerged, making a cutting motion across his throat. The third man was down. In less than a few seconds the STAR officers had control.

With one target down and two targets on the floor, they checked the rest of the apartment for others. There were none. At this point, Reigns had to step back and leave the cops to do their thing. All she needed from them now was to know exactly who had engaged Leong to take her out and why. Then a medic from the STAR team checked out Leong and the other guy and verified that they would both need hospital treatment. Checking IDs, they confirmed that Leong was the only police officer; the other two were hired help. Leong and his accomplice were taken out by the STAR team, Leong to hospital under police guard, the hired man to the SPF headquarters lock-up; once Leong was treated, he'd be taken back to SPF HQ for questioning by Internal Affairs. The third guy would go out on a gurney under a blanket.

Reigns was far too hyped for sleep and once everything at the apartment had been sorted, she grabbed a lift back to SPF HQ and returned to the Interpol National Central Bureau office. Still in the overalls she'd borrowed – the guys had told her to keep them to remember them by – she made some tea and logged in to see if there'd been any intelligence on the images she'd sent through for identification. She also needed to speak with Sheridan to update him on the arrest. She lifted the handset and tapped in the digits on the secure line while she waited for her Intrepid profile to load on screen.

"Sheridan."

"Hey there," she replied. "It's Reigns."

"Hey, kid. How are you?"

She liked that he called her "kid." Rodgers called her that, too, and Sutherland used to as well. The familiarity of it made her feel like part of the family, like the older guys were her brothers looking out for her. That's the way they made her feel, anyway. Except for Morgan. That was something completely different. She wondered if Sheridan knew about her and Morgan.

"I'm OK. I've just come from the arrest."

"How'd it go?"

"We got Leong. The two guys who helped him out were there but one of them tried it on with SPF special ops and they took him down."

"Dead?"

"Yeah," she replied. "Leong was the only cop of the three. Looks like the others were just hired help, locals. SPF Internal Affairs will take care of the interrogation and follow-up. They know what we need out of Leong. I don't want this thing distracting me from tracking Salazar anymore than it already has."

"We're way ahead of you," he said. "Have you checked your messages yet?"

"Not yet, but it looks like they're just coming through now. Hang on." Reigns opened the response message from the Intrepid intelligence team and a stream of information poured onto her screen. She scrolled through, taking in the headline information. "Salazar is still on the move, so the girl seems like our strongest lead right now. She called herself 'Honey' when she came into reception at the Holiday Inn asking for Chaudry, but it says here that her real name is Galina Devushka. Russian passport. Twenty-two years of age. Currently residing in Singapore. Do we know if this address is up to date?"

"I'm told it is. The team have confirmed that she's been living there for the past year and for a girl whose visa information says she's a student, she's living pretty large. That apartment is apparently in a pretty classy area of Singapore, so she must be doing more than just working in a cafe to pay for it."

"Do we know if she's been seeing anyone new – since Chaudry, I mean?"

"No, but if what we know from Dominique is correct and they're making another move soon, then you can bet she's already lining up the next guy, if she hasn't already. Meanwhile, I've asked the team to see if they can link her to any of the pilots of the other aircraft that have been targeted. It shouldn't be too hard if we start with the hotels they were staying at whenever they were in Singapore ahead of their last flights. I'll keep you posted. How do you want to play it from here?"

"I'm going to need a team to watch her. If these guys are behind Leong's attempt on me then I can't risk getting too close to this myself until we're sure about her and I need to act. I've had to involve SPF too much already, so I'd rather not impose on them again if I can help it. Too many people knowing what we're doing – I'm already feeling exposed out here. Do we have any of our teams nearby?"

"I can send you some of our people I've just relieved

from a task in Thailand. They can redeploy direct from there and be with you by midday tomorrow – well, I guess that's midday today for you, right?"

She looked at her watch. It was 1am. "Oh shit, I guess it is. OK, I'm going to get some shut eye back at my hotel and they can reach me there. Anymore for me?"

"No, that should keep you busy for a while. You need anything more from me?"

"No, I'm all good. Just knowing you've got my back is all I need."

Reigns hung up, shut down the computer, stepped out of the overalls and headed, once again, for the lobby. This time there was a squad car waiting for her. She wasn't walking anywhere.

She climbed inside gratefully and sank back into the seat. As she struggled to fight off exhaustion, her mind turned to Morgan.

Chapter Nineteen

CAP D'ANTIBES, CÔTE D'AZUR

Morgan's eyes were locked onto those of the woman standing in front of him. The hair was different. It was dark brown now, still cut in a shoulder-length bob but messy somehow, if that was the right word for it. The face seemed slightly more defined, the cheekbones more prominent, and the body had lost some of its curve but was still sensational. It was the eyes that there was no escape from, despite the camouflage of hair, heavier make-up, gym-toned body and altered wardrobe; even had they been disguised beneath contacts he would have known, but they weren't, they were the same mesmerizing sky blue he remembered. They stared back at him from the face that had haunted his dreams for years, ever since that final, strained farewell at Heathrow. *"I need to put all this behind me,"* she'd said. And here she was, standing in his doorway. Only this time, the beautiful crystal blue eyes weren't full of sadness or regret, there was no longing or pain or conflict, just fear. Fear for him and for her. It was a fear he was all too familiar with in this line of work. The fear of discovery. The fear of being declared a spy when deep in the heart of enemy territory. He wanted to say her name, hug her and tell her everything would be OK but he knew he couldn't. Her expression told him so. This was not a reunion, this was a warning. Here she wasn't Arena. Here they couldn't know each other. They had no history. There had been no love. Morgan knew the score. He would have to work out the personal baggage later. He wasn't looking at Arena. Arena had gone. They were just two strangers meeting for the first time. They were infiltrators within the enemy enclave. And suddenly the fear reached for him. His fear for her safety. All the history flooding back to him. He swallowed the shock, the pain, the elation, the anger and, for the first time since their last physical contact at Heathrow all those years ago, he held out his hand.

"Hello there," he said. "Alex Morgan."

"Major Morgan, I'm so very pleased to meet you," she replied, shaking his hand. She squeezed it, ever so slightly, but for just that fraction longer than required. A subtle, private communication of acknowledgment. Instantly he remembered the softness of her fingers, every joint and undulation. They felt so comfortable nestled among his after so long apart.

He held her gaze throughout the shared seconds of privacy and reconnection, and she held his. Her accent had taken on a decidedly French flavor. He liked it, although it would take some getting used to.

"I'm Dominique, Mr. Zolner's executive officer – his chief of staff, if that makes more sense. I'm here to escort you down to him. He's ready for you now in his private office. Would you like to follow me?"

"I can't imagine why I wouldn't," he replied with a forced smile.

She smiled for a second in response then turned on her heel and headed toward the north wing of the house. She made small talk most of the way along the seemingly endless corridor until they reached a small alcove that accessed an elevator. When they stepped inside she turned and looked at him. Despite the strained smile, her own pain was evident in her eyes. The doors closed and they began to descend.

"I knew it was you as soon as I saw you getting out of the car. I was told to expect an agent and somehow I knew it would be you." She smiled again but it was tight. "It had to be you, I suppose. Destiny ... and all that."

"But, how—" he began.

"Not now, Alex. I'll explain everything, I promise, but right now I have to tell you, we don't have much time. Things have recently escalated here," she whispered urgently, clearly conscious they only had a few seconds. "Yesterday I managed to plant a listening device in his office, that's where we're headed now. I overheard them last night. Not that I necessarily needed the device. They were shouting at each other, Zolner and his father."

Morgan shot her a puzzled look.

"Yes, his father is here," she said. "Masterson has confirmed that the old man you're about to meet is in fact the infamous General Zolnerowich. He's alive and he's here, right now. Apparently General Davenport was none too happy when he found out. I'm told there's history there. Now, this is the clincher. They've murdered a Malaysian who was the assigned intermediary between them and the Malaysian government. They killed him in response to the attempt on the Zolners in Hawaii."

"How?"

"Beheading. I haven't seen it but I heard it being played

as they watched it. They reconstructed an Islamic State execution." She flashed him a glance. "They videoed it and sent it to the Malaysian government."

"Jesus," Morgan said. "So what's been the fallout?"

"I can't work out for sure which one of them ordered it, and that's what's been the source of the friction between them. On top of that, there's now been some kind of new threat directed at the Zolners, from what I can gather it seems to be targeted at Kristina. And that has freaked them both out. I don't know what it is yet. Helldiver is furious but he's also afraid. That's made him *and* her paranoid. He's expecting you to be the answer to all his problems but General Zolnerowich is not happy about you, an outsider, being brought on board. So, be careful, Alex. This will get very messy, very quickly."

The elevator hissed to a stop. She took his hands in hers and held them firmly. "I'll find a way to speak with you alone as soon as I can. Until then, we don't know each other. Please take care."

She let go. The doors opened.

"You too," he whispered and she led him from the elevator. By the sounds of it, they'd walked in on an argument. It was Helldiver. He was berating someone.

"You were a fool to authorize this! It was unnecessary. Unnecessary action brings unnecessary consequences! And now we have them. Now we, me and her, face those consequences, not you!"

"The only thing these people understand is action by force. They were not getting the message. It needed to be personal. And now they are clear. They publicly commit to a ten-year contract for their new range of MiG-29s with you and they will fund the purchase and deployment of the

S-300 air defense missile system for the ISIL forces in the Middle East."

"But this threat is not from the Malaysians!" Helldiver yelled. "It's from our own people. We're not resourced to bite the hand that feeds us!"

Helldiver was standing behind a desk in the center of the room. This must be his private office. The entire eastern wall was colonnaded windows that looked out across the gardens to the sea. Every inch of the room matched everything else about Château de la Lavande that Morgan was trying to shut out – the extravagance was overpowering. He closed his mind to the distraction once again, and watched as Dominique – whom he had only ever known as Arena, his Arena – walked to his left and took a seat off to the side of the desk. How was he expected to function with a clear head when he'd just rediscovered her like a bolt from the blue? She had always been 'the one', and to a certain extent always would be, or so he'd thought. She'd made the decision to move on with her life without him and, eventually, he'd moved on too. But now here she was. Christ!

Morgan moved away from the elevator and crossed the room to Helldiver, noting Kristina Zolner standing nearby, and he could see the head and shoulders of an older man seated in front of the desk. The old man didn't move, only sat still and kept smoking, gazing out of the windows. Rodenko was sitting in a corner, not offering much other than taking up space and stealing oxygen. And there wasn't much of that in the room. The place was filled with smoke and while Morgan could see that the Zolners and Rodenko were all smoking, most of it was coming from the old man. He was puffing like a train.

"Ah, Major Morgan. Finally, someone to make sense of all this mess. Our newest addition. Come in, tovarich.

There is someone I want you to meet. Come. Come, my friend." Helldiver beckoned, walking around to join Morgan. Morgan had the impression Helldiver had been drinking and confirmed it when he grabbed Morgan and hugged him like a bear, slapping his back powerfully and then turning as if to present Morgan to the old man. "This is the man I told you about. This is the guy we need if we are to take on these SVR assholes!"

Morgan watched as the old man finally moved in his chair, awkwardly it seemed, to turn and look at him. He had no doubt that this was the late General Zolnerowich. Clearly no longer dead.

"Who the fuck are you?" Zolnerowich demanded.

"This is Morgan. This is the man who saved my life. Twice. I tell you, he will deal with these fucks who are threatening us."

"They are threatening me!" Kristina Zolner cried suddenly and then resumed smoking.

General Zolnerowich stood and walked slowly toward Morgan and Helldiver, his dark, lifeless eyes never wavering from Morgan. Helldiver was obviously uncomfortable but didn't say a word, leaving Morgan to deal with it. Morgan held the stare, unflinching. He maintained an impassive stance, unperturbed by the old man's attempt to unsettle him. When Zolnerowich had reached him, the two stood eye to eye.

"Is there something you'd like to discuss with me?" Morgan asked. "I believe I was invited, but if you have any concerns about me being here, I'm more than happy to leave."

"You'll leave when I decide you'll leave," said Zolnerowich. "And not before." He made a show of appraising Morgan, as though Morgan was little more than something he'd purchased and was now having second thoughts.

"I tell you, he's good. He stays until we resolve this thing." Helldiver had obviously had enough. "I want him with me."

Kristina Zolner became jittery, fidgeting and pacing in tight little circles at the end of the desk, biting her nails and puffing her cigarette in between. Morgan thought she'd looked concerned when he'd walked in but he put that down to the overall vibe, caused mostly by the presence of Zolnerowich. He certainly had that effect and he clearly unnerved her, but there was more going on. Something that had her scared. The threat must have been personal.

"I don't want to stay here, Hedeon," she said emphatically. "I feel too exposed. Like I'm waiting for them to come for me."

"You're safe, my darling," said Helldiver. "No one can get you here."

At that, Zolnerowich let out a harsh laugh and returned to his seat. "You have no idea, you silly little bitch! If they want you, they will get you. Or have you forgotten already where you came from?"

Kristina's face flushed and all the color drained from it. She downed her drink and began worrying at another nail. "I'm going back to the *Gemini*, now! I'm not staying here like a sitting duck!" With that she stormed from the room.

With a flick of his head, Helldiver motioned to Arena to go with her. Arena followed Kristina Zolner out. Morgan had to stop thinking of her as Arena. It was too dangerous. He could slip up at the wrong moment and they'd be exposed.

"Rodenko. You too. Stay with her. Don't leave her side."

Rodenko glowered at Morgan and stormed out of the room in Kristina's and Dominique's wake.

Helldiver noted Morgan's gaze following Dominique. He laughed and said close to Morgan's ear: "Forget that one, tovarich. She's beautiful, yes, but you could freeze ice on her ass!" He clapped Morgan on the back and announced loudly, "Scotch! Then we must plan."

He walked over to a drinks cabinet and took out a glass. He ladled ice into it from a small bucket and produced a bottle of the fifty-year-old Glenfiddich. He poured a generous measure and handed it to Morgan. Zolnerowich stood, clearly preparing to leave.

"No, you stay, old man!" Helldiver said from across the room. "You got us into this mess. You can stay while we work out how to get ourselves out of it."

"You don't give the orders here, boy!" said Zolnerowich. "You should remember that." He walked out.

Morgan and Helldiver stood by the windows, looking out to the ocean, sipping the scotch.

"Kristina will relax on the boat. She loves to be on the water. Dominique will organize it."

"Where is it?"

"Just a few miles out to sea. The crew are doing some maintenance while we are here at the house," he said. "She'll be happier out there. It will give me time to work this out. They need to know that I don't scare easily. She'll be happier on the water."

Morgan noticed that the drinking was taking its toll on Helldiver and wondered how long he'd been at it. Morgan decided to use it to his advantage. While Helldiver was getting lubricated and unencumbered by the presence of the others, Morgan could get some details.

"When I last saw you, back in Oahu," Morgan began,

"and I asked if you were going to bring me in on whatever it is you're into, you said there'd be 'plenty of time for that.' Well, we're on our own and it seems to me that this is as good a time as any. So if you want me to help, you need to tell me what's going on."

Helldiver took a long pull on the scotch and emptied the glass. He poured himself another and offered Morgan more.

Morgan declined. "I'm no good to you pissed."

Helldiver shrugged, filled his own glass again and walked back to his desk, slumping into his chair.

"Some time ago we embarked on a righteous enter-prise," he began. His words were slurred and he looked tired. This worked for Morgan. "Everybody supported the plan. We were heroes to the cause. The old ways. We were reclaiming our Russian heritage."

Morgan was listening intently but his gaze wandered out across the gardens that overlooked the turquoise waters of the French Riviera. He could see Kristina Zolner and an entourage consisting of Dominique, Rodenko and two of his guys, and a number of household staff all carrying luggage, waddling along toward the private pier at the end of the gardens. He couldn't see it, but he expected that the Riva 33 Aquariva was at this moment warming its screws at the end of the pier, readying to ferry Mrs. Zolner back out to the *Gemini*. When she said she was going back to the boat "now," she obviously meant it.

"But then everything changed."

As those few words registered with Morgan, he saw two men appearing from the southern edge of the gardens near a large stone fountain. At first it seemed harmless enough, gardeners or general maintenance people perhaps, but then the unmistakable movement of each man's right hand to the small of their respective backs had told him that they were reaching for firearms. They were perfectly placed to lay ambush to the group that was oblivious to their presence, walking straight for the boat with no interest in what lay behind them.

Morgan ran from the room and through the closest door, sprinting straight for the two groups. They were at least seventy yards away and Morgan had to bound down deep stone steps and across the lawns to close the gap as quickly as he could. By the time he'd reached halfway and had started calling out, he realized he was unarmed. That's when the shooting started.

Morgan sprinted for the two guys he'd seen first – there could be more. If this was a legitimate hit on Helldiver at his residence then it was very probable that there would be more. The sporadic *crack-crack-crack* of automatics firing and being answered forced him to think of only one person – Arena. She could be whoever the job required her to be here, but she would always be Arena to him.

He ran as fast as he could across the grounds. The group had disappeared where the land dipped toward the pier. He heard some screaming, possibly the household staff who were caught up in it all. He couldn't imagine Arena screaming like that and right now he didn't give a shit if it was Kristina Zolner. She was an ex-SVR agent and whether she was rogue or still on the books, she knew the score. The gunfire was continuing. Jesus! Where was Arena?

Morgan saw the back of one of the hit squad crouching behind a small retaining wall for cover. The response from Rodenko and his crew was halting their progress, and they weren't prepared to react to an assault from the rear. Morgan was closing in. Then he saw the body of one of the household staff: a middle-aged woman in her white uniform now stained with blood. Fuck! He needed a gun. Something. Gunfire erupted to his far left and farther ahead, no doubt the extra members of the hit team he'd anticipated. They were firing toward the pier too. Morgan was just a few paces from the closest guy. At this point he was in greatest danger of being hit by Rodenko's crew. He had to jump down to the level where the guy was firing from. He made the leap.

His shoes crunched onto the stone path that paralleled the wall. The guy heard it and turned. Morgan wasn't close enough to take him on. What would Tom Rogers say about something like this? *"If you're not close enough to strike then you have to extend your reach. Search for a weapon that will do that for you."* A couple of fancy potted plants sat along the top of the wall. He grabbed the closest one he could manage, the fingers of his left hand closing around the top edge. His right came in underneath. Morgan was short by ten feet. The muzzle of an automatic was pointing straight at him, ready to fire. Morgan's body twisted as a discus thrower's might and he hurled the potted plant straight for the gunman. The man had no choice but to move, firing half-a-dozen rounds in Morgan's general direction as he did. Morgan watched as the pot sailed through the air and sensed the aimless rounds as they sailed past him. The gunman jumped clear just as the pot shattered against the wall where he'd been taking cover.

Morgan was instantly upon him and they both fell to the ground in a tangle. Wasting no time, he concentrated his effort on the man's gun hand, going for the Makarov, but the guy wasn't letting him have it. Then Morgan got a break, twisting the gun arm around behind the guy's back. Hanging onto it with both hands, he had the wrist ready to snap. The guy screamed in pain. Using him as leverage,

Morgan got to his knees and then back on his feet. And with the guy's face pressed into the ground and the gun arm and wrist locked in a repulsive angle, Morgan kicked and stomped until he'd rendered the guy unconscious. He tore the Makarov and spare magazines free from the belt rig the guy was wearing and sped off, finally armed, in search of the next one.

The gunfire was continuing, although it seemed to be originating farther away. Mrs. Zolner was still making for the boat. Morgan heard firing to his right beyond a shrubbery about ten yards away. He made his move fast and soon saw the man poised over the hedge firing incessantly toward the pier. Morgan braced and fired four rounds in quick succession. Each one found its mark in the guy's left flank. Morgan ran to check that he was dead. He was. He relieved the body of its hardware and ran back toward the stairs to the pier. Down below the screws of the Aquariva were already rumbling and as he ran, Morgan thought he'd caught sight of Kristina Zolner clambering aboard, but no sign of Arena. Fuck! Fuck!

By the time he reached the ancient stone steps that led to the pier, Morgan could see Rodenko and one of his guys huddled protectively over Kristina aboard the Aquariva, which was now slicing a powerful wake through the water in search of the *Gemini*. Still no sign of Arena or the remaining household staff and Rodenko was down one. Could Arena be alongside Kristina Zolner, under the gaggle of bodies, and Morgan just couldn't see her? A growl of a marine engine that immediately howled as it was pushed unnecessarily into the high revs took his eyes to a second boat, a twenty-foot, center-console runabout, nestled at the base of the pier closest to the end of the stone steps. Morgan recognized it as one of the tenders from the *Gemini*. There were two men onboard, one at the controls and the second unraveling the mooring lines from the cleats on the pier. They were totally focused on the Aquariva ahead of them. Morgan bounded down the steps two and three at a time, fitting a fresh magazine to the Makarov on the move. The 150 horsepower engine bit into the water, churning white froth. The mooring lines were finally freed, racing unattended through the cleats as the boat surged forward.

Morgan made the final few steps as the two in the boat took off after their target, firing wildly at the back of the disappearing Aquariva. There was a bloodlust to their relentlessness, a no-holds-barred fixation on completing their mission no matter what. They'd lost two men and were clearly prepared to die to ensure that their orders were carried out. This reeked of Russian retribution – delivering a message no matter what. Morgan recalled Helldiver's comments: "*This is the guy we need if we are to take on these SVR assholes!*" Why the hell was Russia's Foreign Intelligence Service trying to take out Helldiver? And why were they hell-bent on killing one of their own, or at least one of their ex agents?

Morgan tossed his jacket to the ground, shoved the Makarov under his shirt and behind his belt, took the final few steps and dived from the pier, grabbing for the mooring line in the water before the unfettered end flew free of the cleat. His hands found the wet rope and then, fighting against the pressure of the white water and struggling to catch a breath, he made his way hand over hand along the rope toward the back of the boat. A moment of déjà vu hit him. Where had he done this before? When he felt he was close enough, he twisted his left forearm as best he could around the rope and clamped tight with his hand to avoid slipping off.

As the boat built up speed and turned toward the Aquariva, he narrowly avoided being collected by the corner of the pier. Now he began the impossible task of retrieving the Makarov, but the gun had slipped. There was just an inch or two of the grip clear of the belt for him to get hold of. Nothing was ever easy in this job. After a couple of failed attempts, he got his thumb and fingers gingerly around the grip and then grabbed it as tight as he could, keeping his finger well outside the trigger guard. This was not the moment he wanted the gun to fire. He tore it free, sliding it along his body, out from behind the shirt and finally clear of the water. He was only going to get one chance at this.

When he lifted his head he realized that one of the SVR agents was standing over the engine, firing at him and he was suddenly glad he hadn't accepted the top up of scotch that Helldiver had offered. Right now it was just a matter of who was lucky enough to land the shot first.

Gasping for breath, Morgan locked his right arm straight out in front, pressing his face against his shoulder to line his eyes up with the weapon as he bounced across the waves. The white water was pummeling his arm, streaming past him in great curving wings as he brought the weapon into an impossible aim. He could make out the occasional crack of the weapon above being fired at him. His chances of survival were getting narrower and narrower with every round heading his way. It was now or never.

The boat was gaining speed out on the open water and Morgan knew he didn't have a hope of hitting the agents, so his best option was disabling the engine to enable the Aquariva to get away. He tightened his grip around the Makarov even more, brought his finger back onto the trigger and began firing directly at what he could make out of the fuel filter, the fuel lines feeding the engine and the silhouette of the agent standing over it. He had twelve rounds. He had to make them count.

Fighting against the impossible conditions, Morgan began firing. He squeezed the trigger rapidly, timing each squeeze to coincide with the bounce of his arm against the raging white water. There was some gruesome irony in taking them on with one of their own weapons. He had no idea where his rounds were falling or how close the rounds of the agent were to hitting him. He must be getting close to his twelve rounds running out. He'd lost count. There was too much going on.

Then there was an almighty boom, the dark silhouette of the man disappeared from view and an explosion tore the boat apart and threw the bodies of the two agents high into the air, consumed by a mushroom cloud of brilliant orange flames.

The rope went slack.

Morgan stopped dead in the water.

Chapter Twenty

CHANGI INTERNATIONAL AIRPORT, SINGAPORE

"Patiala Airlines would like to invite passengers flying to Kuala Lumpur and London on Flight 285 to please make your way to gate lounge F34. Your aircraft will be boarding soon. Once again, we welcome passengers flying to Kuala Lumpur and London on Flight 285. Please make your way to gate lounge F34. Your aircraft will be boarding soon."

The announcement carried throughout Terminal 2 at Changi International Airport. The tone was friendly and welcoming and it immediately mobilized most of the hundreds of passengers in the departure lounge. It was a scene that played out at every airport in the world for every flight, every day of the year and had become as routine as catching a bus. At any time of day or night there were literally thousands of planes in the air somewhere in the world. Flight 285's only claim to being potentially more significant than most was that it was an A380 flight and was set to carry over four hundred passengers.

On the flight deck of 285, the captain and first officer were in the midst of their preflight briefings to the other crew members. The interaction between the captain and the others was pleasant but formal, a tone set by the captain, who was new to this crew, having recently come across from Etihad. He had not wanted the distraction of any unnecessary bonding with the crew, so he had remained private and reserved from the moment he'd met them a little over half an hour ago. Thankfully, most of them had responded respectfully, apart from one annoyingly obsequious chief steward who claimed he was certain he had flown with the captain previously, when the steward also worked for Etihad. The captain had been forced to play along in front of the others just enough to appear genuinely engaged but then shut the conversation down before the idiot realized that they had in fact flown together; however, that unfortunate coincidence had occurred when the captain had been flying under his own name, not the identity he had assumed today.

"Have you conducted your preflight inspection yet, first officer?" he asked, maintaining the formality.

"I was just about to, captain," the first officer answered. "Would you care to join me; I thought we might start our respective inspections together?"

"An excellent idea," replied the captain. The attention of the chief steward had nettled him slightly. A little fresh air would do him good. "I'll begin on the port side and you can begin on the starboard side. We'll meet back here."

With the Captain and First Officer conducting their preflight checks, Flight 285 was now in the final stages of preparation for departure which, according to the captain's watch, was scheduled for just over an hour from now.

Chapter Twenty-One

SINGAPORE

Elizabeth Reigns was sitting in the foyer of the Crowne Plaza Hotel, Changi Airport, to all intents and purposes lazily flicking through a copy of *Harper's Bazaar* without a care in the world. She was in a sumptuously upholstered armchair with a pot of green tea on the table beside her and a clear view of the hotel's reception desk and elevators. There was a surveillance team on the far side of the hotel foyer. Circling the hotel were two mobile teams on standby to follow the targets if they left the area in vehicles. An SPF STAR assault team were on standby in the bowels of the hotel and an Interpol liaison officer was poised above a bank of CCTV screens in the hotel's security operations room with Inspector Chan, the SPF STAR commander.

So far Intrepid surveillance had connected Galina "Honey" Devushka to a new target, a Patiala Airlines pilot by the name of Abdullah Rahman. Rahman was a man with a similar personal history to the one they'd pieced together on Farooq Chaudry: middle-aged, adult children, strained marriage and, apparently, generally disheartened with his life. He was perfect fodder for the honey-trap that Salazar had developed and, with Galina Devushka as the enticement, obviously perfected. The greatest concern for Intrepid was that, unlike the previously targeted flights – Katak Airlines 0712 and Chimbu Airways 376, both of which were A320 aircraft, and Patiala Airlines 550, which was a Boeing 777 – Rahman was an A380 pilot with comparatively hundreds more passengers under his control and, therefore, potentially hundreds more passengers at risk. The ramifications of another incident occurring were beyond inconceivable. It simply could not be allowed to happen.

From the paucity of intelligence they'd been able to crunch over the past twenty-four hours – mostly CCTV footage, credit card statements and cellphone data – it was obvious that Salazar and his team cultivated the targeted pilots over many months, with background research occurring many months before that, which meant that Galina Devushka's relationships with them must have overlapped. Rahman had been lured well over six months ago and by now was thoroughly besotted with "Honey." Reigns felt her skin crawl when she considered that this young woman was sleeping with these doomed men concurrently, knowing that she was sending them and ultimately hundreds of others to their deaths. No doubt there was an origin point for Devushka's damage somewhere in her history that they would uncover during the post-operation wrap-up. And no doubt Devushka would use that as a defense when she was eventually answering for her part in all this. At the core of all Intrepid's responsibilities, it was this element – the what-made-people-tick part – that Reigns knew held the greatest interest for her.

Frustratingly, the intelligence was changing every day.

Two days ago Intrepid knew that Helldiver was preparing to launch another attack imminently. However, the phone chatter and behavior among the recruitment team had escalated ten-fold over the past twenty-four hours, and the likelihood of the next attack was now considered immediate. Overnight something had happened at Helldiver's residence in France. The details available to Reigns and her team were sketchy but the result was that everything had been brought forward. Clearly, Helldiver's escalation strategy was based on ego rather than intelligent consideration. In terms of thwarting the attacks against the airlines, the counter-strategy Intrepid had adopted was to beat the plan at its source: targeting the pilot selection-and-replacement phase, or the enticement-and-radicalization phase as Reigns preferred to consider it, while Morgan would unravel the leadership end.

Right now Devushka was upstairs with Rahman. They'd been up there a number of hours so, Reigns hoped, there should be some activity very soon. They'd be cutting it very fine if Rahman – or rather, his replacement – was going to make his next scheduled flight on time. Intercepts of Devushka's cellphone indicated she was expecting to rendezvous with Salazar at the hotel at 8pm, which was only ten minutes away. The surveillance teams were all equipped with numerous images of Salazar, Rahman and Devushka and had become intimately familiar with what the main players looked like. Based on the murder and replacement of Farooq Chaudry at the Holiday Inn, the team's focus was confirming who, if anyone, Salazar turned up with. If it was a Rahman lookalike, they'd move in.

Like clockwork, Carlo Salazar appeared in the foyer, alone. He didn't bother with reception, he knew where he was headed. Rahman's room was on the eighth floor. Reigns kept reading and sipping her tea. She watched Salazar's reflection in a glass panel as he loitered near the elevators. She saw him make a sweeping glance around the foyer, pause, then take out his cellphone and tap on the screen. Less than a minute later a man entered the foyer carrying an overnight bag. He appeared to be of Malay ethnicity, medium height, balding, with a slight paunch. Even from here she could see the obvious similarity with Rahman. He made a study of the foyer and then headed straight for Salazar. Bingo! There was an acknowledgment between the two, subtle but obvious if you were looking for it.

Following not far behind the Rahman lookalike was a young man, Slavic looking. Reigns recognized him from the CCTV footage at the Holiday Inn. This guy was the muscle. He did the heavy lifting, literally, and was most likely the one to have put a bullet in the head of Farooq Chaudry, and possibly others. He ignored Salazar and headed for the staff-only corridor. She couldn't see if he produced a pass to gain access to the corridor but she had to presume that he did.

Reigns' cellphone buzzed. Rather than being a standard phone, which is what it looked like, the handset had been configured to operate on a secure radio frequency.

"That's all three." It was Damon, leader of the surveillance team.

"Roger," she replied. "Stay put and keep your eyes out for any additional players. Blue?"

"I'm here. What's the play?" asked Chan, leader of the SPF STAR team.

"We have all three heading into the elevator now. Your guys in position?"

"They're all set. Just say the word."

"Roger. Standby."

Up on the eighth floor the CCTV cameras followed Salazar and the Rahman lookalike from the moment the elevator doors slid open, tracking them along the corridors until they reached Rahman's room.

"He's listening at the door now," said Chan from the security operations room. Reigns had the phone pressed to her ear but kept thumbing through her magazine, occasionally sipping on the tea. "They're waiting," Chan continued. "Here we go. The third guy has just come out of the service elevator on eight. He's dressed in a set of the hotel's laundry contractor coveralls, making his way to the room. And, yes, he has a trolley."

"OK," said Reigns. "The moment they enter that room, they're all yours."

"Copy that," Chan replied.

A tense few moments ensued as Reigns was forced to sit quietly in the foyer apparently oblivious to any real-life drama unfolding within the hotel.

"Standby," she heard Chan say. A pause. "OK, they're in. We are GO!"

Reigns calmly finished her tea, closed her magazine and placed them both down on the table beside her. With the phone still up to her ear, she went to the elevator. When she got in and pressed eight, an urgent voice brought the phone to life.

"Go ahead," she said.

"This is Blue. We're in the room. You better get up here ASAP. This guy's saying some crazy shit."

"On my way."

The ascent to the eighth floor took an age and Reigns was ready to peel the doors open herself the moment the ping announced she'd arrived. She ran to the room.

As she rushed in she saw a dozen STAR officers: half

with guns drawn, the others cuffing Salazar, the Rahman lookalike, the Russian muscle and Galina Davushka, aka 'Honey'. Lying flat on his back on the edge of the bed wearing nothing but a sheet that had been pulled over him was the real Rahman. His eyes were shut and he wasn't moving. The lead officer from the assault team turned when he saw Reigns.

"Is he dead?" she asked.

"No, ma'am. He's been given some kind of sedative that's put him out for a while but he's not dead. I guess he was probably going to get the same treatment as the last guy, once they got him out of the room and ready for the dumpster."

"So what's this one been saying?" She looked at Salazar, who was face down on the floor sporting a freshly applied set of handcuffs.

"You're not going to like it."

"You're too late," Salazar said. "The real double is about to fly. You're too late!"

Reigns' blood ran cold. At that moment, the Interpol liaison officer and Chan ran into the room. Reigns turned to them both.

"I'm going to need whichever flight Rahman was scheduled to captain out of Changi today stalled without any fuss. Can you do that?"

"Of course," replied the Interpol liaison officer. "As you requested, we haven't alerted the airline yet in case the information made it to the captain, but we have all the details of the flight. It's 285 to Kuala Lumpur then it continues on as 775 to London Heathrow. It's due out in less than an hour."

"Which means that right now the actual, chosen Rahman lookalike is probably sitting in the captain's seat doing his preflight and getting ready for take-off with more than four hundred people boarding, and none of the crew would even know that he's not the real Captain Abdullah Rahman. Jesus! OK, do whatever you have to do to stall that aircraft. The crew cannot know they're being deliberately stalled."

"Understood," said the Interpol liaison officer who then disappeared from the room, tapping at his cellphone.

"Patiala Airlines has to do whatever it takes to keep that flight on the ground," Reigns called to the retreating back. Then she turned to Chan. "How quickly can you get me to that aircraft without drawing any attention to us?"

"Fifteen minutes."

"OK. I'm going to need these three later for interrogation," she said. "Can you arrange for them to be held?"

Chan looked at the STAR assault team leader, who nodded in response.

"Thank you," she said. "Let's go!"

Reigns and Chan ran from the room, collecting Interpol liaison on the way. By the time they'd reached the SPF STAR assault vehicle in the hotel's loading dock, Reigns had issued redeployment orders to her surveillance teams and Chan had arranged backup to make the arrest at Changi Airport. Interpol liaison was working the phones with the airline and Changi Airport administration. The moment they'd all buckled into their seats, the police driver stamped his foot to the pedal and had them racing to stop the flight.

Reigns checked her watch. Thirty minutes to take-off. She tried to imagine exactly what was happening on the flight deck of 285 right at that moment – the co-pilot briefing the captain on the preflight inspection, the flight plan, the weather ahead; while the cabin crew would be dealing with the confined chaos of boarding over four hundred souls – ensuring every passenger was seated in accordance with their allocated seating and carry-on luggage was stowed safely in the overhead compartments. Meanwhile, the man in ultimate control of their lives was at that moment preparing to destroy them all.

As their vehicle reached the airport's outer limits it was met by an SPF Airport Police Division car and they sped in convoy straight to Terminal 2. Soon the cars skidded to a halt and Reigns and the others raced to Gate F34 where 285 was set to depart. She checked her watch again. Ten minutes. Shit! All she could think about was whether or not the airline had managed to stall the plane without giving anything away to the pilot. She couldn't guarantee it, so all she could do was get there. As she closed in on Gate F34 she saw a team of STAR officers emerge from a doorway twenty feet ahead of her. She saw the recognition on their faces when they saw Inspector Chan running with her.

"F34!" Chan called to them. They sprinted ahead. They knew what needed to happen. They all just had to get there.

She saw the illuminated F34 sign appear and watched as the STAR officers disappeared out of sight toward the plane. She sprinted after them, racing through the now empty departure lounge. The pounding of boots thundered through the space as the police hit the airbridge. Reigns could hear the high-pitched whine of the A380's Trent 900 Rolls Royce engines as the flight deck prepared for imminent departure. *You think you're home and hosed, you bastard! Well no, you're not! Not on my watch!*

She was on the airbridge, thundering down behind the STAR team with Chan hot on her heels. The Interpol liaison was now with Airport Management, dealing with the inevitable fallout no matter which way it went – success or failure. Reigns saw the team at the door to the aircraft. It was closing, inches away from being sealed shut. She saw the first team members' hands reaching for the edges of the door, grappling it awkwardly back from the stunned cabin crew. The door was heaved back open and the dark blue tactical uniforms of the heavily armed officers streamed into the aircraft. Reigns was just a few feet behind. There was yelling from the cockpit, shouted commands, loud in the confined space – then screaming from the cabin crew and inevitably an uproar of fear and uncertainty from the passengers who were close enough to realize there was a problem. A major problem.

Reigns ran onto the aircraft to find the STAR officers manhandling the captain from the cockpit and hurling him along the line of officers until he arrived bloodied and disheveled in front of her and Chan. She looked down at him and he stared defiantly into her eyes. His body was rigid with tension as two STAR officers held him tight on either side, his arms bent up high behind his back. Reigns ignored his bravado and the contempt written all over his face. That was for him to deal with. She had no time for ego. She withdrew her cell from her pocket and studied his face minutely, comparing it to the images of the real Captain Abdullah Rahman on the screen, but she knew already.

A broad, relieved, utterly satisfied smile brought her face alive from the tension of the past few days. She held his gaze steadily, unwavering in triumph.

"Good job, everybody," she said. "This is our guy."

Chapter Twenty-Two

CHÂTEAU DE LA LAVANDE

Morgan was swimming back to shore when there was a rumble of twin 800 horsepower diesel engines close by and then a sleek blue hull flashed past him like a shark fin in the water. The Aquariva was racing back to the Château de la Lavande and as he followed its course he could just make out Helldiver standing on the edge of the pier. The man was dead still. Morgan was too far away to make out his facial expression but he could sense that it was grim. He turned in the water and looked back at the burning carcass of the tender that was billowing the last of its black smoke in a single narrow column up into the sky. The remnants of the hull that had survived the explosion were all but submerged and it was only a matter of time before it sank beneath the waves. There was no sign of the two agents. Nobody could have survived an explosion like that. He must have hit the fuel filter with those last few rounds from the Makarov. The tender would have had the capacity to carry about thirty gallons of fuel and judging by the extent of the explosion it must have been pretty close to full when it went up.

Morgan pushed off again, swimming for shore and watching with interest the events unfolding on the pier. He could make out Rodenko and one of his guys lifting Kristina Zolner's limp body from the Aquariva. That didn't look promising. Helldiver was looking on without a hint of movement. What was the story? Then the security guys laid Kristina down upon the pier and the three of them simply stood around looking down at her. Dead? Must be. None of them were making any attempt to revive her or even tend to her injuries. How odd that Helldiver had made no attempt even to hold her or check for himself whether she was alive or dead. After a few moments, Helldiver turned, waved a hand of command to the crewman at the helm of the Aquariva, and then wandered back up to the house alone. Rodenko and his offsider were left to deal with the body.

Morgan saw the Aquariva heading toward him and didn't know if he was going to be run down or rescued.

And still no sign of Arena.

Morgan felt an unexpected tightness in his chest. It was a feeling he hadn't experienced since the day he said goodbye to her at Heathrow and she'd walked through the customs frontier and disappeared so completely from his life. Or so he'd thought. Anxiety. Pain. Loss. Regret. All of those things swirled around in his mind, squeezing and tightening with every pass. But this time there was an added element. Morgan thought he'd dealt with losing Ari long ago. Now, faced with the very real possibility that she may be lost to him forever, he realized he hadn't.

The Aquariva throttled back with a loud rumble, slowing to a halt just a few feet away. Torn, his mind awash with long buried memories of Arena and sudden guilt-laden flashes of Beth, Morgan kicked off toward the tender. He reached up to the waiting hand of the crewman, clambered awkwardly aboard and slumped exhausted upon the long bench seat.

...

Chapter Twenty-Three

Morgan jumped across to the pier from the Aquariva and left the crewman to tie her off. Rodenko and his offsider were still standing over the body of Kristina Zolner.

"Are you two just going to stand there all day looking at her or are you going to take care of her?" he asked.

"She's dead," said Rodenko. "What's to take care of? The meat wagon is on the way. Stay out of it."

Morgan ignored Rodenko and walked between the two men to get to the body. He kneeled down beside her, turned her on her side for a moment and examined the obvious damage with an experienced eye. She had been shot in the back at least three times. The rounds had caught her down the left flank, in the neck and directly over the lung and kidney on that side. The bullets must have found their mark as she and her bodyguards ran down the steps to get to the boat. She was dead. That was for sure.

"I said, stay out of it," Rodenko barked. "He's waiting for you."

Morgan laid her back down made his way up the steps

to the gardens and found his jacket where he'd dropped it. He looked at it and then his trousers, shirt and shoes. Another suit trashed. He reached the top of the steps and was suddenly hit with the sinking feeling that he would find Arena somewhere in the gardens in a similar condition to Kristina Zolner; nothing more than collateral in the race to send a message to Helldiver. When he reached the edge of the gardens he walked to where he'd the seen the other bodies – Rodenko's guy and the woman from the household staff. He found them, checked them, confirmed they were both dead, laid his jacket over the woman and kept looking around. There were no obvious blood trails on the grass and no groans of pain anywhere close by. Fuck! His only option was to work his way back to the house and then see what was going on with Helldiver.

When he reached Helldiver's office, he found the billionaire there in a rage. The bottle of Glenfiddich had moved from the cabinet to the desk. Helldiver was holding a glass in one hand and hurling anything that was within reach across the room with the other. In the background, standing well clear of the affray, was Arena, white as a sheet. Thank God! Morgan was ready to run to her but she caught his eye and shuddered almost imperceptibly to caution him. He reluctantly stood down. She was OK. She was alive. That was all that mattered but the tight feeling in his chest didn't ease.

Helldiver saw Morgan enter.

"You know, those fucks from the SVR have done this! They killed her at my home!" he yelled at Morgan. He pointed to the cellphone lying dormant on the desk. "And now, they are recalling me. Me! They are sending a plane to collect me tomorrow. They expect me to roll over and play fetch like a dog. They expect me to travel back to Moscow with my tail between my fucking legs." He emptied his glass, slammed it back onto the desk and refilled it.

"I don't understand," Morgan said, feigning ignorance. He was reminded of the conversation that was left hanging when he spotted the agents stalking Kristina Zolner in the gardens. Helldiver had been on the verge of unloading the background. *A righteous enterprise. Heroes to the cause. Reclaiming heritage.* Morgan needed to know for sure. He needed to know the extent of the connection to the Russian government. That would definitely explain the global impact of the strategy. Why else would a billionaire want to employ jihadist kamikazes to bring down all those airplanes and kill hundreds, maybe even thousands, of people? "The SVR. Why the hell is the SVR recalling you? What do they have to do with any of this?"

Helldiver slumped again in his seat and rubbed his hands across his face and through his white hair. He waved a drunken finger at Morgan and began to laugh in that way that drunks do. "You're the only one I know who runs toward the danger, Morgan," he slurred. "Do you know that? The only one. The others all run away. If I'm going to beat this, I need you on my team. You understand what I'm saying?"

"Yes," he replied. "I understand."

"So, are you on my team, Morgan?"

Morgan walked closer to the desk so that Helldiver could see him more clearly.

"If you want me on your team and you want to take the fight to whomever it is that is after you, then leave that to me. If there's one thing I know how to do better than anything else I'm employed for, it's taking the fight to an enemy and winning. If that's what you want me to do then, yes, I'm on your team."

Helldiver stood and faced Morgan, holding himself against the desk. Morgan could see that he was mustering everything he could to sound as sober as possible.

"These fucks want me dead but they can't kill me because this face is too well known and I know too much. So they killed her instead." He took a deep breath, wavering slightly. "They're not telling me what to do. I'm not going to be treated like their fucking dog. So, we will fly to Moscow tomorrow but on my plane and on my terms. I will tell them!"

"What's your plan?" Morgan didn't place much stock in rash decisions made while under the influence but somehow he had a suspicion that Helldiver would follow through no matter how drunk he was.

"Dominique will arrange everything. I've told her. We leave on my jet in the morning."

Morgan glanced at Arena. Her face was full of concern but she was still in character, supporting her employer's wishes. But Morgan knew her, remembered her well enough to know she was torn. Questioning the extent to which she should be proceeding with her orders or bringing Helldiver down here and now. But bringing him down wasn't her job, wasn't her call. It was for Morgan to decide and he needed to see this through. If that meant taking Helldiver back to Moscow to see where this had all started, then that's what he would do. Arena would just have to go with it.

Meanwhile, if Helldiver was hell-bent on going to Moscow in the morning then Morgan would have to play the advance-party card. That way he could get the lay of the land ahead of Helldiver's arrival and, as urgently as possible, reestablish contact with Intrepid HQ to see if there'd been any developments.

Back down at the pier Rodenko and his offsider were loading the body of Kristina Zolner back onto the Aquariva. They'd weighed down her body with large rocks from where the pier met the shoreline. When they had her back onboard, the engines rumbled once again. They took her body out to where the tender had exploded and dumped it in the ocean.

Chapter Twenty-Four

ST. JAMES'S PARK LAKE, WESTMINSTER, LONDON

General Davenport stepped out onto Broadway. The sun was streaming down and in a rare moment of indulgence, he closed his eyes and took in a deep breath, basking in the warmth of the sunshine, enjoying a beautiful London summer's day just like any normal person might. Normal person? Perhaps one day.

He strode purposefully, turning right past the Ministry of Justice and along Queen Anne's Gate toward his destination, all the while thinking through the myriad issues that had dominated his thoughts and plagued his memories since receiving the news and seeing the image that Sheridan had presented to him two nights ago.

He'd managed to contain the anger that had so thoroughly consumed him at the sight of that simple, pixelated image, the face of a ghost from the past. Yet, not really a ghost. Not dead, as he had been led to believe for the past ten years, but in fact very much alive and well. Zolnerowich. General Igor Sergei Zolnerowich. In that instant, the operation to bring down Helldiver had ratcheted up in significance by about a thousand percent. Because, while the son was a formidable adversary in his own right, the implications of the additional influence of his father were unimaginable. The man was an unconscionable butcher who had only sought to embolden that reputation over the many years since Davenport had last seen him in Aldershot. "*The West condemned us for Afghanistan*," he'd said back then. "*But one day, colonel, you'll wish you left us alone to finish the job. Mark my words.*" So, he was still alive and therefore, without the slightest doubt in Davenport's mind, still pulling the strings. He had to be.

Soon, Davenport crossed Birdcage and arrived at St James's Park Lake. At the park, he took his time wandering along the paths amid the trees, shrubberies, squirrels and waterfowl, and crossed the Blue Bridge, scanning for his contact. Eventually he found her sitting on a bench just where she said she'd be, watching tourists taking photos of a pelican.

Asya Namdakov was a senior official stationed at the Russian Embassy in London, listed under a suitably obscure title within the Scientific and Technical Cooperation section. Davenport had known her for many years, dating back to his deployment to Kosovo in the mid-nineties and his various visits to the continent during the intervening years. She was a career intelligence officer, just a few years younger than him. She'd got her start in military communications and technology in the dying days of the Soviet Union, and she had gone on to their foreign service, stationed at various diplomatic posts around the world as a technology adviser. One thing led to another, as it so often did in the espionage game, and she'd found herself permanently assigned to the Ministry of Foreign Affairs, where she had carved out a career as a signals intelligence guru. She was only about five-two or -three, and comfortably proportioned, but despite her relatively small size, she was a powder keg, not to be underestimated. He smiled as she noticed him and stood.

"Thank you for meeting me, my dear," he said. They hugged and kissed each other lightly on each cheek. "Rather ironic don't you think? You sitting here, watching a bloody pelican." They began to walk.

"What on earth do you mean, Reggie?"

"Didn't you know? These pelicans are directly descended from the original birds that were a gift from the Russian ambassador in the seventeenth century."

"How interesting," she replied. "Did you know that pelicans wait for their prey, patiently, quietly, watching until it comes near the surface and then—" she clapped her hands together, "—they snatch them and eat them. Maybe not so ironic that a Russian gave them to you, I think."

Davenport laughed, surprised at how relaxed she seemed, especially as she was meeting him at such short notice. He said so.

"I am not worried, Reggie. I believe I already know what you want to discuss and I suspect – I hope – that our discussion may turn out to be mutually beneficial. So, I have nothing to hide."

"Very well, Asya. Then I'll get straight to the point. Two nights ago I was sent a photograph that was recently taken in France. Of all things, I happened to be in Lyon at the time. It was a face that I haven't seen in over twenty years. A face I thought I would never see again: General Igor Sergei Zolnerowich, looking very much alive and well."

"So," she said sharply. "Now you know."

"Yes. Yet, all this time, I was under the impression he had been killed by the SVR in 2005."

"Unlike the Koreans, we don't broadcast our political assassinations in the international press, Reggie. In the case of General Zolnerowich, it was staged. As you now know, he is not dead."

"Very well," said Davenport, and took in a deep breath. "Confirming that information makes what I need to discuss with you much clearer, for me at least. I will understand if you can't discuss everything I'm about to raise with you, but I would appreciate at least some clarification here and there."

She smiled but remained silent.

"For some time now we have been investigating certain individuals who we believe are responsible for the recent string of air disasters that, you'd be aware, have been reported widely in the press, specifically, Patiala Airlines flights 550 and 190, Chimbu Airways 376, and just last week Katak Airlines flight 712. Last night one of our agents managed to stop another attack; an attack which could potentially have resulted in significantly greater loss of life than any of the others. Our early intelligence drew our attention to a Russian businessman with significant resources and international connections. Our interest was due, in part, to an association between him and a pilot recruitment consultant known to us thanks to his extremist sympathies."

"You say 'due in part.' What was the other thing that drew you to this Russian businessman?"

"His name. Not the name he's given himself, but his real name."

"Of course. You are speaking of Zolner, yes? The son of the soldier, General Zolnerowich. The one who calls himself the 'Helldiver.' And this recruiter of pilots: the Argentine, Salazar, yes?"

"Yes, that's correct."

"Go on."

"On the basis of our earliest information, it appeared that this man Helldiver was operating in isolation. So, the strategy behind his actions in bringing these aircraft down confounded me. I could not see any reason for the attacks beyond basic extortion, but why kill all those people just for money? He's already a billionaire and, despite his ancestry, he has no personal history associated with violence or mass murder – not that I'm aware of, anyway. So my thoughts turned to an association of some kind that might support the theory that the attacks were part of something bigger.

"Then a few days ago we had a breakthrough when we confirmed the identity of Helldiver's wife, Kristina Zolner. She is not a Turkish heiress as they would have us believe. She is in fact an Armenian by the name of Khristya Bedrosian, a former or possibly even a currently serving officer of the SVR. We have ascertained that Ms Bedrosian is the protégé of SVR Director Vasily Latushkin, who we also know was a previous deputy director of the SVR's Directorate S, responsible for illegal intelligence and maintains an active interest in that area to this day. Their SVR association suggests the high probability of an ongoing collaboration; an argument supported by the very close association that once existed between Latushkin and Helldiver's father, General Zolnerowich; back to the days, in fact, when the young Latushkin was protégé to Zolnerowich. Confirming that Zolnerowich is still alive convinces me that this group is both capable of devising and implementing the plan to attack these airlines, and most importantly, they are motivated to ensure its success."

By now their walk had found them free of the tourists

around the bridge. Buckingham Palace was in clear view and an empty bench beckoned. They sat down.

"Is that all you have so far? I know you well, Reggie. I suspect you have more to add."

"Perhaps," he replied. "But first, I would appreciate your views on my theories."

"Very well. You have taken me into your confidence and I will take you into mine. When you reached out to meet with me, I was already aware of most of what you have told me, but there is more. Much more. Some of what I will tell you is official, some is not; but rest assured the reason we are speaking at all is that we are working to the same end. I can help you and you can help me. You understand, yes?"

Davenport nodded.

"Some time ago, influential people, old Communists within the Russian government and our intelligence services – Vasily Latushkin among them – embarked upon a campaign to reinvigorate our energies toward destabilizing the West, specifically the United States and her principal allies. The foundations of the operation had already been laid by the United States many years ago when we were in Afghanistan. All that was required was support and encouragement. *Hearts and minds*, I think you call it. In the eyes of the hardliners, the operation was an unprecedented success and the reaction of the West will be known to you as the War on Terror. The plan was progressing well, exceeding expectations, in fact, and then Bin Laden was killed. Suddenly, the efforts of the extremists in the Middle East began to falter, and the US began the withdrawal and handover to the Afghan government. I'm sure you appreciate the irony, from our point of view, of the West being embroiled in a decade-long war against the very forces they helped to defeat us in Afghanistan thirty years ago. But this changed situation, the US withdrawal, was counter to the hardliners' plans. They wanted the distraction of the war against the Islamist extremists to continue. It took the attention away from Russia and its plans for expansion. Or so they had hoped. A new strategy was devised to maintain pressure on the West by forcing them to recommit to the Middle East, placing even greater strain on America's relationships with her allies in seeking their commitment to supply more troops. But most importantly, nothing could be traced back to the Kremlin. So, the task was, how do you say … out …?"

"Outsourced," Davenport offered.

"Yes, outsourced."

"Zolnerowich?"

"Yes. By now the hardliner Latushkin had been appointed head of the SVR and he handed the task to his mentor, General Zolnerowich. As you can imagine, Zolnerowich was only too pleased to accept. The story of his assassination was leaked to ensure that he could proceed with the task without any connection being traced back to him or to the government. Zolnerowich was funded to bolster the organization he had established some years before and, with Latushkin's blessing, he was sent off to keep the United States and her allies in the Middle East by any means possible. He would be self-sufficient to ensure that he was distanced from the Kremlin. Of course, we now know that Zolnerowich exceeded his orders and has become a law unto himself."

Zolnerowich was funded to bolster the organization he had established some years before. The name Renegade immediately flashed through Davenport's subconscious. He didn't share that thought, this was not the time, but he knew that he was right.

"And Helldiver?" he said.

"The perfect intermediary to ensure that the plan could be implemented by his father, albeit once removed. Helldiver is a favored son of Russia; an oligarch who enjoys the friendship and support of those in the highest levels of government and society."

"An eccentric billionaire who can travel the world as he pleases, indulging his passion for wreck diving and living the high life, without interference," Davenport added. "And this plan to destabilize the West?"

"When you wish to create fear and mistrust globally, you must first strike at the foundations of international alliances. Al Qaeda was defeated and a new enemy was required, one even more evil than Al Qaeda."

"Islamic State," Davenport said, barely able to believe what he was hearing. "How very like Zolnerowich."

"Precisely, he'd been cultivating them for years; but of course that was not enough for Zolnerowich. He took it further, beyond his orders. An additional layer was required to cement Islamic State as the ultimate enemy. Without the endorsement of the Kremlin, he devised a plan to create fear and uncertainty in the skies, to remind the West of 9/11 and all that followed. This time however, they would attack the national carriers of Muslim nations who, in the eyes of the extremists, had not done enough to encourage global jihad. Under the premise that the extremists required funding, fighters and equipment, the hijackings were designed to coerce those governments into greater support of jihad while also creating fear and uncertainty across the world."

"Meanwhile, the Russian government is progressing its expansionist agenda across Europe and reclaiming former Soviet territories while the US and her allies are overcommitted elsewhere and unable to do anything more than wave an angry finger." Davenport's memory of Zolnerowich's final words to him that day in Aldershot came back to him as clearly as if he was standing beside the man once again and hearing them for the first time: "*In twenty years, we will be reclaiming every inch of Russian soil back from the separatists and the West will thank us for it.*"

"But, as you know, Reggie, government priorities change as quickly as they are implemented. Often without notice. Putin has now made his plans for Europe more than clear to the West, already showing NATO that he is not afraid to push the friendship, and he is fully committed to his plan to reinstate Russia as a superpower once more, restoring the balance that once existed during the days of the Soviet Union."

"The new Cold War."

"Of course, and so, despite earlier support for this Islamic State destabilization operation, Putin's strategy has advanced well beyond that and the government is satisfied that their objectives have been achieved. The US and her allies are committed again to fighting the extremists and the conditions are set for a return of Russia to superpower status."

"So this destabilization operation is no longer required?"

She nodded.

"Then why is Zolnerowich persisting with it, Asya? Flight 712 was brought down only last week. Required or not, this operation is still in play."

Namdakov remained silent. Her expression told Davenport that there was more going on on the Russian side. More than she was prepared to say.

"Your government has tried to shut him down but he's not toeing the line. Is that it?"

"General Zolnerowich and his son, Helldiver, are no longer in favor in the Kremlin," she said. "He was told to close the operation down. He did not. Zolnerowich thinks he is above direction. He is not. He was told there would be consequences. I can tell you that in the past twenty-four hours there have already been consequences in the south of France. Zolnerowich has been recalled to Moscow. The son, too."

"What has become of Latushkin?"

"Latushkin will be dealt with."

"And the attempt on Helldiver in Hawaii. Your people?" She nodded. "Although it was hastily arranged and I understand contractors were used. If it had been our own people it is highly probable that Helldiver would not have survived."

"You said when we sat down that you considered our discussion could be mutually beneficial. You have trusted a great deal of extremely helpful information with me, Asya. You have taken me into your confidence and for that I am very grateful. So tell me, what can I now do for you?"

"You can stop Zolnerowich and his son, Helldiver. And we will help you do it."

Chapter Twenty-Five

Alex Morgan touched down at Sheremetyevo International Airport at 2240 hours on Aeroflot flight SU2473 from Nice. The flight had been a reasonably pain-free four and a half hours. He managed to get out of the house almost immediately in order to make the flight in time. Obviously that meant leaving Arena behind but he had no choice – he needed to get into Moscow well ahead of Helldiver's arrival. Arena had arranged everything, including actively supporting Morgan's argument to a very drunk Helldiver that it was necessary he went in first in order to ensure they had a foot on the ground and weren't flying in blind. The arrangement was that Morgan would personally be standing on the tarmac at the arrivals hangar awaiting Helldiver's private jet at midday the following day. If he wasn't there then they could expect trouble and, if possible, abort. Helldiver had reluctantly acquiesced.

Unfortunately, Morgan wasn't able to get any more than a few stolen moments with Arena before he raced to the airport. They'd managed to arrange for Arena to ensure that her controller made contact with Morgan in Moscow – personally if possible. Meanwhile, Morgan sent off a brief but crucial communiqué to Intrepid HQ, outlining what had happened and what he knew so far. As so often happened in the clandestine world, the long fuse of intelligence gathering inevitably resulted in an explosive period of intense activity to bring the issue to a conclusion. Traditionally, that had been the very moment when General Davenport would insert his agents. And that was where Morgan found himself once again, after months of supposed exile – less than twenty-four hours into his phase of the operation and already the lit fuse had begun its explosive trajectory toward the finale.

Sheremetyevo airport was pretty standard in terms of any recently upgraded modern airport. Morgan was taken from the aircraft to the terminal by bus, walked upstairs to the arrivals pier, through passport control and, having been cleared, moved through the terminal to collect his luggage. Everything was unremarkable. Morgan didn't notice any of the tourist brochure minutiae common in airports these days; he traveled so often and to so many places that he only paid attention to things like passport control processes and staff, the general layout, notable RV points in case he had to meet anyone, suspicious people and exit routes. Otherwise, they were no more significant to him than a bus stop. Sheremetyevo was no exception. It was the history of the airport that came to Morgan. It had been built at the height of the Cold War in 1959 and still came with the inherent danger of falling into the hands of the KGB that had routinely faced Western agents who had attempted to gain access to the Soviet Union through this portal during those years. Morgan found himself walking in their shoes, facing those same dangers – not at the hands of the KGB but its successor, the SVR. He'd already seen the extent to which SVR agents would carry out their orders with no apparent regard for the risk to themselves or their colleagues. The significance of the fact that Morgan himself had, as recently as a few hours ago, killed four of them was not lost on him. Nor was the highly likely possibility that he was known by the SVR to be on Helldiver's payroll and therefore a person of some interest to them. The only information he'd received that had given him any solace was from Intrepid HQ: top cover had been arranged but he should proceed with reasonable caution on arrival in Moscow. He was to make his way directly to his hotel and he would be contacted first thing in the morning. That was it. Clearly something was going on but it was either too early to advise him with any certainty or the details hadn't been sorted out yet. He would just have to grin and bear it, maintain the pretense of being Helldiver's advance party and see what happened.

For the first time in a very long time, Morgan was wrestling with his conscience. Over the months of his self-imposed exile, he'd been harboring thoughts of turning his back once and for all on the path on which his life had led him as a soldier and, now, an agent. He'd even been giving serious consideration to convincing Reigns to join him. The idea held strong appeal to him, resonating with a deep-seated need to settle, somewhere, someday. Sooner rather than later. But that had all come to a screeching halt the moment he'd opened the door of his room back at the Château de la Lavande to find Arena standing there. Jesus. Ever since that moment, his thoughts had been consumed by Arena, all the while feeling that he was somehow betraying Beth.

His first priority was getting a taxi into the city and the

Hotel Baltschug Kempinski. He made his way outside with his luggage, wrestled within the usual melee of the taxi network and found the ride Arena had pre-ordered for him. Pre-ordering was apparently the most efficient way to arrange a taxi when traveling to Moscow from the airport and, having done so, Morgan had to presume the driver could very likely be on the SVR payroll. Either way, as they spent the next forty minutes driving into Moscow, the guy who picked Morgan up was convincing enough in his guise as a professional taxi driver. Morgan soon discovered that Moscow was not a very hilly city and so the chances of seeing any major landmarks on the drive were not good – until you were basically driving alongside them, he thought, especially at this time of night.

When he arrived at the Hotel Baltschug Kempinski on the edge of the Moskva River in central Moscow, he found the behavior of the reception staff a little disconcerting. As he'd walked into the building while the porters retrieved his luggage from the cab, he was welcomed warmly by a young woman and a middle-aged man – until he mentioned his name. At that point there was a change, it was subtle but it was there, and it was the very thing that a secret agent was trained to observe when most people would not have noticed a thing. The eagerness of their combined welcome had not altered one iota, nor the breadth of their smiles, nor even the patter of their seamless transition to English when welcoming a foreigner. The shift was in their eyes and in their body language. It was nothing more than a minute tightening of the reins of personal comfort. It told Morgan that the staff had been ordered to look out for this man and to make a call the moment he arrived and certain people were to be informed. At this point, Morgan knew that all the desk staff wanted to do was check him in, get him seen to his room, make the call, and be done with it. And once they were done with it they'd be hoping that nothing bad would happen during their shift. But this was Moscow and anything could happen. All Morgan could do was go with it.

He could feel the eyes on him already – from across the lobby or across the river, he couldn't tell. He just knew and he knew that the desk staff couldn't be rid of him quick enough. It was obvious that the young woman had been dealt the short straw. She was to be charming to the late-arriving foreigner who, for whatever reason, was a person of interest to the authorities, while the middle-aged man, possibly her senior, would remain discreetly to one side, smiling when required, until Morgan had left the reception desk and then, Morgan guessed, the man would be the one to make the call. Morgan decided to make their job easier by being as swift as he could while registering his details. The closer the young woman got to handing him the access cards for his room, the calmer both she and the man became. They could see the finish line and Morgan was silently cheering them on.

The girl handed him the courtesy envelope for his room, the man waved over a porter, and Morgan turned and headed in the direction of the elevator with the porter eagerly trying to get in front of him in order to lead the way. By the time they'd reached the top floor and he was shown into a room alongside the premiere suite that Arena had arranged for Helldiver, Morgan was braced and ready for anything they could throw at him. He waited until his luggage arrived. He tipped both porters handsomely, closed the door behind them and then began the process of inspecting his room.

He'd no sooner taken off his jacket and was about to remove his tie when there was a knock at the door. He took a deep breath, stood slightly to one side with all his weight on his leading leg, flicked the room's entrance light off and opened it.

The moment the door cracked and the light from corridor spilled inside, the gun appeared.

Chapter Twenty-Six

There were two of them. The first was the rookie – whose sole purpose was distraction. He was to engage Morgan for the vital first seconds of the confrontation just enough to ensure that Morgan's A-game couldn't be fully deployed against the second man. The gun arm leading into the open door was the giveaway. All Morgan had to do was resort to a quick and dirty disarming technique that involved securing the weapon with the right hand and then, with a rapid grab, pull and twist, breaking the wrist, taking the weapon and following through to incapacitate the attacker. The proximity of the second guy meant the follow-through option was not available to Morgan; all he could do was make the most of breaking the rookie's wrist as badly as possible and deliver a well-placed kick to the guy's face before he bore the brunt of the second man's attack against his exposed flank.

Then all Morgan could see was the barrel of a heavy caliber automatic coming straight for his face. The hand carrying it and the silhouette behind was equally heavy and

Morgan knew that overcoming the second man was not going to be as easy as the first. A flat-footed kick to Morgan's left side came dangerously close to breaking ribs, but he ducked beneath the weapon and came at the gun arm from the outside. The guy's elbow was at Morgan's head height, which meant he was at least six-five or six-six tall. Morgan got his right forearm up on the inside of the guy's wrist and then slammed his left palm directly at the elbow joint, but he knew already this guy wasn't going down easily and that the tried-and-tested maneuver had failed before he'd even thought to use it. His strike recoiled off the guy's arm and the joint remained unmoved.

Suddenly the gun barrel was coming around again. Morgan and the second man were facing off within the confined space of the room's foyer, standing awkwardly over the first guy, who was whimpering about his fractured wrist. Discarding any kind of finesse with his counter-attack, Morgan dropped into a crouch, keeping below the gun, and came up with all his weight under the second man's ribs and right armpit, forcing him sideways and, inescapably, across the top of his whining comrade. The man stumbled and he and Morgan fell their way clumsily back into the suite. Morgan fell down heavily on top of the second man and was in the process of getting back on his feet when the rookie finally recovered and came in over the top, kicking wildly in manic retribution. Morgan couldn't get any purchase on the floor, was copping blows left, right and center, was struggling to get clear of the two of them when he became aware of an even bigger commotion coming in through the open door behind him. Jesus! More of them.

Two shots were fired from a silenced automatic. The rookie fell instantly. All Morgan could see now was the reaction of the big guy, his face just inches away, looking up from the floor, past Morgan, straight at whoever had just pulled the trigger. The eyes were wide with anger and frustration and as he began to mouth the word "No!", Morgan was pulled clear by unseen hands and two more shots were fired.

Tumbling away from the body, Morgan made a grab for the big guy's dropped automatic but a barked command from behind stopped him mid-reach.

"*Nyet, shpion!*" The voice was used to being obeyed.

Morgan got slowly to his feet, raised his hands in the air and turned to face the man behind the order. The man who had marked Morgan as a spy and killed the two men currently lying dead at Morgan's feet. He was standing less than four feet away, pointing a silenced Makarov at Morgan's face. Either side of him, four more men stood, all of them between Morgan and the door, all no doubt similarly armed and not the types to be negotiated with. One of them dropped back into the darkness of the unlit foyer and closed the door. Morgan knew what was about to happen.

What struck Morgan most of all was that they were in uniform, but not the type of uniform you'd necessarily recognize as one unless you saw a bunch of them together. They were all wearing leather jackets, all black and well worn, with T-shirts just visible at the neck, jeans and heavy boots. None was the same when considered in isolation but together they were almost identical. Physically, all of them were distinctive by their ordinariness: about Morgan's height, around six feet, medium build, neither slender nor heavy set. Their complexions were fair, almost pale, and they all wore their hair close-cropped, high and tight like US Marines. Only, these guys weren't Marines. Not in this part of the world. Apart from the leader standing in the middle of the room, who had now leveled the barrel of the

Makarov to point directly at Morgan's chest, they'd all had recent military or paramilitary service. The leader also had at some point, that was a given, but most of his time had been spent in clandestine service – it was written all over him. He had that incomparable quality that said he was used to having ultimate control when on his turf and Moscow was very much his turf. Morgan was an outsider, a foreign spy, and maybe that was why he was the only one of the three original targets still on his feet, alive. Although how long that particular luxury would be afforded him he had no idea. As Morgan prepared to ask, the lead man returned the automatic to the holster under his jacket and took a step back. One of the troops remained by the door while the other three stepped forward, each removing a cosh from within their jackets. They closed in on Morgan.

Sometimes you just have to take it. No matter what's being thrown at you and no matter how bad it's going to hurt. You have to stand there, prepare for the worst and accept that your options have just run out. In those moments, someone else is calling the shots. All you can do is try to survive it and see how recoverable or not your situation is if you make it through to the other side. As the three men closed in on Morgan, he braced to withstand an old-fashioned beating but he wasn't going down without trying to balance the damage.

Eventually, despite his best efforts, that proved impossible. Morgan could do little more than defend himself until the sheer weight of numbers began to overwhelm him. He gained some kind of sadistic satisfaction when he realized that the fourth man had been requisitioned from door duty to join his colleagues just as Morgan's resistance was at its most intense. But soon his only option was to lock his fists and arms up around his face and head to protect himself against the relentless onslaught of cosh strikes. Fortunately, he could sense that his attackers were tiring too. Their tempo began to slow and, apart from the occasional kick and punch, the blitzkrieg they'd just put him through finally stopped.

Then the four of them withdrew just as there was a knock at the door. Morgan rolled from his side and onto his back, spitting blood, trying to get his breath back. Were the efforts of the cosh quartet just the fucking appetizer? And were the new arrivals about to deliver Morgan the main treatment? He was so completely dazed that he couldn't make sense of any of it. He blamed concussion, which was a good sign, because he was at least lucid enough to recognize it for what it was. He wiped the blood from his mouth, nose and cheeks along the sleeve of his shirt and pulled himself up enough to sit and face the door.

His greatest concern now was that the leader didn't seem in any way fazed that someone was at the door, despite the fact that there were two dead bodies bleeding into the hotel carpet in full view of the corridor, along with four men holding coshes standing over a bloodied foreigner who had obviously just taken a serious beating. Not a good sign. Concussion or not, Morgan was preparing himself for more of the same.

When the door opened and he heard the leader say, "Ah, finally, tovarich!" in a friendly, almost jovial tone, he thought things couldn't possibly get any worse.

When the man at the door walked in and Morgan could see him clearly, he didn't know whether to grab for a gun or get to the drinks cabinet.

Chapter Twenty-Seven

"Jesus, kid," said Masterson. "You look like shit. Those guys really worked you over good."

Morgan and Masterson were sitting together in a new suite, still in the Hotel Baltschug Kempinski, only this one didn't have the dead bodies or Russian agents that the last one did. Masterson was dropping ice cubes from the minibar fridge into a hand towel before handing it over to Morgan, who held it against the right-hand side of his face. Masterson dropped more ice cubes into two glasses, each of which was doused with a few liberal fingers of vodka. It was almost 2am and Morgan was beat.

"So what time did you check in?" asked Masterson, seemingly unperturbed by what he'd walked in on.

"Sometime before midnight," Morgan mumbled against the ice pack.

"And the two stiffs," replied Masterson. "When did they turn up?"

"Almost the same time. I'd barely had time to check out the view. Speaking of which." Morgan stood carefully and, taking a couple of painful steps, retracted the heavy drapes that ran across the north-facing windows of his suite. Red Square was instantly revealed in dramatic fashion and Morgan felt an almost adrenal rush at the sight of it. "You were here," he said eventually, "back in the dark old days, right?"

"Once or twice," Masterson replied from his chair. "Although, I gotta tell you, this business has a ring of the dark old days, all of its own. Thirty years ago, they would have used metal pipes, not coshes, and that would have been just the tenderizer. You would have ended up with a bullet in the back of your head and a long final swim down that river you're staring at. Things are a little more civilized these days."

"Civilized?" Morgan turned and gestured at the damage he'd sustained.

"I said 'a little.'" Masterson took a drink. So did Morgan. The two remained silent for a while.

"So, tell me," Morgan began, "how is it that you end up here out of the blue?"

"You asked for me. Your instructions to Dominique were pretty clear: *Have your controller make contact with me in Moscow.* So, here I am."

"You're Dominique's controller?"

"That I am. Is that a problem for you?"

"No, it's just …" Morgan paused.

"I know the history, Morgan. Mickey Sheridan filled me in. You need to deal with that right now if this thing is going to progress. And it is. So, whatever feelings you still have for her, for Arena, then you need to get it off your chest or one of you may end up on the wrong end of another Makarov before this day is done. And I know you don't want that to happen."

Morgan took another drink. Masterson reached across with the bottle and topped him up.

"I'll deal with it," Morgan replied. "It just took me completely by surprise. I mean, her operating in our world. It wasn't anything like I expected her life had turned out. All this time I thought she had gone back into humanitarian work and was married and having kids with some safe-bet, intellectual UN type or a university professor. I had no idea she'd be in the middle of something like this."

"That's because you're thinking about it totally from your perspective. Think about it from hers. Her history makes her perfect for this line of work and her university pedigree and contact with the current chief of MI6 seals the deal. She may have been damaged by that job in Malfa-jiri, but name anyone you know in this game who doesn't get fucked up by their first real taste of the life. She just had to go off and get her head straight and when she did, she knew what she wanted to do."

"But who is she working for?" asked Morgan. "I heard Europol."

"You heard right," Masterson replied. "The General arranged it years ago, apparently. You should really get those kinds of details from Sheridan. Short version, as I understand it, she couldn't or wouldn't work in the UK after that whole Abraham Johnson thing, so Davenport got her a gig at Europol. Then, when he needed her a couple of years later, she was ready."

Morgan came back to the chairs and sat down. He felt like he could sleep for ten years but knew there was work to be done.

"OK, let's leave that where it is," he said. "What's going on with your Russian friends down the corridor? Who are they, and why aren't I dead and floating down that river?"

"Well, my take on the first two is that they were sent in by someone who isn't happy with your involvement. From what Arena managed to tell me earlier, that's most likely Zolnerowich. Helldiver obviously wants you around but his old man doesn't. Zolnerowich still has some pull back here, not for much longer mind you, so he arranged a hit. God only knows how many people he's had put away like that over the years. In the early days he would have done it personally. Not now."

"So then who were the guys who came in and took care of Zolnerowich's hit team – and then had a crack at me?"

"They're SVR. I've known Hermescec – the guy who just shot those two assholes – for the best part of thirty years. He's one of my back-channel contacts over here. He's a survivor. He has a knack for successfully calling the direction the winds of political change have blown here in Moscow and he's always managed to come out unscathed. This time around he's correctly noted that the current director of the SVR, his boss, General Latushkin, is about to be replaced. This Helldiver thing has become such a mess for the Kremlin that Hermescec was only too willing to step in to clean it up."

"And I guess that's where you come in, right?"

"Correct," Masterson replied. "Everything about this operation has changed in the past twenty-four hours and now it's a forensic-level rout of the main players. Helldiver has to go, along with his old man."

"So if we're now in cahoots with the Russians, why the fuck did this Hermescec guy and his comrades do me over? Hardly fucking détente."

"News travels fast in this business, kid. You know that. He got word that you'd killed four of their guys in Antibes earlier today and what you got was a little bit of old-fashioned Russian retribution."

"Why didn't they just kill me and wait for me to be replaced?"

"Call it professional courtesy," Masterson said, smiling. "And a personal favor to me."

"Oh, great! I'm much obliged," said Morgan. He raised his glass. Masterson responded in kind. "So what am I supposed to do now? Seems like this thing is already wrapping up."

This time Masterson stood and walked over to the windows, looking out across his own history in the home of the old enemy. He sipped his vodka. "This thing is light years away from being wrapped up, Morgan. Not with Helldiver and Zolnerowich still at large. This is where it all gets seriously old school. Shit is going to go down tomorrow that you're probably not going to be very comfortable with, but you'll have to get comfortable with it – pretty darn quick."

Morgan remained silent, listening and watching, his admiration and respect for Masterson's experienced guidance underpinning the urgency of his need to understand the new environment he found himself operating in.

"Tomorrow, as far as your responsibilities to Helldiver are concerned, everything remains unchanged. You'll turn up at the private hangar to greet him as per the current plan and, importantly, just as he's expecting. And then you'll deliver him straight into the hands of the SVR. After that, he's no longer your concern."

"How am I supposed to do that?"

"Don't worry. They'll let you know. For now, just make sure you're shipshape for his arrival back in Moscow. He thinks he's flying into town to tear Latushkin a new one, but he has no idea that Latushkin is already out. As of this afternoon, there's a new guy calling the shots at the SVR. When Helldiver sets off from Nice in—" he consulted his watch, "—just a few more hours, he'll be on a one-way ticket."

"What about Zolnerowich?"

"Hopefully he'll be on the same plane. If not, there'll be a team going into the Antibes house the second Helldiver is with you. We don't want to risk any tipoffs, so timing will be crucial. Don't worry, we'll have eyes on you at the airport, so we'll know the second Helldiver is off the plane and getting into that vehicle with you."

"And Arena?"

"All she has to do is make sure Helldiver gets on the goddamn plane."

"What's General Davenport's position on all this – delivering Helldiver to Moscow instead of The Hague?"

"I guess you can ask him that question yourself some time. Meanwhile, you better get some shut eye and hope that the swelling goes down at least enough not to scare Helldiver back onto his jet when he sees you. Everything has to be smooth sailing tomorrow, Morgan. If he smells a rat he'll aim to disappear and things will just get a whole lot messier than they already are. All you have to remember is the hundreds of people who have died in the past twelve months as a direct result of his actions. The casualty rate will only continue to climb if he isn't stopped now. As for his father, that old bastard should have been killed years ago. So." He turned back to Morgan. "Are we good?"

"Yeah, we're good."

Masterson put his empty glass down and walked out.

Chapter Twenty-Eight

Morgan was standing on the tarmac at Sheremetyevo International Airport just outside the private hangar that was ready to receive Helldiver's Gulfstream IV. It was sunny but there was a hint of dark cloud off in the distance and a light wind was starting to get some kick. The plane was at that moment winding down its engines and the aircrew were already lowering the steps for the passengers. Russian customs officials were in place. Morgan knew that they were on the SVR payroll and that Helldiver would be given only the most cursory attention on this occasion, potentially his last. Behind Morgan were two cars – a standard Mercedes GL SUV for the security team and Helldiver's favored Bentley Mulsanne long-wheelbase limousine, which Arena had arranged and which had picked Morgan up from the hotel and brought him to the airport. The only thing that would be different from previous pickups was the driver: the guy who normally drove Helldiver in Moscow had apparently come down with a sudden bout of gastro and so it was necessary for the limousine company to replace him at the last minute. They had been very apologetic when they called Morgan at the hotel ahead of the vehicle's arrival. Morgan told them he completely understood and that he would explain the situation to Mr. Zolner, if it came up. The moment Morgan got into the vehicle and met the replacement driver, he knew that he too was on the SVR payroll. On the tarmac the driver remained behind the Bentley, ready to open the doors for the passengers as they were cleared by Customs. The Mercedes SUV was being driven by one of Rodenko's local security people, and he met them at the tarmac. Morgan stood well forward of both vehicles, level with the nose of the Gulfstream. Despite Masterson's encouraging final words about the swelling going down on Morgan's face, it hadn't, and so Morgan had decided to own it and pin the incident squarely, by implication, on the shoulders of Zolnerowich. He needed Helldiver to be distracted enough by news of Morgan's misfortune to ensure a smooth transition from the aircraft into the motor car.

The steps were being lowered and Morgan recognized Famke as she descended ahead of the passengers, giving Morgan a beautiful smile as she took up her post at the bottom of the steps. Arena exited first – thank God – and gave him a very reserved smile just as anyone would expect from colleagues familiar with each other in a professional sense. He saw her thank Famke as she stepped onto the tarmac and walked toward Morgan. He maintained an air of confidence so that if there were any eyes on him from the aircraft then he would give them no reason for concern. Arena was met by the Customs officials, who checked her passport, asked her their questions and got her to acknowledge and sign their forms. She remained with them, no doubt to assist with Helldiver's entry formalities.

Rodenko emerged from the airplane with all the usual bravado of the bodyguard expecting to stop bullets with his puffed-out chest. He walked down the steps and into the depressing anti-climax of the waiting bureaucracy and was eventually also cleared. He walked to the car, ignoring Morgan, and made straight for the new driver.

"Where the fuck is Kurylenko?"

As agreed, the driver didn't reply, instead deferring to Morgan, who turned and said, "He's sick. Got the shits. The company had to replace him at the last minute. They cleared it with me first. I said it was OK."

Rodenko made a point of trying to stare the man down as he inspected him as best he could in front of the Customs officials. Then he took up his position covering the car.

Finally Helldiver emerged. The drunkenness of the previous evening had evaporated although the trademark arrogance was still front and center. Morgan wondered if the man suffered hangovers. He hoped so. Helldiver looked squarely at Morgan as if to say, "*Is everything OK? I'm relying on you to tell me right now.*" As Morgan stepped into the lime-light, ready to play his part in delivering the man to the gallows, he thought of Masterson's advice to remember the hundreds of souls who'd lost their lives under Helldiver's plan to reclaim his heritage and be a hero to the cause.

During the night, after Masterson had left, Morgan had re-familiarized himself with the news reports of the four downed aircraft – Katak Airlines 712, Patiala Airlines 550, Patiala Airlines 190, and Chimbu Airways 376. He'd trawled through the hundreds upon hundreds of names of those who had lost their lives, studying photographs and replaying the most recent news reports. It was an endless stream of heartbroken people, grieving relatives from all over the world, who only wanted one thing: justice for their lost loved ones. It was all that he needed. Helldiver deserved to get what was coming to him, and that was all there was to it.

Morgan exuded confidence. Everything about his nonspoken cues told Helldiver it was perfectly safe to step down from the plane and walk across to the Customs officials. Helldiver smiled grimly at Morgan from the steps before proceeding down to the tarmac and across the last few feet to be cleared for entry into the sovereign territory of the Russian Federation.

With the formalities complete, Helldiver walked straight to Morgan, shook his hand and the two engaged in a brief exchange of targeted questions and specific assurances against the whine of the twin Rolls Royce turbofan engines as they finally shut down. Apparently satisfied, Helldiver made his way to the Bentley. He noted the new driver and shot Morgan a quizzical glance. Morgan simply shook his head slightly, indicating that it was all good and that he was across it. It was at this point that Helldiver finally noticed Morgan's damaged face. Morgan indicated that he would explain en route to the hotel.

Thankfully, Rodenko climbed into the front passenger seat of the SUV, leaving Morgan and Arena to join Helldiver in the Bentley. Arena climbed into the front with the driver and Morgan got into the back with Helldiver. Once they were inside, the driver ensured that all the doors were closed firmly but quietly and then expertly got them underway without a word.

"What the fuck happened to you?" Helldiver asked.

"I was paid a visit at the hotel last night, not long after I arrived," Morgan replied casually. "A welcoming committee of some sort; I presumed they'd been sent to warn me off by someone who doesn't really want me on board."

Helldiver thumped the armrest between them with his fist.

"Don't worry," Morgan continued. "It was directed at me, not you. If I thought it was designed for you I would have immediately recommended that you abort the trip."

"How do you know it wasn't a hit?"

"You don't take someone out with a cosh unless you're really patient and they're really compliant," Morgan replied. "There were two of them. They'd been told to deliver a message and they did. I sent them back with my response."

Helldiver looked at Morgan and smiled. "Dead or alive?"

"Alive," Morgan said. "No need to start the trip off hiding bodies."

They fell silent for a few moments. Morgan could see that Helldiver was taking in the familiar territory. He wondered what was going through the man's mind, not that he would ever in a million years be able to fathom the thought processes of a narcissistic megalomaniac. He wasn't even sure if that's what the experts would classify a person like Hedeon Zolner; it was just the way that Morgan had decided to pigeonhole him. He was curious to understand exactly what Helldiver had planned to say when he eventually confronted Latushkin and wondered if the man still felt the same way now that he was through the drunken tirade and actually on the ground on the home team's turf. Of course, Morgan knew full well that there would be no confrontation with Latushkin. It was then that his mind returned to the next issue, which was when and how the takedown would occur. He found himself worrying again about Arena's safety and immediately a sharp stab of guilt hit him hard as he realized that his feelings for Elizabeth Reigns had been put to one side. Jesus. This was not the time to be analyzing his feelings for these two women, both of whom were very much responsible – in some ways at least – for who he was today.

They were traveling along the M11 route south to Moscow and were about the cross the Vodnik when Morgan noticed a black UAZ Patriot SUV moving quickly into the lane ahead of them. The Bentley's driver remained unmoved. He maintained his speed and the UAZ matched it perfectly. Helldiver was oblivious, caught up in his thoughts and the confrontation he was no doubt playing out word for word in his mind's eye. A second UAZ Patriot overtook them, identical in every way to the one in front. Morgan noticed it now taking its place in the convoy ahead of the first one. He wondered if Rodenko had noticed when, checking to the rear of the Bentley, another vehicle appeared, this time a large truck, heavy and powerful, wedging perfectly between the Bentley and Rodenko's Mercedes SUV behind them.

"Everything OK?" Helldiver asked, obviously sensing Morgan's growing tension.

"It looks like we're getting an escort," Morgan replied calmly.

"Do you know anything about this?" Helldiver demanded of the driver in Russian.

Sitting beside the driver, Arena shifted uncomfortably and shot an accusing look across at him. The man replied in the negative, feigning a very well-practiced astonishment at the suggestion, assuring Helldiver – as far as Morgan's sketchy Russian would allow – that he was completely unaware of what was occurring. Morgan stepped in, thanking the driver and recommending that he follow the direction of the convoy and not try anything untoward. The driver acknowledged gratefully.

"An escort does make sense, given who you are and who you're here to see," Morgan said.

He felt the most minute drop in speed. It was subtle, extremely so, just a few miles per hour, and was instantly matched and maintained by every vehicle in the convoy. Morgan then noted that the lorry was dropping out of sight and with it, Rodenko's Mercedes. In their place a third UAZ Patriot appeared directly behind, identical to the two in front. The four vehicles raced along as one without any obvious anxiety from Helldiver. Morgan remained outwardly relaxed, he needed Helldiver to remain exactly as he was, comfortable that this unexpected development was actually expected. The routine traffic that had been racing past their open flank, Morgan's side, suddenly eased and a large black limousine, a Russian made ZIL-4112, emerged predatorily from the traffic and closed in tightly on the exposed flank of the Bentley. The ZIL was new but with its ominous box-like design and blackened windows it could easily have been lifted from the streets of Soviet-era Moscow or the pages of a le Carré novel. The severity of its stark, old world appearance and the uncertainty of the next few hours traced a cold finger of death directly down Morgan's spine. They were boxed in.

"A further development," Morgan said calmly and Helldiver's attention was immediately drawn back to him. Morgan motioned with his head toward the ZIL. "It looks like General Latushkin has elected to hold your meeting outside of the city."

Helldiver stared past Morgan at the black windows of the ZIL. It was impossible to see inside yet Helldiver seemed reasonably unperturbed, if only a little curious.

"This is just like Latushkin," he said. "Trying to rattle my cage. He seems to have forgotten that he would not be director of the SVR if not for my father. And he has me to thank for the properties and mistresses he retains in Spain and France. Perhaps I will remind him."

Morgan felt a second speed change, this one even more subtle than the last. Another followed just a few minutes later and then another and by now Helldiver was again quizzing the driver, who expertly maintained his nervously apologetic demeanor.

Then the box was tightened and the convoy eased onto the hard shoulder in unison, preparing to leave the highway

Chapter Twenty-Nine

The convoy pulled away from the highway and turned down a narrow gravel road between a silent honor guard of crumbling gray buildings. Already the sun was withdrawing behind the heavy rainclouds, which had been threatening earlier and were now settling in, lending an eerie darkness to the scene. With every crackle of the rocks beneath the tires, the road channeled them farther away from the busy highway. The road seemed endlessly long, a feeling exacerbated by the slow progress they were making. As each building passed from view, Morgan couldn't help but feel that a succession of impenetrable gates was being slammed shut behind them, permanently. The sense of foreboding that oozed from the staged drama of this power play by the new director of the SVR was not lost on him. These guys had been doing this a long time; they knew how to unnerve people. Morgan wondered for a moment about Masterson and made a mental note to grill him some more on his days of operating solo behind the Iron Curtain.

Their funeral procession finally broke free of the old

buildings and drove on through fields of dry tussock and stone for four or five more miles before cresting a hill and descending into an abandoned shell that had once been a warehouse, with rotting concrete walls twenty feet high and a roof that was now nothing more than a latticework of collapsed steel trusses and rusted sheets of corrugated iron that had, over many years, fallen autumnally like huge leaves to the ground.

Now Helldiver was showing serious concern, and Morgan could sense that Arena was equally anxious. She was rigid and silent in the front seat and had not engaged once during the drive from the airport, busying herself instead with her cellphone, emailing and occasionally making calls regarding Helldiver's imminent arrival at the Hotel Baltschug Kempinski. Morgan had tried to catch her eye in the wing mirror on their side of the car a number of times but to no avail. All he wanted to do was reach between the seats and squeeze her hand. All she had to do was hold on a little bit longer.

The convoy formed a rough circle, the Bentley in the center, and stopped. The Bentley's driver shut down the engine and got out without a word. The ZIL eased up alongside and stopped with the finality of a blade being embedded to the hilt in soft flesh. A dozen men climbed out of the Patriots, removed automatics from beneath their suit coats and took up positions around the limousine.

"Everybody just stay cool," Morgan said.

One of the men from the Patriot crew opened the rear passenger door of the ZIL and a man emerged. He was tall, lean, bald and middle aged and dressed in a dark suit. He moved unhurriedly as he approached the Bentley.

"This is not Latushkin," said Helldiver, his voice barely

audible. The bravado of flying into Moscow to lay down the law to his masters had all but evaporated.

When the man was within ten feet of the Bentley he made a gesture and all of their doors were opened. The men who had opened them all moved as unhurriedly as the first man, who was obviously in charge.

Helldiver took the lead, removing himself from the Bentley to stand facing the man in charge. There was less than five feet between them. Morgan and Arena got out on the far side of the car and were directed at gunpoint to stay there.

"Where's Latushkin?" Helldiver asked and, with a hint too much arrogance added, "I don't know you."

"Latushkin has been retired," the man replied. "I am his successor."

"Where is my security detail?" Helldiver asked. Morgan thought the question was clumsy, almost clutching at straws.

"They have been retired, too. As will you, very soon."

"Perhaps you'd like to explain to me exactly what is going on? Latushkin and I had an arrangement. We had agreed to meet today to sort things out. If he is out and you are in then I expect that you will be aware of this arrangement. Yes?"

"No, I have no knowledge of any arrangement and what's more, I have no particular interest in one. You demand a great deal for a man in your position. I recommend that you modify your behavior around me. I am significantly less tolerant than Comrade General Latushkin. Now, did you or did you not receive directive number Mike Juliet Victor two nine exactly one week ago today, ordering you to cease and desist any further action in regard to this operation you were running with Latushkin? And did you then ignore that order and arrange the beheading of a third-party foreign official while on US soil?" The man's voice was full of threat and menace. "Did you proceed to implement a subsequent and unnecessary attack on a civilian aircraft, which was to have been brought down two days ago?"

"I will be more than happy to discuss all your questions directly with Latushkin."

Morgan knew that wouldn't go down well at all. Helldiver was making this very primal and very difficult, very rapidly.

"My father and I are personal friends of the president, whom I believe you report directly to. Perhaps you should check again before you end up on the other side of this conversation. My father—"

The other man gave a short, sharp, braying laugh. Then he was silent again. The forced smile faded away to dust.

"You simply do not understand ... *Helldiver*." There was condescension in his voice. This man was in no way emotionally invested in the conversation; he was holding all the cards and toying with the billionaire. "Your father fled France this morning. You and he have considered yourselves beyond our reach for many years. You were wrong to think that way but he knew how far he could push before our patience would snap. And that is why we are here, Mr. Helldiver. Our patience has run its course. Comrade General Latushkin accepted his fate and died honorably. Your father, however – well, he has run away to save his own skin."

The man held out his hand and one of the Patriot men walked over and placed a gun in it. Arena's hand came up to her mouth as she let out a muffled gasp that only Morgan could hear.

"Your father understands the old ways."

With that the man raised his hand, leveled the gun and

fired. The bullet struck Helldiver in the center of the forehead. It happened so quickly he had no time to plead or bargain. The spray of blood and debris exploded across the pot-holed concrete floor and the body crumpled, dropping from sight on the other side of the Bentley. The man took two paces forward, emptied two more rounds into the body and handed the warm gun back to its owner.

"And sometimes the old ways are best," he said to Morgan and Arena. Then he got back into the ZIL and the big car drove away.

The driver of the Bentley appeared and gestured for them both to get back into the car. They did. He got behind the wheel and handed Morgan an envelope. Then he started the car and they rolled silently away.

Chapter Thirty

LONDON, ENGLAND

Reginald Davenport sat back into the welcoming arms of his sofa. His tie and cuff links were finally off for the day and his shoes weren't far behind. It had been a hell of a week but his agents had brought to an end a reprehensible endeavor and thwarted at the eleventh hour what could have been another disaster in the air. Not to mention the numerous other Intrepid operations going on around the world, but the Helldiver operation had been the most significant in recent months. Yet, there was still a nagging sense of anti-climax sitting uncomfortably in the pit of his gut. Something like unfinished business, but what was it? He massaged his temples and allowed his head to rest against the cushion he'd placed behind it. He was awaiting word from headquarters on the latest out of Moscow. Sheridan was in contact with Morgan and the two were compiling their report, which would come through as soon as it was done. In the meantime the operational headlines would have to do. Details would be good, but Davenport understood better than anybody that field agents weren't always able to sit around writing reports on laptops. All he'd heard so far was that Helldiver had been executed and Zolnerowich had fled.

Zolnerowich had fled. That was the issue sticking in his craw. He was dismayed – after everything he'd thrown at this operation, that particular piece of news was extremely disappointing. Of course, there was great solace in the knowledge that the attacks against civil airlines had been stopped and the recruiter, Salazar, and his accomplices had also been rounded up.

But the unresolved issue about where he had hoped the operation would lead them had yet to be resolved and was the cause of his greatest frustration. He knew they were on the right track; forty-plus years of service in his very particular operating environment had told him so. Global history, in this case at least, had become intrinsically linked to his personal history and it was his familiarity with certain individuals and their respective modus operandi that had piqued his interest and driven him to set Intrepid on such a potentially perilous course. He had thrown himself at the challenge of pulling together so many disparate threads. Deceiving Morgan into believing he was on an indefinite leave of absence while carefully arranging for him to be infiltrated into the Helldiver machine was only a part of it. One never knew where the majority of effort would be required in these long-term undercover operations involving so many different players and angles all over the world. His identification of Arena Halls as a valuable asset had proven a wise decision. Having her placed within Europol to prepare her for being seconded to the Zolner global empire had resulted in invaluable intelligence, which can only ever be achieved by selecting the right person for the job. Halls had been the right choice from the outset. Her ability to demonstrate her inestimable value to Zolner had seen her rise through the ranks of his corporate machinery until she became a trusted insider. The fact that she was never subsumed into the non-public-facing side of the business had not curtailed the extent of the information that she was able to send through via Masterson. It was her information that had eventually led to Morgan's involvement. But it had taken almost two years to achieve.

Davenport knew he could never have conceived of an alliance with the Russians in order to bring down Helldiver. Their willingness to participate was indicative of their concerns over Zolnerowich and his son – monsters of their own creation. Yet, despite all of the conspiracy theories, some of which had come very close to the truth, the general populace would really never know what the apparently isolated issue of civil aircraft falling from the skies had to do with global politics and the aspirations of individuals. Individuals who could influence the future of entire generations – and ultimately the world. Headlines heralding the new Cold War were as routine now as past headlines concerning the extremists. The Russians had achieved their objective: the West had become distracted once again by the Middle East and the shadow of the old Soviet Union had been resurrected. An Iron Curtain could very well, once again, descend across Europe.

Davenport couldn't help being reminded of the way things had been during his time with the Special Air Service and his introduction to the world of clandestine operations. Never knowing who to trust was the central theme of the time, and he dreaded a return to those uncertainties, although he knew deep down that absolute trust was a quality very hard earned indeed, and the importance and inherent fragility of its value would always be exploited by those motivated by self-interest.

In danger of being overwhelmed by the scale of it all, Davenport shut down those thoughts and contemplated what he might do for dinner. He wasn't inclined toward the prospect of remaining at home, something about the ongoing nature of the operation had unsettled him and so he would be better off out; either at a restaurant – where the bustle of people enjoying their meals and good company would be a welcome distraction, or there was always his club – but that would inevitably turn to shop talk and that wouldn't be helpful. Perhaps he might call one of his sons and see what they were up to.

His phone rang.

"Hello, V," he answered. "How are things across the river?"

"Very well thank you, Nobby," Violet Ashcroft-James, the Chief of MI6, replied. "And how are things with you, well I hope?"

"Oh, all of the usual nonsense, I'm afraid. And to what do I owe this delightful surprise?"

"Don't be awful, Nobby. I know it's been an age since we last spoke and that's been entirely my fault. So, here I am rectifying it. I thought it would be nice for you to do something spontaneous."

"I must say, your timing is impeccable, my dear. I'm intrigued. What are you proposing?"

"I was down at Warminster today for a meeting with some people from the Ministry of Defence and rather than returning to the city, and as it's a Friday, I've decided to stay at my house down here in Surrey. I'm going to have a few local friends over for supper, all very interesting, nice, normal people, none of whom have any involvement in our line of work, so I thought you might appreciate a change of scene."

"Do you mean this evening, V?" he asked, looking at his watch. It was almost 6pm. "It sounds very nice, but I'm afraid I wouldn't get down to Cobham until about eight. Would that be too late?"

"Of course not. Eight would be absolutely perfect. You can take one of the guest rooms. Pack an overnight bag, get in that old Jaguar of yours, and get moving straight away. I won't take no for an answer."

"Very well. You've always been good at dragging me out of my comfort zone," he said. "I'll get myself sorted out here and will see you in a couple of hours."

Davenport put down his phone. How extraordinary.

Chapter Thirty-One

HOTEL BALTSCHUG KEMPINSKI, MOSCOW, RUSSIAN FEDERATION

There was a tap at the door. Morgan opened it. Arena was standing there looking at him with those incredible blue eyes. He was instantly transported back to Sydney, how many years ago – four or five? Seeing her that first time after Malfajiri, her face framed by those few inches of open hotel room door. Room 109, that was it. Her hair was blond then. She'd been wearing a T-shirt, track pants and sports socks. And she'd been reading *The Count of Monte Cristo* which she knew was his favorite. He was reading that very book right now, had begun it before he even knew that their agent in France named Dominique was in fact his – his what? His Arena. He used to call her Ari, then.

"Can I come in?" she asked. She looked lost – or was it distance?

Whatever it was, she looked incredible. She was wearing a casual business suit, ready to travel back to Paris. Morgan was even getting to like the new dark hair. God, he was distracted by her so easily.

"Sure," he replied. "Come in. Can I get you anything?"

"No, I'm fine," she said, walking in. "Actually, scratch that. I'll have a glass of wine. Something white."

"What time's your flight?"

"A few hours. They'll be collecting my bags from my room soon and there's a car booked for me in about half an hour. They'll call me here. What about you?"

"Same. Few hours." Morgan went to the bar fridge and found a bottle of sauvignon blanc. He poured her a glass and, out of character, one for himself. Morgan would only drink white if there was nothing else or if he just had to. This was a just-had-to moment; he needed to fortify himself. She still had the same impact. He couldn't hide that from himself. He felt the same way he did all those years ago and all it took was for her to walk back into his life again, in a bizarre reversal of the scene they'd played out at the Hyde Park Regency in Sydney, with her this time walking into his room.

Ari had taken a seat by the windows and was looking across the Moskva River directly at Red Square. Morgan handed her the glass of wine and joined her on the adjacent seat.

"Hell of a day," he said.

"You think?" she said, then laughed nervously. He noticed her hand trembling slightly. Shock. Understandable. A man had been murdered in cold blood right in front of her by a senior government official, the same government official who'd guaranteed them both safe passage out of Russia as long as they each flew to their respective home ports immediately. How concrete was the man's guarantee? Morgan watched her for a moment, wondering about her life.

"You OK?" he asked.

"I suppose so. I guess, to some extent, I've been

expecting it the entire time I was undercover. There was such a brutal inevitability to the way in which it all ended, but I guess seeing it like that, first hand, witnessing it, really brought home the reality of what I've been in the middle of all this time. Especially what he's been up to. All those people."

"I realize it's little consolation, but he had it coming," Morgan said. "That won't make what you saw today just go away and be suddenly OK, but while you're trying to make sense of it, process it, perspective can help."

She nodded and sipped her wine. "They really dealt with it, didn't they?" She motioned across the river to Red Square. "Just as we all secretly imagine they do still deal with issues like that, here. The old ways."

"Old ways is right. Can you imagine the head of any agency in the West turning up and blowing someone away like that? It's very personal for them, even though they make it seem like it's not. It's as though the message must be conveyed directly, man to man, in order for it to be very clearly understood by all concerned. Even all those under-lings standing around watching and, eventually, cleaning up the aftermath."

"I meant to ask, what was in that envelope the driver gave you when he got back in the car with us?"

"It was a printout of the passport that Zolnerowich is traveling under, his new identity. They're gifting him to us. I've sent the details on to headquarters. They can start looking for him all over again. At least this time we have a head start, and we know for certain that he's actually alive. He'll show up soon enough."

Ari looked at him, nodding, and then turned in her chair, away from the view across the river, to face him. They held each other's gaze for some time, Morgan didn't know how long, but neither of them faltered. It felt natural, the way things were intended to be. The way they should have been for years.

"I heard about Dave Sutherland," she said. "I'm so sorry. I know you were close."

"Thanks," Morgan said. The reminder of his friend's death took him by surprise. "It's the nature of this business, I suppose. You just never know."

"I wouldn't even be here if not for you and Dave," she said. "I wish I could have made it to his funeral."

"He would have understood."

They fell into an awkward silence. The past, their shared past, was trying to surface, but there was just too much to unravel. Not here; not now.

"You know, Alex, when I said goodbye to you that day in London, I told you it was because I had to put distance between me and what we went through in Malfajiri. I thought I would be able to cope with it, but I couldn't. And having you around me and becoming so much a part of my life, I was torn between my feelings for you and knowing that every time I was with you I was constantly reminded of that dreadful place. It was so unfair. I felt that I had no other choice but to leave, which, of course, meant leaving you and London behind me. So, I did, but I can tell you it wasn't easy. In fact it was almost impossible. I just had to go through with it. It was a self-preservation thing."

Morgan sat quietly, sipping on his wine, watching her.

"But then, it must have been a year later, General Davenport tracked me down in Switzerland where I was doing some contract work for the British Embassy. I was thoroughly bored and he came in out of the blue with a job offer and the ability to do some good. And that, mister, is all your fault."

"How on earth can you blame that on me?"

"Because I felt that it would somehow make me feel close to you again. Like we were on the same team."

"A phone call would also have done that."

"It wasn't as easy as that for me," she replied. "By that time, I just presumed you would have worked me out of your system and moved on; whereas I thought about you all the time, almost everyday, to be honest. Barcelona. London. Your place in Farnham. But seeing you again, the way you've looked at me these past couple of days, I feel like nothing's changed for you and now I feel like such a fool."

Morgan couldn't believe what he was hearing. After all this time. "Why would you feel like a fool?"

"Because now I know I still love you – I never stopped loving you – but my fear drove me away and kept me away from you when I should never have left, and now it's too late."

"It doesn't have to be, Ari," Morgan found himself saying. "I'd walk away from all—"

"I'm afraid it does, Alex," she said. A single tear rolled down her cheek. "I'm married now."

Chapter Thirty-Two

"Our friend Zolnerowich arrived in the UK via Gatwick yesterday, traveling under those passport details the SVR gave you and suddenly General Davenport's gone off the grid," said Sheridan. "At this point we believe Davenport's in Surrey, but – with Zolnerowich on the loose – until I have eyes on the boss or receive his personal verification, I have to assume there's a problem. That's why we're heading there now. Your tactical gear is in the back."

"Jesus," replied Morgan. "What the hell is going on?"

Morgan and Sheridan were in the back of a specially modified Transit van that had a dual cabin in front connected to a weapons and equipment storage area in the back. A member of Intrepid's driving team was at the wheel, while Morgan and his chief of staff were in the back seat. Morgan had just returned from Moscow on one of Intrepid's Gulfstream G650 ultra-high-speed jets, one of an exclusive fleet specifically modified for Intrepid by Gulfstream's Special Missions Program Office, and Sheridan had collected him from Heathrow.

"Davenport left the office earlier than usual this evening to return to his home in Mayfair. Mrs. Jolley thought he was looking strained and so she called me. I walked in, took one look at him, agreed with her immediately and we packed him off home so he could relax while I watched the shop. His driver delivered him to his house a little before six. When I sent your report through to him at eight, I rang to let him know it was in his inbox. I got no answer. I tried again a few minutes later, still nothing. I issued a preliminary alert and we followed all the protocols; I even checked back with Mrs. Jolley, who was already at home but she had no idea where he could be."

"So, what's dragging us to Surrey?" Morgan asked.

"The GPS emergency locator in that old Jaguar of his went off a little after eight o'clock. It took a while to filter through the system back to me. The location received via the GPS was just outside a place called Cobham in Surrey."

"Cobham. Why the hell would he be in Cobham at this hour on a Friday night?"

"Ashcroft-James, chief of MI6, has a country house in Cobham."

Morgan snapped a look at Sheridan. The street lights along the M25 flashed across their faces. Sheridan's expression was not encouraging.

"I asked Commissioner Hutton at the Metropolitan Police to verify the whereabouts of Ashcroft-James for me without letting anyone know who was asking or why. He came back almost immediately and confirmed that she is in Washington, DC. She's been involved in meetings with their Homeland Security people this past week and isn't scheduled to return to London until tomorrow. He double-checked it with his people and as far as the Met is concerned, that's where she is."

"So, you're working off the premise that the boss has been lured there under false pretenses?"

"On the basis that our chief has never been off the grid ever before, I am. Ashcroft-James has a property on Old Lane at the edge of the village. It's about five acres and her home is located on the northeastern corner of her land. Reigns is currently on the ground and is moving in by foot across the property. Once she's checked it out, she'll send you her exact location so you two can RV there."

"Jesus, Beth must be on her last legs. I saw her report from Singapore when I was flying back. She's been through the ringer and all I've done so far was fucking nursemaid Helldiver and deliver him to the Russians so they could put a bullet in him."

"She is. That's why she's your backup on this if it goes pear-shaped. Once you get eyes on that residence, I need to know ASAP whether or not I'm walking up to the front door and asking to speak with the General personally or we're calling in the Marines."

"You can call in the Marines when you're in the US," said Morgan with mock indignation. "Over here you call in the Paras."

"OK, OK," Sheridan replied amiably. "I don't care who we gotta call as long as we get the boss back in one piece. Commissioner Hutton is on standby to provide any operational support we need, including police, army, you name it; and he'll provide top cover with Whitehall if need be. Meanwhile, he's spoken with the chief constable of the Surrey Police and she has dispatched a number of squad cars to standby in the village. If you need 'em, I'll call 'em forward. So now would be a good time for you to crawl in the back there and get kitted up. I'll let you know when we're getting close."

"Roger that." Morgan pushed open the central connecting door between their two seats and disappeared into the rear section of the van where the tactical gear was ready for him.

He had processed his conversation with Arena during the flight back from Moscow and, for now at least, he decided it was best left as it had been for many years – parked in a part of his mind that didn't require constant attention or speculation. It was just too hard to comprehend. Right now, there were two people who needed him; two people for whom he would sacrifice everything in a heartbeat. And, at this moment, one of them was stuck in a field in the dark and on her own, ready to take on whatever was going to be thrown at her in order to save their boss. Morgan knew she'd been through enough. He'd read between the lines of her operational report to understand the real detail.

Reigns needed him and right now that was Morgan's only thought.

He just hoped they could get there in time to find Davenport.

Chapter Thirty-Three

"Nice of her," Zolnerowich said, "to arrange my safe passage onto your little island and then lend me her private retreat so I can lay low for a while. So very English of her, wouldn't you say?"

"Yes, she's a real dear," Davenport replied. "Although I doubt very much that her invitation was intended to include the rest of your friends, but then again you always did like an audience."

Zolnerowich only smiled. He walked up to the chair Davenport was tied to and pulled on the ropes, specifically tightening the one that was wrapped around Davenport's neck. Davenport didn't flinch but the added discomfort and difficulty it caused him to breathe was apparent. They were in the drawing room of Ashcroft-James's country home and in addition to Zolnerowich, there were four other men, dangerous types, all upwards of forty, whom Davenport presumed to be ex-agents still loyal to their old master. Davenport was madly trying to piece together the details of the connection between Ashcroft-James and the Russians. It wasn't unheard of that the chief of a British intelligence agency was 'in bed' with the enemy. Davenport had long held his suspicions about her but he had no idea how far back her betrayal would eventually be traced. It was the constant fishing for information during the Night Witch operation and the eventual selling out of Morgan as an Intrepid agent that could have only, in those circumstances, come from her that had further heightened his suspicions. When he'd received her call earlier that evening he'd willingly taken the bait. He'd needed to know. He just hoped he'd activated his emergency locator in time for his team to act.

"So how do you think I should deal with the man who has been responsible not only for tearing down my life's work, but also for arranging the delivery of my son to his executioners?"

"Oh, I'm sorry. You're actually mourning the death of your boy now, are you? Seriously, Zolnerowich, you don't expect me to believe that. The two of you have orchestrated the deaths of thousands of innocent people in your combined lifetimes. Hardly the fodder for a proud family legacy. So let's not waste any time lamenting his passing here. My man delivered him to the SVR on my orders and they killed him. It saved my agent the job. Now, let's move on, shall we?"

Zolnerowich merely inclined his head and closed his eyes. Two of the men stepped forward and began beating Davenport about the head and upper body. Davenport felt every one of his six decades with each blow but refused to show any sign of pain or fatigue. The beating lasted a number of minutes and then stopped, leaving him breathless and bleeding. When the two men stepped back, Zolnerowich was standing once again in Davenport's eye line.

"I see you outsource your valor these days, comrade," said Davenport. "I suppose with all the money you've amassed at the expense of other's lives, you can afford just about anything. Although this really is a new low, even for you, paying thugs to beat up an old man."

Zolnerowich remained silent.

Davenport turned his head toward his assailants. "And you two must feel very proud of yourselves," he said.

One of the two made a move to attack him again but a bark from Zolnerowich stopped him in his tracks. The room fell silent. Davenport had made his point and so took the opportunity to regain his breath and composure as he dealt with the pain.

"Many years ago, you and I faced off in East Berlin," Zolnerowich said eventually. "You had come across the border to kill me with one of your SAS assassination squads because I had killed one of your agents in West Berlin. Do you remember?"

"I remember. Tiergarten." Davenport remembered every detail of the operation. It had haunted him for years. "And, on that occasion, we weren't trying to kill you at all. We were attempting to bring you in but we were sold out and three of my men were murdered. Two bodies were recovered. One was not."

"You were sold out. Yes, indeed. You were sold out. Have you ever wondered by whom?" Zolnerowich was grinning broadly. Enjoying every moment.

The answer to that question had eluded Davenport for so long he had all but given up wondering.

"It's quite incredible the lengths that an impressionable young woman will go to in order to impress those whom she believes share her misguided idealism. Equally, there is great value in the gentle cultivation of a potential agent over a prolonged period of time. Particularly, when that agent is on a fast-track career path in the Ministry of Defence and her lover is an officer in the Special Air Service. Questions at the beginning are innocent enough; personal questions about her, her family, her life. Trust is established. Then friendship. It was the height of the Campaign for Nuclear Disarmament. Emotions ran high and young intellectuals had very strong views. So then the questions become more specific – does she have a boyfriend? What does he do? It must be hard being away from each other so much. Is he away now? Where might he be? I'm sure you understand, general."

Davenport's expression remained unchanged. Inside he was a defeated man, his greatest fear realized. The woman who at one point had been the love of his life had, throughout the tenure of their intimacy and their lives since, been his enemy. Worse, she had not only betrayed Davenport, but Davenport's friends, and ultimately her country. Who knew what damage she had caused as her star continued to shine in Whitehall? Promotion followed promotion until she was named 'C', chief of the Secret Intelligence Service, MI6.

"Destroying your mission in Tiergarten was as simple as a phone call to my little angel in Whitehall. I shot the two troopers dead. They had no idea. But I wanted a head to take back to my masters in Moscow. A bright young sergeant. I arranged to take him across the border into East Berlin and then the plan was to fly him to Moscow. But, as so often happens in the field, things did not go to plan." He laughed again.

At this point Davenport was numb with anger. Not only was his mind alive with memories of his time with Ashcroft-James, but now he could see, as clearly as if they were sitting beside him, the faces of the three soldiers he had sent to their deaths during the failed operation thirty years ago.

"We took your man – what was his name?"

"Blair."

"We took your man Blair up in a Fokker F27 and during my preliminary interrogation, he became aggressive and managed to break free of the bonds around his wrists. I was young and impetuous in those days and eager to impress my superiors with some raw intelligence when I landed. So, in order to show my disapproval, I hung him from the door of that aircraft and threatened to throw him out if he didn't cooperate. And do you know what he did, general?"

Davenport just looked at Zolnerowich.

"He fought off the two men who were holding him and jumped of his own accord. I've always admired him for that. It took real guts to do that, don't you think?"

"Of course. Sergeant Blair was an extremely brave man. I would have expected nothing less."

"I'm so glad you feel that way, general, because I can think of no more fitting an end for the great Davenport than to be hurled to his death from an aircraft. Just like your man, Blair."

"How very original of you," Davenport answered defiantly. "Remarkable, really. You reach the rank of general in the armed forces of the Russian Federation. You amass billions of dollars of private wealth, using your son as the instrument of your extortion of your own country's resources, but then the only seemingly original idea you

CHRIS ALLEN

come up with, you've stolen from a brave young man who
sacrificed his own life to protect the interests of his country
thirty years ago. No doubt you'll outsource the hurling
element of my demise to one of these clowns, too."

Davenport felt them all bristle, including Zolnerowich,
but again he had made his point. If he was going to die
tonight he wasn't going to be bloody well polite about it.

234

Chapter Thirty-Four

Morgan found Reigns in the heather very close to the house. She, like Morgan, was dressed in black tactical gear and armed with their standard Sig Sauer P226 and an assortment of other weapons. Their balaclavas were rolled up as beanies.

"Hey, long time no see," she whispered as Morgan crawled in beside her. "What brings you out into the English countryside on this balmy Friday evening?"

"There was nothing good on telly," Morgan whispered. "Nice house. What do you think it's worth?"

"More than you and I will ever see put together. How does a senior public servant afford a place like this?"

"Old family money, I'm told. What's the latest? And is that the boss's Jaguar I can see parked down the far side of the house?"

"It is indeed. There's also a Land Rover Defender out front and if you look carefully through that open gate in the fence behind us, you'll just see the silhouette of a light aircraft, I think it's a Cessna 206, parked on the end of

Wisley Airfield; it's an abandoned World War Two strip. There's a field between us and Wisley, but no other fences once you're through that gate. Country folks don't leave gates open on their properties. I reckon it's been left open for convenience, by non-locals. I'm only guessing, but it's not a stretch to consider that Zolnerowich came here by air from Gatwick."

"Anyone in it?"

"I can't be sure but I may have seen the glow of a cigarette a couple of times," she replied.

"Jesus, how close is it?"

"A few hundred yards, if that. Close enough to get to easily through the open gate." She pointed. "The strip was the first thing I checked out when they dropped me off up the road. That's when I realized that the gate was open."

"Any sign of the boss or anyone else, like Ashcroft-James?"

"Neither of them, but before you showed up I'd been watching two men dressed in black overalls doing regular patrols around the house."

"A Secret Service protection detail?"

"No, they're not giving me that vibe. Not professional enough – one is carrying a shotgun and the other's probably got a sidearm, I can't tell from here. But mostly they're slovenly, if that makes sense?"

"Totally," he replied. "How often are they doing their thing?"

"Every thirty minutes. They're due again in about ten."

"We better get a wriggle on then. Anything else?"

"I've done a circuit of the whole outside area of the house and there are lights on throughout, what you'd expect to see of a home that's occupied, but most of the rooms that are lit are downstairs at the front. I haven't gone in too close, because I know she has CCTV that's linked back to the Met and Surrey Police."

"Sheridan's looking into that now via Commissioner Hutton. They'll be reviewing the past twenty-four hours' worth of recorded footage and, as we're about to go in, he's confirmed with Hutton that the CCTV will go offline from eleven pm." He checked the luminous dial on his Tag Heuer. "In five minutes, and it'll stay offline until we're clear."

"OK, so how do you want to play it?"

"Which door are the sentries using to come in and out?"

"This side, near the back, off the kitchen." She pointed. "The lights are off down there but that's where they've been coming from."

"Sounds like the perfect place to start. Reckon you can get that Land Rover ready to go? If we find him in there, I'm expecting we'll need to get out as quick as we can."

"Sure. Just say when."

"Watch me go in, give me a couple of minutes inside and then get it going. Give it a lot of revs once you do and keep it running. I'll try to deal with their reaction but just keep your eyes peeled in case anyone slips through the net."

"You got it. Check comms with Sheridan?"

They fitted their earpieces and checked their radios. Morgan went first.

"Alpha-Alpha and Callsign Two, this is One. Comms check, over."

"One, this is Alpha-Alpha," Sheridan replied. "Loud and clear, over."

Reigns confirmed she was loud and clear with both Morgan and Sheridan then began to move cautiously around the shadows on the edge of the residence toward the Land Rover, maintaining a visual on the rear kitchen door.

Morgan made his way across the pebbled driveway that skirted the house from the front and around to the side entrance. At first he was careful not to make too much noise but then decided he was comfortable with the idea of drawing them out, and ran across. The pebbles crunched under every footfall. When he reached the kitchen door he pressed his back up against the wall beside it and waited. He saw a gardening shovel to his right and grabbed it. He checked his Tag. Almost 11pm. Anytime now.

Within a minute the door to the kitchen opened and a man appeared, dressed in black overalls, a cigarette hanging from his lips and a shotgun in his hands. Morgan had the shovel poised and ready. The moment the man cleared the step and his foot hit the pebbles, Morgan swung the flat back of the shovel blade with everything he had straight at the man's face. It impacted with a sickly slap and crack. The man dropped the gun to grab at his face and began to fall backward against his comrade, but before the man completely lost his footing, Morgan brought the curved edge of the blade down hard across the top of the man's right boot. Morgan could feel the damage to the guy's foot instantly telegraph its way up the handle. The man howled in pain and fell to the ground in a heap. His head slammed against the stone step and he was silent. Morgan dropped the shovel, reached over and pulled his comrade outside, throwing him down on the driveway. He grabbed the dropped shotgun and slammed the butt into the guy's temple. Two down. Morgan relieved them of their side-arms and tossed the shotgun into the shadows. Then he raced inside.

The howl from the first guy had obviously drawn some interest – Morgan could hear a ruckus developing ahead. The raised voices of men reacting to an uncertain set of circumstances. The tone and urgency may have been the same as English speakers, but these voices were speaking in Russian. Morgan raced toward the voices, through the kitchen and along an unlit corridor that connected with the main living areas of the house. Outside, the Land Rover Defender coughed to life and then began revving loudly. *Good girl, Beth.* Bang on time. As Morgan approached the end of the corridor, he could hear the heavy footfalls of men in boots rushing across the floorboards of the entrance foyer, heading for the front door, for the Land Rover. Heading toward Beth, as planned.

As he reached the foyer, there were two men with their backs to him preparing to rush outside. One got the door opened and the other was hot on his heels. Morgan intercepted them, ASP baton in his hand. With a flick of his wrist he extended it out to its full length. The gratifying click as the telescoping high carbon steel blade locked into place told him the weapon was ready. Morgan brought his right arm around and then drove the weapon down in a wide arc to strike at the side of the first man's right knee. The impact immediately checked the man's speed and he fell sideways into a potted fern. Morgan was following through when he was grabbed around the neck from behind. With the ASP still in hand, Morgan brought the weapon up and struck his assailant directly across the head, hard. The pressure on his neck released. Morgan raised his left foot high and then drove it down, scraping the man's shin from kneecap to the top of his foot, then he spun and finished the guy off with a lateral strike with the ASP against the side of his head. The flowerpot guy was now back on his feet and dragging an automatic from a shoulder holster. Before the gun was fully withdrawn, Morgan had struck the gun-hand with the ASP and driven his left fist into the man's nose. Reigns appeared in the doorway. She was closing her baton and Morgan could see that the first guy to make it through the door had obviously run into Reigns and was now face down and immobile on the front porch.

"What now?" she said.

Morgan was about to answer when he heard the spluttering of an engine coming to life not far from the house.

"Oh, shit!" said Reigns. "That Cessna is getting ready to take off."

"Fuck! OK, see if Sheridan can get a vehicle onto that strip to cut them off at the far end, and bring the Land Rover around the back. Keep the lights off."

Chapter Thirty-Five

Reigns ran out through the front door, calling Sheridan on the move. Morgan ran through the corridors toward the back of the house and, following his instinct, soon found himself in a large drawing room that opened onto the gardens. He scanned the room as quickly as he could, searching for any signs of Davenport. At first glance it was as expected, elegantly appointed with Regency furniture and expensive looking artifacts and paintings. He'd had his fill of the rich over the past few months and expected he would for quite some time to come. The thing that struck him most was that the room had very obviously been recently occupied – it still had the stale air of tension about it and was thick with cigarette smoke. Men had been in this room. Violent men. He'd seen some of them already; they were currently strewn semiconscious outside the kitchen and across the front entrance, and were about to be rounded up by the Surrey Constabulary. But there were more and they'd escaped. The French doors that led onto the gardens were open and a light wind stirred the curtains. Just as he was about to rush outside, his attention was drawn to the center of the room. He knew that they'd been right to move in. An old chair had been knocked over and there was a pile of discarded ropes laying in a mess around it. But the ropes weren't what had piqued his interest. There were small circles of blood around the chair and ropes, which then streamed in a diminishing line toward the open doors. And just beside the chair, in a crumpled heap where it had been thrown at some point during the evening, was a Harris Tweed sports coat that Morgan recognized immediately. His eyes blazed as he reached for it and lifted it up to be sure. A rattle of keys in the right-hand pocket confirmed everything. The keys were for the Jaguar parked outside. The Jaguar that belonged to General Davenport. Morgan pocketed the keys, dropped the jacket on a nearby sofa and sprinted from the room. In an instant the lights of the house were behind him and he was running through the darkness, heading straight for the open gate in the fence line at the back of the property. The rumble of the Cessna was building now and Morgan knew it was minutes, if not seconds, away from taking off. He sprinted with everything he had, stumbled and fell more than once on the uneven grounds of the gardens, got up and kept going. To his right he heard the roar of the Land Rover as it sped from the front of the property, along the pebbled driveway and then bounced onto the lawns that paralleled the rear perimeter fence. He and the Land Rover were racing to the same point: the gate.

"Hit your lights and don't slow down!" Morgan yelled into his radio and the lights blazed to life. He kept up his speed and in moments was level with the Land Rover and reaching for the passenger side door handle. He grappled it open and jumped inside.

"Get us on that strip."

"Did you see any more of them?" she yelled back. "Any sign of the General?"

"No, but they had him back there, bound to a fucking chair. I found his jacket and there was blood on the floor."

"Jesus!"

"I'll tear these fuckers apart, Beth. I fucking swear it."

The Land Rover raced across the lawns, through the open gate and onto the field that separated the house from the airstrip. Reigns expertly pushed the Land Rover over the uneven ground, maintaining a steady course straight for the southeastern end of the strip. What they saw in the Land Rover's headlights caused Reigns to slam her foot down, and Morgan realized he was pressing his right foot flat to the floor, too.

Directly ahead of them in the aircraft was Zolnerowich, reaching back out of the aircraft to drag someone onboard. That someone was Davenport. It looked as though his wrists were bound. Despite what he'd already been through he seemed, from a distance anyway, as stalwart as ever and was resisting, as best he could, all their attempts to get him inside the aircraft. The General was being manhandled from behind by one of Zolnerowich's thugs. He was a big unit, no doubt the Russian general's primary muscle, and he was clearly getting frustrated with Davenport's defiance. Despite Morgan's rage, it was a relief to see the old man putting up such a good fight. Not that he expected anything less.

They were almost at the strip. The scene at the Cessna was becoming even more clear now. Then Morgan saw the thug, clearly at the end of his tether, produce a handgun, raise it above his head and bring it down on the crown of Davenport's skull.

"Oh, God!" Reigns cried.

Beside her, Morgan was rigid with tension.

Davenport's body slumped back against the thug and then he was bundled clumsily inside with Zolnerowich dragging his legs in as the thug clambered in over the top of him. The Cessna began to turn around and line up for take-off. Reigns got the Land Rover over the lip of the tarmac and slammed her foot down again as soon as she had traction on the hard-standing. The Cessna straightened and as they drew even closer they could both hear the whine of the revs over the sound of the Land Rover's engine.

"Drop the lights again and get me along their port side, Beth. Under the wing. Go! Go!"

Reigns didn't flinch or second-guess. She doused the headlights and lined the Land Rover up against the portside wing light of the Cessna. Morgan clambered between the front seats and into the back. He had his Sig Sauer in his hands and was mechanically checking that it was ready to fire. Reigns had the Land Rover at fifty-five miles per hour and was building to match the Cessna's take-off speed. The Land Rover was powering across the surface of the strip and was almost level with the tail of the plane. Morgan knew they were close to take-off speed which, at their current rate, he estimated would be around seventy knots for the Cessna, eighty miles per hour for the Land Rover. He looked over Reigns' shoulder. Seventy miles per hour. She had them perfectly aligned. It was time. Morgan opened the door, climbed out of the Land Rover and pulled himself up into a standing position with his feet on the running board and his hands hanging on tight to the edge of the metal roof-rack. The Cessna's front wheels were just skimming the tarmac now and the engine was screaming to take off. Reigns knew exactly what Morgan needed her to do. She got them under the portside wing tip just as the front wheels of the Cessna lifted off. Morgan was buffeted by the winds racing against his body. He would only get one chance at this. *Come on, Reigns. Come on. Now!*

At that moment, Reigns inched the Land Rover to the right just enough to put Morgan within reaching distance of the wing's strut. The Land Rover's engines was howling back at the Cessna. The Cessna was crying to take to the skies. The wing strut rose and was level with Morgan. He turned his body, braced his feet against the running board for a split-second of solid purchase and leaped for the wing strut.

Chapter Thirty-Six

Alex Morgan wrapped his arms around the wing strut just as the Cessna 206 became airborne. The addition of an extra two hundred pounds at the moment of take-off caused the Cessna to lurch to port and the pilot to overcorrect, raising the portside way too high and dipping the aircraft well to starboard. The tip of the starboard side wing came dangerously close to scraping the tarmac but the maneuver helped slide Morgan down the strut to the fuselage. He hit the paneling heavily and almost lost his already tenuous grasp on the strut. The bonus was that the slide took him beneath the eye-line of the pilot and the level of the windows. He knew that the pilot would have been madly looking for the source of the interruption to his take-off and that, in the back, Zolnerowich and his guard dog would have been grappling with Davenport. What the fuck were they up to and, more importantly, where were they planning to take the General?

The Cessna was under control again now and beginning a steady climb. Soon the lights of the houses surrounding

Wisley Airfield were well beyond reach and as they rapidly ascended hundreds of feet into the air, Morgan suddenly realized he was dangling on the outside of an aircraft at night without a parachute or any real thought of how his rescue of Davenport would play out. If he'd come up with this as a solution to a training scenario when he was being considered for Intrepid, Davenport would never have taken him on. Still, here he was. He had no choice but to make it work.

The Cessna continued to climb and from what he could gather, it was ascending in a classic corkscrew, straight up, common to skydiving clubs, where the aircraft would essentially land, pick up parachutists, gain the target height above the strip, throw them all out and do it again. In this case, that wasn't a good sign. He had to get inside.

Morgan checked his grip at the base of the strut and then, dangling for a moment, lifted his legs across to the top of the wheel cowling. When he hooked his foot around the top of the cowling's strut and squeezed the fingers of his right hand through the portside door handle, he let go of the wing strut altogether. He slid into a sitting position on the wheel cowling, wrapping his legs around the wheel strut as tightly as humanly possible. Slowly, he changed hands so that his left was on the handle and then rechecked the safety strap across the top of the Sig Sauer on his thigh holster. Morgan rested his head for a moment, facing aft against the cold metal fuselage. He took two long, deep breaths and then yanked the door open, pushing it as wide as he could against the blast of the wind, and threw himself awkwardly inside.

Halfway through the door, Morgan copped a boot in the side of his face. He almost lost his grip but managed to wedge his right elbow in hard inside the frame of the door.

As a second kick came at him, he ducked his head to floor level and got his entire body inside. The thug was upon him, not trying to fight but to get Morgan back outside the door. What ensued was little more than a clumsy schoolyard brawl, unskilled and frantic, with each man attempting to overwhelm the other within less available space than an average phonebooth, each with the sole objective of ejecting the other out of a opening less than half that of a normal door. Morgan was aware of a lot of yelling and cursing in Russian as he squirmed his way free of the half nelson that the other guy had him in.

Morgan was through with these guys. He was here for one reason and that was to recover his boss, the man who had returned to him the life's purpose he had so badly craved for the duration of his exile. For months he'd been on the security detail of a man who had killed hundreds of innocent people without a second thought, just to sell MiGs and build his personal fortune into the astronomical billions range. He'd witnessed Helldiver and his wife living a life beyond the dreams of most of the inhabitants of the planet and indulging in excesses that Morgan found abhorrent. He'd witnessed the summary execution of the man at the hands of his clandestine masters and learned that the old ways were never really old at all: they were a constantly evolving beast that never aged, never weakened, never relented. And now these same people were striking down the man who represented the polar opposite of everything they stood for. The man who had created an agency that drew the best people from all over the world to fight on behalf of the majority of the planet's inhabitants who could never fight for themselves. To defend the right of every individual, regardless of race, color or creed, to live their life safe from the threat of harm or fear. Right now, that man was in a crumpled heap on the floor of the Cessna, beaten into submission because he wouldn't toe the line.

There was one thing Morgan had learned about these people during the course of the operation that he would carry with him forever, and that was that they only understood the power of the old ways. They only respected the old ways and would only ever respond to the old ways. It was their live by the sword, die by the sword philosophy that delivered to Morgan, in that moment, the only real option left.

The thug was still grabbing at Morgan, trying to drag him by his feet to get him back near the flapping door. Morgan could feel the hands trying to get a firm hold around his ankles and he could hear the grunting as all the unexpected exertion was getting the better of the man. Morgan allowed the guy a second to secure his grip on Morgan's legs and then, focusing his attention on the silhouette of the head and shoulders in front of him, he withdrew the P226 from his leg holster, thrust the barrel directly into the center of the thug's forehead, and fired. The grip seized for a moment and then suddenly released.

Morgan kicked free of the mess and turned his attention to Zolnerowich, who was at that moment scrambling to find the gun his man had dropped.

"No, general. Unless you'd like to be shot like a dog, too, I'd recommend against it," Morgan said. "Your journey ends here. Get out of that seat and come forward."

Zolnerowich hesitated at first but then a look came over his face that, in the dim half-light of the cabin, seemed strangely compliant for a man with a reputation for being so familiar with death. It was as if with the flick of a switch he had acquiesced and had turned over his fate willingly to Morgan. But Morgan wasn't buying it. Something else had prompted the change. Then there was a sudden surge in power and the engine groaned in protest. The pilot. Morgan turned quickly and saw the pilot leveling an automatic at him between the front seats. A shot was fired, followed by another and both rounds sang past Morgan as he threw himself clear.

Zolnerowich grabbed for the gun on the floor and got a hand around it. He came at Morgan, trying to aim, but the plane was being buffeted by winds and the pilot wasn't really concentrating on flying. Morgan couldn't shoot for fear of hitting Davenport, but Zolnerowich was old and his movements awkward and Morgan was wondering when he had last pulled a trigger himself when the gun in the old Russian's hand exploded twice. One round hit the roof near Morgan's head and the second winged past him and hit the body of the thug. In the confined space he felt the pressure of its trajectory as it narrowly missed his left arm. There was another explosion and then a loud groan from the pilot and the aircraft immediately nose dived. Once again the engine protested loudly. Morgan grabbed a seat to keep himself upright and Zolnerowich tumbled against him. Morgan pushed him away, trying to get to his feet, but Zolnerowich was also trying to steady himself — against Morgan. There wasn't time for this. The aircraft was falling and would be dangerously close to an unrecoverable dive in seconds unless he was able to get to the controls.

Morgan got up on one knee and reached forward to the front seats but the old Russian grabbed his arm, attempting to pull Morgan down. Morgan realized that Zolnerowich was trying to take them all down together. The old ways. One in, all in. The old fool was crazy but deceptively strong. He kept grabbing at Morgan, and with the Cessna now almost vertical, they had both fallen forward against the back of the front seats. Morgan was desperate. The howl of the engine underscored the urgency with which he knew he had to recover the aircraft if he and Davenport were to survive. The old Russian became crazed, as though the noise of the dying aircraft was feeding a death-frenzy within him. He clawed at Morgan, still trying to keep him from the controls. Morgan felt as though he was caught in a huge web he couldn't get free of and, like a trapped insect, was predestined to accept his fate. He had no idea how far they'd fallen but he knew he'd parachuted from much higher altitudes and didn't like their chances if this went on much longer. He twisted against the starboard wall of the fuselage and with both feet together, kicked Zolnerowich as hard as he could in the chest. The old man fell back against the flapping door, grappling without success for a handhold. It was now or never. Morgan pulled himself up, braced, and kicked again with everything he had. In less than a second, the door snapped open like the ejection port on a weapon as it's fired and Zolnerowich was gone.

The aircraft was starting to spin and all Morgan could see now were the lights of the houses dotted against the blackened background of Surrey.

He threw himself between the front seats and scrambled for the controls.

Chapter Thirty-Seven

It was midday, give or take, the June sun was high in the sky over London and the drive through the streets of Mayfair, along Park Lane and around behind the Palace to Belgravia, was really something – a stark contrast to the events of the past thirty-six hours. A lot had happened, including an extraordinary amount of cooperation by a number of law enforcement agencies, all ably coordinated by trusted friend and ally Sinclair Hutton, commissioner of the Metropolitan Police. In fact, it would not be an over-statement to acknowledge that the final phase of the Hell-diver operation, the phase that was about to occur, could not possibly have happened without him. Numerous arrests had been made, bodies recovered and repairs made to a certain private residence all within the traditionally tranquil surrounds of Old Lane in Cobham. Not a word had made its way to the press yet and, cherishing any opportunity to have one over the clandestine services, the Metropolitan Police and the Surrey Police had pulled out all the stops to ensure that all official reporting had been placed under a restricted caveat for seventy-two hours in order to keep it off the Whitehall grapevine. Which, of course, was critical to the operation's ultimate success.

As the car approached Eaton Square, Davenport was filled with a combination of dread and elation. He put the dread down to being a symptom of a soft heart and the elation being proof that there was still sufficient ruthlessness in him to keep him in the game a while longer yet.

"It's very kind of you to accompany me, Mr. Masterson," said Davenport. "I'm afraid this is likely to be rather unpleasant."

"It's my absolute pleasure, general. I'd do just about anything to drive this old Jag of yours around London. Including the odd confrontation, here and there. Besides, if you don't mind me saying, this is long overdue."

"Quite. Still, it's important that you're involved, given the work you've been doing for me on this over the past few years. Your investigations have ensured that all of these most recent developments can now be included within the legal briefs we've compiled. Without your work, I fear we'd still be five years away. Here it is, on the right."

Masterson eased Davenport's treasured navy blue 1968 S-Type Jaguar to a stop in front of a magnificent five-story terrace faced with white stucco located at the eastern end of the square near St. Peter's Church. He got out and came around to open Davenport's door. Following the events of Friday evening, Davenport's face was battered and bruised, and a number of his ribs were suspected of being fractured and had been strapped by his doctor. He was walking with a cane mainly due to the general punishment he'd received but also to the difficulties he had been experiencing in breathing as a result of the broken ribs. With great tact and discretion, Masterson assisted him in getting out and standing confidently on the footpath. There was a car with plainclothes officers from Scotland Yard in the street outside the residence. Davenport strode up to the door, Masterson following protectively behind him. When he reached the door, Davenport gave it three sharp raps.

A young man in a suit who Davenport recognized as a member of the Scotland Yard Special Branch answered the door and showed them into the drawing room. Davenport sat down and Masterson hovered by the front window overlooking the street. The young policeman left them and went off to announce their arrival.

A few moments later an uncharacteristically reserved Dame Violet Ashcroft-James appeared. Davenport stood as she entered the room. Masterson paid her only cursory interest, choosing to remain at the window.

"Good afternoon, Nobby," she said. She didn't approach to embrace him, which had been their usual custom over the past thirty or more years during private or professional meetings. "Can I offer you anything? Or anything for this gentleman?"

Davenport declined on behalf of them both.

"Perhaps you might sit down, Violet," he began. He wasn't about to allow her to waste time with superficial pleasantries. Now that he was here with her, facing her and preparing to present his accusation in person, he realized that the dread he'd been feeling had vanished. Now, there was only resolve.

"Very well. Although, I'm not accustomed to being told what to do in my own home. Perhaps you might cut to the chase. As you no doubt already know, I have been made aware of the allegations made against me. Allegations, I might add, that came from you. Am I right?"

"Yes, that's right. And that's why I'm here."

"Well, I don't see what difference it makes. The damage has been done and my career is in ruins. It's only a matter of time before the tabloids get wind of it."

"I appreciate that you are holding your ground and, at some point in the near future when you are called to officially answer for your crimes, you will no doubt profess your innocence. That, of course, is your right. So, rather than playing any silly games and behaving like a petulant schoolgirl, perhaps you'll allow me to say what I've come to say and then I'll leave."

Ashcroft-James sat forward in her chair, legs crossed at the ankles, her raven hair brushed back and held with a clip. Her face was cold and devoid of humor. She knew the score and would remain silent, knowing that anything she said could potentially harm her. Davenport didn't intend to share any new details with her, he just wanted her to hear it all directly from him. He had provided all the evidence he and Masterson had collected directly to Commissioner Hutton earlier that morning, having also met with the Prime Minister and the Minister of Defence on the previous evening and provided a detailed briefing. The decision had been made. Her appointment had been immediately suspended, pending a full and thorough investigation. She had been placed under house arrest and all of her access to external communication sources had been barred.

"Are you familiar with the gentleman behind me? His name is Masterson."

"Yes, of course, I know of Mr. Masterson by reputation, but I don't believe I've ever had the pleasure. How do you do?"

Davenport didn't see how Masterson responded. It was probably little more than a perfunctory nod. Ashcroft-James returned her attention to Davenport.

"I am aware of the type of work Mr. Masterson does. In fact, I believe he's even been engaged by my own service on occasion. But why is he in my house?"

"For some time I've suspected your involvement in certain activities which I believe compromise your responsibilities as chief of the Secret Intelligence Service. There were a number of issues, minor at first, that made me curious. I don't intend to bore you with them all now but they will be made available to you in due course to review with your legal team. It was your actions at the time of the Malfijiri civil war that were the catalyst for my interest. To that end, I engaged Mr. Masterson to assist me in piecing together the information as I saw it. I needed an objective and experienced eye to take the suspicion and find within it the kernel of fact that would hopefully lead to evidence. Your eagerness to derail Abraham Johnson's operation in Malfajiri on behalf of Renegade, for example, was not what I would have expected from the chief of SIS. So eager were you to ensure that his plan could not continue that when the efforts of your own agency failed, you came to me, hat in hand, under the premise that you had an agent who had gone rogue. I said at the time that I had the distinct impression that my organization was being used to help you clean out some MI6 deadwood. What I did not realize was that you were manipulating the facts in order to bring down a competitor. This Renegade Group really has had the lion's share of aspirants. When I realized that two of our most senior civil servants were both vying for appointment to its ranks, I had no hesitation but to begin gathering my evidence. And that's precisely when I brought in Mr. Masterson and the reason he is standing here in your house today."

"This really is quite tiresome. Do you have anything more to say?"

"I'm almost done. I've had my eye on Renegade for some time now, thanks to you and Johnson. And, with Mr. Masterson's assistance, I was able to identify this Helldiver character as one of its principal combatants. The fact that he was the son of Zolnerowich only served to strengthen my resolve to target him as the entry point for my people to finally unravel the Hydra that is, or rather was, Renegade. Of course, I had no idea that Zolnerowich was still alive and none of us could ever have conceived the operation Helldiver was in the midst of when we began to put our plan into effect. Our infiltration of his organization commenced over two years ago and we very quietly, very patiently, cultivated our asset until that asset reached the most senior ranks of his inner circle. That is how we learned about the attacks upon the airlines and ultimately, the connection of Renegade back to the old enemy, Mother Russia.

"Of course, throughout all this, we were still building our evidence against you. You've been very clever and have managed to cover your tracks very effectively over many decades, which we now know you have done with considerable help from your masters in Moscow. And this rushed and very clumsy attempt of yours to deliver me into the hands of the Renegade chairman himself, Zolnerowich, while you're overseas – did you really think I was naive enough to believe it was a genuine invitation? I was prepared for a showdown of some sort, Violet. And I will admit to thinking that you would have been there. Of course, you weren't and, well, Zolnerowich and I had a lot to catch up on. I was made aware of just how far back your treachery began. You'll just have to live with the shame of it when it all comes out, and it will. You have betrayed the trust of a great many people, Violet, not the least of whom are your own children and others who have had regard for you these many years."

Davenport got up and Masterson walked over to join him. Before leaving, Davenport turned to face her one last time.

"You may not be aware yet that Hedeon Zolner was shot a few days ago by the SVR in Moscow and his father fell from a plane two nights ago over Surrey. The body was recovered yesterday morning, not too far from Cobham."

"And what has any of that to do with me?" she asked.

"You should consider yourself lucky," replied Davenport.

Chapter Thirty-Eight

Alex Morgan wandered out of the shower, heading back to his room to get dressed, and stopped dead in his tracks. Elizabeth Reigns was on his bed wearing nothing but her underwear. She was lying on her front, her feet up behind her, reading a magazine. Morgan couldn't help but stop and admire her. She was svelte and lightly tanned and possessed the classic beauty of her Asian-American heritage. Her long black hair fell down one side of her face and when she looked up at him and smiled, her soft features were framed perfectly by it.

"If that's *Guns and Ammo* you're reading, I may just propose," he said.

"What if I said it was *Jane's Defence Weekly*?"

"Let's fly to Vegas right now. How many kids do you wanna have?"

"You are such an idiot," she said and went back to reading.

"So, seriously, Reigns," he said from the door. "What are you reading?"

259

She lifted it just enough for him to see the cover.

"*HELLO* magazine! Jesus. Are you kidding?" Morgan laughed. So did she and then she hurled the magazine at him and sat up. Morgan dodged it just in time.

"I may be able to kick your ass, Morgan," she said. "But I'm still a girl, you know. Or hadn't you noticed?" She rolled her body out slowly, laid her head back among the pillows and stretched until her toes curled over the edge of the bed, using a pair of endlessly long legs and a thong to captivate Morgan's attention. There was something primal in the pull she had over him and her almost nakedness presented so wantonly before him reduced Morgan to his most carnal. She carried her beauty unashamedly and Morgan realized in that moment that they had become much more to each other than just buddies with benefits, as they'd started out. Through all the confusion of Arena's sudden and unexpected reappearance in his life, coming back to Reigns somehow made everything feel exactly as it should.

He walked over to the bed and Reigns pulled the towel from his body. Morgan lay down beside her and began kissing along her neck, slowly working his way over her breasts and down to her thong. Reigns body arched under his touch and she groaned a deep lascivious purr from the back of her throat. She reached down and ran her fingers through Morgan's thick brown hair, her nails scratching at his scalp. Morgan looked back at her and smiled as his teeth teased the fine lace edging of her thong.

"You can do whatever you want," she breathed, looking into his eyes. "But only if you promise not to be gentle."

Ranger: Chapter One

Day 1 - Thursday

Upper Huallaga Valley, Amazon Basin, Republic of Peru

The jungle was almost awake now. The rain had started again and the legions of wildlife that had been dormant for the last twelve hours were breaking their silence. Soon, the darkness would completely withdraw its protection and the first grey light of a cloud filled sky would reach down through the canopy. This was the time soldiers called stand-to. The time when nature does its shift change. Every man is awake and a defensive posture assumed. Weapons face out and no one makes a sound above a whisper – and then, only if absolutely necessary. For the uninitiated it's a time of uncertainty and vulnerability, when the senses struggle to adjust to the transition between darkness and light, silence and noise. For the expert, it represents the perfect moment to exploit weakness.

In the midst of it all were eight men, all of them experts in jungle warfare, crouched in a tight defensive circle, weapons at the ready. Six of them were members of the US Army's Special Operations Command South; specifically, Green Berets of the elite 7th Special Forces Group (Airborne) and one half of an Operational Detachment Alpha from Bravo Company, 2nd Battalion, or ODA 751. With them were two other men. Not Green Berets, but agents of Interpol's highly secret black-ops unit – the Intelligence, Recovery, Protection and Infiltration Division, otherwise known as Intrepid. Out here in the jungle there was no difference – Intrepid agent or Green Beret, everyone was a warrior. All of them wore Crye Precision combat uniforms in US MultiCam Tropic pattern, and were strapped from head to toe in exoskeletons of tactical equipment. They were armed with suppressed M4 carbines and 9 millimeter Berettas. In the center of the group, the Intrepid agents and the ODA commander sat in a huddle, whispering under the rain. Their features, etched by the glow of an infrared torch, reflected back at them from the folded section of map sheathed in a waterproof map case. They'd stopped to confirm their navigation before moving in, just fifty yards southwest of a clearing that opened onto their target. Around them, the rest of the team faced the jungle. No one made a sound above the hushed tones of the final planning.

The Intrepid agents Alex Morgan and Hermann 'the Key' Braunschweiger, having served in the British Parachute Regiment and Germany's GSG-9 respectively, were completely at home on combat operations. With the support of the 7th Special Forces Group – a favor called in by Intre-

pid's new Chief of Staff, ex-Green Beret Mickey Sheridan –
they were moving in to extract a colleague, Intrepid agent
Ricardo Pedrosa. Formerly a lieutenant of the *Brigata Para-
cadutisti Folgore, Italia* – the Italian Paratrooper Brigade
Folgore, Pedrosa had been teamed with special operations
officers of the *Policía Nacional del Perú* – the Peruvian
National Police – to bring down an illegal narcotics operation run by former members of the Shining Path group who
had, according to the US Department of the Treasury's
Office of Foreign Assets Control, struck an alliance with
Daesh.

Shining Path was formerly a Maoist insurgent organization that emerged in the '80s, driven to deliver Peru to a
Communist dictatorship. After the arrest of its founder,
Abimael Guzman, in 1992, Shining Path lost some of its
ideological steam and instead evolved into a criminal narco-
terrorist group responsible for trafficking cocaine
throughout North and South America, running its operations largely via a slave trade, most of whom were the children of Shining Path members. Recent intelligence
identified links to Daesh, specifically a money trail from the
illegal narcotics operations leading to Daesh cells operating
in South and Central America. This arrangement was reci-
procated by Daesh advisors providing training, which in
turn had facilitated a revival of Shining Path's traditional
subversive influence in Peru, albeit without the original
Communist philosophy.

Pedrosa had been dispatched to infiltrate the organization, establish the connection to the Islamic extremists and,
if possible, follow the links and the money back to the
Daesh cells. But just a few weeks into the mission, he'd
disappeared. Soon after, one of the Peruvian National

Police narcotics agents who'd been working with Pedrosa reached out to her contact at the US Drug Enforcement Administration office in Lima, citing that Pedrosa had been sold out by a corrupt cop and had been redeployed to a Shining Path outpost farther up in the Amazonian high country to be killed. Word filtered back via the DEA to Interpol, whereupon the information reached the desk of Intrepid's chief, General Davenport. Morgan and Braunschweiger were immediately dispatched to extract their agent.

Peru is the largest producer of cocaine in the world. On any given day, thousands of Peruvian teenagers negotiate their way on foot through some of the most hazardous regions of the country, carrying an average of thirty pounds of cocaine on their backs through dense jungle and mountainous terrain to covert airstrips where their cargo is stashed until eventually retrieved and loaded onto an aircraft for transport further along the chain. In Peru, two pounds of cocaine is worth around $1200. Street value in the major capitals of the world, mostly the United States and Europe, can be anywhere from twenty to sixty times that amount.

According to the Peruvian narc, Pedrosa had been tasked to lead a team of these *mochilero* – backpackers – and would be killed once he'd delivered his team and their cargo to a destination located in the high country of the Upper Huallaga Valley. The trek would take two weeks. What Intrepid knew so far was that Pedrosa had reached his objective less than twenty-four hours earlier, and was now in a house believed to be the home of the local Shining Path commander – a routine turnaround point for teams of *mochilero*, and a base camp from which slave labor would be deployed to various plantations and labs throughout the surrounding area. It was also the location that Morgan, Braunschweiger and the Special Forces ODA were closing in on.

Over the past forty-eight hours, a series of covert aerial surveillance runs were conducted utilizing MQ-9 Reaper, a hunter-killer UAV capable of sustained, high-altitude surveillance tasks and, able to deploy with a significantly greater ordnance payload than its predecessor, Predator. Controlled via a ground control station crew back in Lima who fed the information back to the ODA, the Reaper had confirmed the location and layout of the house, approximate numbers of Shining Path members – who the Green Berets referred to exclusively as Bandits – and their slave laborers. And, as at 1700 hours last night, Reaper had also confirmed that Pedrosa was definitely there and staying in the main house. The house was located on a hill bordered to the north by a creek line, steep and dense with an almost impenetrable barrier of secondary jungle undergrowth. The slave laborers – there were about thirty of them: men, women and some children and, since yesterday, a dozen or so *mochilero* – were housed in a long, open-sided building with a thatched roof, which sat above the ground and was accessed by ladders at either end. It was on the edge of the jungle on the north-western side of the compound and enclosed by a high cyclone-mesh fence. By night the one gate that provided access and egress was padlocked.

The main house was currently occupied by the local Shining Path commander and approximately ten or twelve of his people – including Ricardo Pedrosa. It was located on half an acre of cleared land providing 270-degree views to the east, south and west but only over limited distance, no more than twenty or thirty yards at most, giving the occupants just seconds of warning in the event of an attack from the edge of the jungle. The only road to the house ran in from the east along a narrow, meandering ridge line that widened slightly about a hundred yards away to double as a clandestine airstrip; cleared to allow for the short touch-down and take-off of the irregular but regular enough light aircraft that delivered money and collected coca for ship-ment to Colombia and then, as cocaine, distribution into North America. Hence the cooperation between the US and Peruvian governments that had facilitated a large US military contingent to be semi-permanently based in Peru, and hence the ease with which the assistance of the US Special Forces had been secured.

Preparing to assault the house, Alex Morgan knew there was no guarantee that Pedrosa would even be alive when they found him – if they found him. But they had to try. At least time was on their side, because according to the whistleblower's statement, Pedrosa's murder was planned to coincide with the arrival of an aircraft at midday. So, they still had about six hours left.

"The lead Blackhawk pilot says they're on schedule for the extraction," said the detachment commander, Captain Kirby, his voice barely audible above the building rumble of the early morning rain. The dense foliage that cocooned the soldiers and their equipment was humming under the growing onslaught of what would soon be a downpour.

"Given the amount of time they've been in the air, that'll put 'em due east of us, about here," replied Morgan, indicating a point on the map with the tip of a SOG Force SE38 knife, the same knife he'd used to kill Zupan, the big Serb who'd almost killed him on Corfu a few missions ago. Morgan checked his TAG Heuer. "It's almost zero-five-hundred." He produced a sketch plan of the compound also sheathed in a plastic case, which included the main house, laborers' accommodation and the sentry post.

"My second team with Master Sergeant Muldoon will be in position by zero-five-thirty," said Kirby. "They'll sit tight until we're ready. Once we give them the green light, they'll take out the sentry post and then they'll cover the airstrip."

"We've made good time getting here, but it will be slower going between here and the back of the house," said Braunschweiger, indicating on the sketch. "You should get moving."

"HUA," replied Kirby, using the well-known US Army acronym for *Heard. Understood. Acknowledged.* "Coming up out of that creek line on the north side will be steep and the undergrowth much thicker. We'd better haul ass."

"As soon as you and Muldoon's guys are in position," said Morgan, "let us know. We'll set off in ten minutes and will prop here, west of the house." The tip of the blade indicated a point on the map. "It'll be sunlight at zero-six-ten; we all need to be in position by zero-six-zero-five, latest."

"Affirmative," Braunschweiger replied.

"You got it," said Kirby. "Let's go get your boy."

Kirby and three Green Berets moved off without a sound, melting away into the jungle. Braunschweiger and the two remaining Green Berets, Spring and Devereux, immediately closed in around Morgan. Every man knew what his responsibilities were. There wasn't anything to risk unnecessary conversation about. The four of them sat in silence and when ten minutes had passed, they set off.

Pushing through the last fifty yards of heavy jungle, moving closer toward their objective with every step, Morgan began mentally preparing for whatever would be thrown at them once they launched the assault. Alone with his thoughts, the jungle closed in around him as he and his team advanced with agonizing slowness through the secondary re-growth. Every sense was alive, processing, prioritizing and deciphering the constant stream of environmental data that changed with every step forward. With his right hand locked onto the M4 and his left reaching ahead, making slow progress through layer after layer of vines and debris, Morgan's eyes searched through the vegetation for anything out of the ordinary. Anything that wasn't meant to be there – the straight edge of a rifle barrel, the shine of a metallic surface, or the whites of a man's eyes. He laughed to himself, he'd be lucky to see a tank in these conditions. The now hammering rain made it almost impossible to hear anything above its roar, but every man in the team was trained and experienced in doing just that, listening for the mumble of a voice or the cocking of weapon. There wasn't much chance of smelling anything in a downpour, but never say never, he thought.

The operation to extract Pedrosa would be conducted in three phases.

Phase one would commence with an assault by Master Sergeant Muldoon, callsign One-Eight-Zero-Alpha, and his team on the Bandits' sentry post a hundred yards to the east of the house, which covered the covert airstrip and the approach road. Muldoon's assault would have two objectives: firstly, to neutralize the three sentries located at the outpost and, secondly, to deliberately draw as many Bandits as possible to respond to the assault on the sentry post, thereby reducing opposition to the rescue of Pedrosa back at the main house.

Phase two involved Morgan and Braunschweiger clearing the house and, ultimately, recovering Pedrosa.

Kirby, callsign One-Eight-Alpha, and his team, would split into two to cover the northern side between the jungle and the house, and the southern side, specifically, the open ground between the house and the edge of the jungle, thereby creating an impenetrable channel down either flank of the building while Morgan and Braunschweiger, with Spring and Devereux, would enter the house in pairs from the south-western end, clearing room by room.

Phase three would be the extraction by helicopter of Morgan, Braunschweiger, Pedrosa and any Special Forces casualties requiring evac. Meanwhile, in a follow-up operation, Kirby, Muldoon and the regrouped ODA 751 would remain in place for the separate task of taking control of the drug courier aircraft that was due at midday.

Just like that. Yeah, right, thought Morgan. Just like that.

The rain eased then stopped suddenly, and an all-consuming silence fell upon them.

Morgan reached the clearing, spotted the house and slowly went to ground, still shielded by the embrace of the heavy undergrowth. The rest of the team followed suit. Inch by inch, Morgan, Braunschweiger, Spring and Devereux each crawled to the edge of the jungle and watched intently for a full five minutes allowing their eyes to adjust, taking in the layout of the compound. There were plumes of smoke tentatively emerging from smoke stacks in the main house and the slave quarters. The breakfast fires were going. With the rain gone, the smell of strong coffee and cigarettes wafted across to them, yet there was no obvious movement. There was no one outside and no activity within the buildings. Was it too quiet? As if reacting to his uneasiness, the *crack-crack* of a lone assault rifle followed by the immediate and unmistakable roar of responding heavy-caliber ammunition sliced through the jungle from the direction of the sentry post. Morgan's eyes snapped at his watch. Zero-five-five-seven – too early. Fuck! Nothing ever goes according to plan.

"Let's move," said Morgan. But he didn't have to say it. Instinctively, all four of them were already moving, fast, breaking cover through the dense undergrowth at the edge of the jungle and running toward the south-western end of the main house.

"Muldoon's team," said Devereux. "They've been sprung at the sentry post."

Morgan hoped that Captain Kirby and his guys were in position. If they weren't, things could get tricky. It was almost daylight now, just enough to see by, but up ahead the house lights were finally coming on. Breaking away from the protection of the jungle, they sprinted across fifteen yards of open ground. By now, the gunfire down at the sentry post had evolved into a full-scale firefight. Morgan and Braunschweiger headed straight for the door at the closest end of the main house. Spring and Devereux followed. They had to find Pedrosa, fast. But no sooner had they covered the open expanse of the clearing than they were engaged by a Bandit with an AKM crouching behind the far corner of the house. Down here they called AKMs *cuerno de chivo*, which in Spanish means "goat horn," because of the curved shape of the infamous weapon's magazine. Whatever they called them, the guy pulling the trigger on this one wasn't the best shot in the world, but his rounds were striking the ground close enough for the odds to favor him sooner rather than later.

Still on the move, their pace unchecked, Morgan and Braunschweiger fired in unison at the Bandit's muzzle flash. Their rounds easily tore through the wooden sheeting of the building, splintering it and silencing the gunman. He fell into view, the weapon falling from his hands, and both Intrepid agents fired another short burst into the body. *To be sure, to be sure*, as Tom Rodgers, Intrepid's chief combat instructor would say, complete with dodgy Irish accent. One down.

Without warning the heavy downpour resumed just as a second deafening burst of gunfire sliced through the deluge to their right. For a moment it seemed surreal. Surely there was nobody out there? But two Bandits suddenly appeared behind their dead compadre, firing wildly in the direction of the Intrepid agents. Then the Green Berets, Spring and Devereux, were there.

"We got this!" Spring shouted over the hail of gunfire and Morgan and Braunschweiger kept going. The rounds that were cleaving through the air just inches above their heads were answered by the Green Berets and silenced. Two more down.

Now the Intrepid agents were running in a low crouch over the last few yards of open ground to the house, their weapons raised, ready to fire again. Rain was cascading down their faces, through their eyes, drenching them, turning the soft brown clay at their feet to rivers of mud. They were ready for anything, their eyes focused on the entrance to the main house.

The door was flimsy, like the rest of the building, and yielded easily under the Key's unforgiving shoulder charge – his preferred method of entry from his GSG-9 days, hence the nickname. The two agents burst in and found themselves in a large communal sleeping area where half-a-dozen straw mats were strewn across the floor. The heavy footfalls and yelling of panicked men running to the opposite end of the house echoed down the central corridor, but two men, too slow to respond to the gunfire outside, were still on their backs, grappling with their AKs and bringing them clumsily around to fire at the door. Morgan and Braunschweiger opened fire, killing them instantly. With Spring and Devereux hot on their heels, the four soldiers poured into the building, giving chase to the rest of the crew, who were making their way to the action outside. A padlocked door appeared on the left of the corridor. Braunschweiger charged at it and the hasp-and-staple latch was ripped from the frame. Outside there was an explosion of gunfire. Kirby's team had engaged the Shining Path Bandits who were running to join the battle at the sentry post.

"He's here!" bellowed Braunschweiger. "Ricco!"

As Morgan followed Braunschweiger into the room, another Bandit appeared at the far end of the corridor, raising an AK. Spring fired straight across Morgan's back and took the man down, not before a burst of 7.62mm short ammunition spat from the AK and into the walls and roof above their heads. The Green Beret ran forward and emptied a second short burst into the body to ensure the Bandit was dead, then stood post at the northern end of the corridor. Devereux covered south.

"Ricco! Ricco! It's us," said Morgan.

The man on the floor was alive but only just. His breathing was shallow and his pulse had the cadence of a funeral march. He'd been huddled in the corner, wrapped in a blanket that smelled like it was meant for a stable. Morgan was holding his face, trying to see if his eyes would open. Pedrosa was barely conscious, exhausted no doubt by the beatings he'd obviously endured through the night. He was dressed in little more than rags and roped to a D-ring in the wall. Braunschweiger tore the D-ring from its fastenings and lifted his brother agent into the center of the room so they could get a better look at the damage he'd sustained.

Then, as Morgan tried to bring Pedrosa back to consciousness, the big Austrian cut away the ropes that bound his wrists and ankles. Pedrosa gave a sudden yell, his arms and legs flailing in every direction. His friends took the punches and kicks until they finally calmed him.

"Ricco," said Morgan again. "It's me, Morgan, and the big guy's here, too."

"Morgan?" Pedrosa's voice was a rasp. His eyes opened. Recognition. "Morgan."

"That's right, mate. It's Morgan and here's the Key."

Braunschweiger leaned into view. A broad grin broke across Pedrosa's battered face.

"*Guten morgen, mein Herr*," said Braunschweiger, returning the grin. "If you've finished with your beauty sleep, liebling, now would be a good time to get your fat, lazy ass up so we can get the fuck out of here."

Pedrosa coughed blood, laughed, and then coughed up some more. With the help of his friends, he pulled himself into a sitting position. He stifled a howl of pain and his breathing became more intense and forceful as he fought against the agony that accompanied any movement.

"They've broken some ribs," he said through shallow breaths. "And I think my ankles are both broken."

"I'm on it," said Spring from outside the door. "One of you guys take over here and I'll get to work."

Without another word, Braunschweiger took over in the corridor, covering them to the north, as Spring – the ODA's medical specialist – took his place beside Pedrosa, administered morphine and then set to work on the injuries.

"We have the package," Morgan said into his radio while helping Spring as he tended to Pedrosa.

"*Roger that*," replied Kirby. "*We're secure out here. Bandits neutralized. All of mine are accounted for and good to go. You?*"

"Same," Morgan replied. "All good to go. Package in need of evac, ASAP."

"*Understood. Evac inbound. Move to RV now.*"

"WILCO," said Morgan. "We're on the way."

Grab your copy...
vinci-books.com/ranger

About the Author

Chris Allen is an author, senior executive, leadership mentor, public speaker, veteran and father. He is a member of the Australian Crime Writers Association (ACWA).

The formative years of Chris's career began in the Australian Army, initially as a soldier before being selected for commissioning as an officer. His service included airborne forces, military intelligence, attachments to the New Zealand Army, the British Parachute Regiment and deployments to Africa, South East Asia and Central America. After almost fifteen years of military service, Chris was medically retired at the rank of Major.

Chris's post-military career continued to reflect his commitment to service. He led security and logistics operations for CARE International in East Timor during the 1999 emergency. Later, in the wake of the September 11 attacks of 2001, he oversaw the upgrade of Counter Terrorism First Response (CTFR) measures at Sydney Airport. And in 2003 when protestors painted 'No War' on the sails of the Sydney Opera House, he was headhunted to take over the protection of the iconic landmark. In 2008 he was appointed Sheriff of New South Wales, one of Australia's most historic law enforcement appointments.

In more recent years, Chris has continued his career as a senior executive, broadening his experience across a diverse range of roles within Commonwealth and state government departments, and the not-for-profit sector.

Today, Chris lives on the New South Wales south coast with his sons, Morgan and Rhett.